"A powerful and 1930s Europe that both illuminates and captivates. I was so invested in Barbara and her family's plight that I could not stop turning the pages. Mario Escobar has penned an unforgettable novel of love and fortitude—and books!"

—SARA ACKERMAN, *USA TODAY* BESTSELLING
AUTHOR OF *THE CODEBREAKER'S SECRET*

"Deftly captured and eloquently told, Mario Escobar's *A Bookseller in Madrid* is an important, powerful tale bringing tragic circumstances and resilient characters together in an often-overlooked time in Spanish history. This story is an impressive testament to literature's ability to provide comfort, strength, and hope even in the darkest of times."

—GABRIELLA SAAB, AUTHOR OF *THE LAST CHECKMATE*

"Within the harrowing landscape of both the Spanish Civil War and World War II, Escobar shines a light on hope and humanity through Elisabeth Eidenbenz and her work to create the Elna Maternity Hospital and the Mothers of Elne, saving countless mothers and their newborn children. Descriptions and prose, both startling and lyrical, bring you into the scene and into the lives of both Elisabeth and Isabel as they strive to survive, thrive, and care for others in this gripping tale of destruction, war, and the endless potential within the human heart to endure, sacrifice, and rejoice."

—KATHERINE REAY, AUTHOR OF *THE LONDON HOUSE*
AND *A SHADOW IN MOSCOW*, ON *THE SWISS NURSE*

"Mario Escobar shares the true story of Janusz Korczak, a respected leader and speaker whose life was dedicated to children . . . Escobar's account draws readers in with compelling, emotional, mind-searing descriptions while delving into human nature, evil, prejudices, and forgiveness."

—HISTORICAL NOVEL SOCIETY
ON *THE TEACHER OF WARSAW*

"In *The Teacher of Warsaw*, Mario Escobar tries to recreate Korczak's complexities, which have largely been erased by his martyrdom during the Holocaust . . . *The Teacher of Warsaw* is a nuanced fictionalization, and it may motivate readers to learn more about the real man behind it—whose tragic circumstances left him unable to save the Jewish children in his care."

—JEWISH BOOK COUNCIL

"In *The Teacher of Warsaw*, Escobar's intimate, first-person delivery is flawlessly researched. Its historic timeline unfurls with heightening drama from the vantage point of one selfless man dedicated to the wellbeing of Polish children in harrowing wartime conditions against all odds and costs. It's a sobering, memorable story taking the reader through tragic events in occupied Warsaw, from September 1939 to May of 1943. An important, sensitive look at the triumph of the human spirit over evil, *The Teacher of Warsaw* is based on a true story and epitomizes the very best of poignant historical fiction."

—*NEW YORK JOURNAL OF BOOKS*

"Through meticulous research and with wisdom and care, Mario Escobar brings to life a heartbreaking story of love and extraordinary courage. I want everyone I know to read this book."

—KELLY RIMMER, *NEW YORK TIMES* BESTSELLING
AUTHOR OF *THE WARSAW ORPHAN*,
ON *THE TEACHER OF WARSAW*

"A beautifully written, deeply emotional story of hope, love, and courage in the face of unspeakable horrors. That such self-sacrifice, dedication, and goodness existed restores faith in humankind. Escobar's heart-rending yet uplifting tale is made all the more poignant by its authenticity. Bravo!"

—TEA COOPER, *USA TODAY* BESTSELLING AND AWARD-WINNING AUTHOR OF *THE CARTOGRAPHER'S SECRET*, ON *THE TEACHER OF WARSAW*

"This is a powerful portrait of a woman fighting to preserve knowledge in a crumbling world."

—*PUBLISHERS WEEKLY* ON *THE LIBRARIAN OF SAINT-MALO*

"In *The Librarian of Saint-Malo*, Escobar brings us another poignant tale of sacrifice, love, and loss amidst the pain of war. The seaside town of Saint-Malo comes to life in rich detail and complexity under German occupation, as do the books—full of great ideas and the best of humanity—the young librarian seeks to save. This sweeping story gives us a glimpse into the past with a firm eye toward hope in our future."

—KATHERINE REAY, BESTSELLING AUTHOR OF *THE LONDON HOUSE* AND *A SHADOW IN MOSCOW*

"Escobar's latest (after *Auschwitz Lullaby*, 2018) is a meticulously researched story, recreating actual experiences of the 460 Spanish children who were sent to Morelia, Mexico, in 1937. Devastating, enlightening, and passionately told, Escobar's novel shines a light on the experiences of the victims of war, and makes a case against those who would use violence to gain power. Although painful events in the story make it hard to read at times, the book gives a voice to so many whose stories are often overlooked, while inspiring the reader to never give way to fear or let go of one's humanity."

—*BOOKLIST*, STARRED REVIEW, ON *REMEMBER ME*

"Luminous and beautifully researched, *Remember Me* is a study of displacement, belonging, compassion, and forged family amidst a heart-wrenching escape from the atrocities of the Spanish Civil War. A strong sense of place and the excavation of a little known part of history are reverently handled in a narrative both urgent and romantic. Fans of Arturo Pérez-Reverte, Chanel Cleeton, and Lisa Wingate will be mesmerized."

—RACHEL MCMILLAN, AUTHOR
OF *THE LONDON RESTORATION*

"An exciting and moving novel."

—*PEOPLE EN ESPAÑOL* ON *RECUÉRDAME*

"Escobar highlights the tempestuous, uplifting story of two Jewish brothers who cross Nazi-occupied France in hope of reuniting with their parents in this excellent tale . . . Among the brutality and despair that follows in the wake of the Nazis' rampage through France, Escobar uncovers hope, heart, and faith in humanity."

—*PUBLISHERS WEEKLY* ON *CHILDREN OF THE STARS*

"A poignant telling of the tragedies of war and the sacrificing kindness of others seen through the innocent eyes of children."

—J'NELL CIESIELSKI, BESTSELLING AUTHOR OF
BEAUTY AMONG RUINS AND *THE SOCIALITE*,
ON *CHILDREN OF THE STARS*

"*Auschwitz Lullaby* grabbed my heart and drew me in. A great choice for readers of historical fiction."

—IRMA JOUBERT, AUTHOR OF *THE GIRL FROM THE TRAIN*

"Based on historical events, *Auschwitz Lullaby* is a deeply moving and harrowing story of love and commitment."

—*HISTORICAL NOVELS REVIEW*

A BOOKSELLER IN MADRID

ALSO BY MARIO ESCOBAR

The Forgotten Names

The Swiss Nurse

The Teacher of Warsaw

The Librarian of Saint-Malo

Remember Me

Children of the Stars

Auschwitz Lullaby

A
BOOKSELLER
IN MADRID

A Novel

MARIO ESCOBAR

HARPER MUSE

A Bookseller in Madrid

Copyright © 2025 by Harper Focus

La Librera de Madrid

Published by Harper Muse, an imprint of HarperCollins Focus LLC.

Translator: Gretchen Abernathy

Scripture quotations are taken from the King James Version. Public domain.

This book is a work of fiction. All incidents, dialogue, letters, and all characters, with the exception of some well-known historical figures, are products of the author's imagination and not to be construed as real. Where real-life historical persons appear, the situations, incidents, and dialogues concerning those personas are entirely fictional and are not intended to depict actual events or to change the entirely fictional nature of the work. In all other respects, any resemblance to persons living or dead is entirely coincidental.

Any internet addresses (websites, blogs, etc.) in this book are offered as a resource. They are not intended in any way to be or imply an endorsement by HarperCollins Focus LLC, nor does HarperCollins Focus LLC vouch for the content of these sites for the life of this book.

Library of Congress Cataloging-in-Publication Data

Names: Escobar, Mario, 1971- author. | Abernathy, Gretchen, translator.
Title: A bookseller in Madrid / Mario Escobar; [translator, Gretchen Abernathy].
Other titles: Librera de Madrid. English
Description: Nashville: Harper Muse, 2025. | Summary: "An exciting and rigorously documented novel by one of the most translated and read Spanish authors in the world. This hopeful and inspiring story in the face of the horror of intolerance is, above all, an indisputable tribute to literature"—Provided by publisher.
Identifiers: LCCN 2025001419 (print) | LCCN 2025001420 (ebook) | ISBN 9781400347445 (paperback) | ISBN 9781400347476 (hardcover) | ISBN 9781400347452 (epub) | ISBN 9781400347469
Subjects: LCSH: Booksellers and bookselling—Fiction. | Spain—History—Civil War, 1936-1939—Fiction. | Madrid (Spain)—Fiction. | LCGFT: Historical fiction. | Novels.
Classification: LCC PQ6705.S618 L5313 2025 (print) | LCC PQ6705.S618 (ebook) | DDC 863/.7—dc23/eng/20250310
LC record available at https://lccn.loc.gov/2025001419
LC ebook record available at https://lccn.loc.gov/2025001420

Printed in the United States of America

25 26 27 28 29 LBC 5 4 3 2 1

To the booksellers, ever at the vanguard of culture, who protect the sacred temple of the conscience and fight to keep books from disappearing.

To the bookseller in Concepción who eyed me suspiciously when I entered his store, and who wielded his smoke pipe like a flaming sword to protect the borders of humanity's lost paradise.

Contents

CONTENTS

Part 2: Of Books and Children

Part 3: One, Great, and Free

CONTENTS

A Note from the Author

A Bookseller in Madrid is a work of fiction born out of the desire to draw readers into the harsh reality of the Second Spanish Republic, the Spanish Civil War, and the early years of Franco's rule. Nearly ninety years after the outbreak of the bloodiest conflict in Spain's history, it's time for us to calmly review the past.

All wars are bad, but civil wars are perhaps the most tragic. The wounds from fratricidal fighting endure, and the simple fact of time passing does not cure them. Every city, every town, and every household in Spain holds a family tragedy related to the war, a story that reminds them of the humiliation and injustices their loved ones suffered. People tend to face such suffering in one of two ways: with attempted amnesia, which renders the memories helpless, or with hatred, which stores up resentment toward those who took away loved ones, a nation, or freedom. Novels are a sort of practice round for real life. They can help us reconcile with the past and put ourselves in the shoes of those who lived it.

The terrible ideological battle that a few years later dragged the world to the brink of destruction was also waged in Spain. The fear of the spread of Communism in Europe, especially in Germany, made it easy for Fascism to extend beyond the borders of Italy. Meanwhile, Western democracies had inadequate answers to the challenges of the new political and economic scene. Spain had initially emerged stronger from the Great War. After the military dictatorship of Miguel Primo de Rivera, the country attempted to transition to democracy. Yet the success of the Republic was brief. Social divisions, economic inequality among regions, insufficient agrarian reform, rapid changes to which a large sector of society did not adapt, violence, and international pressures kicked the country's second attempt at being a republic to the curb.

Bárbara Spiel is the protagonist of this fictional story about a young German woman who opens a bookshop in Madrid during the tumultuous 1930s. Representative of a generation of young idealists who struggled to keep another worldwide con-flagration at bay, her work is in line with the very real tenacity of Sylvia Beach and Adrienne Monnier. These women, who sought to change the world through books, were the founders of the Parisian bookstores Shakespeare and Company and La Maison des Amis des Livres, respectively.

The story of Bárbara Spiel details the turbulent, exciting Madrid of the Second Spanish Republic, ever changing and full of rapid social transformation but also of violence and danger. During the war, the Republican government retreated from the besieged, relentlessly bombed city to a safer zone, which opened the door for extremist factions to take control and subsequently purge their ideological enemies. The arrival of Franco's troops brought hunger, fear, and the persecution of intellectuals. In *The Hive*, Camilo José Cela poignantly describes the disenchantment of the capital in the postwar years:

Something like sorrow floats in the air and strikes into people's hearts. Hearts don't hurt and can suffer for hour after hour, a whole life long, without anyone ever knowing for sure what's happening.

A Bookseller in Madrid is about dreams, about the capacity of human beings to face adversity, and about life that finds its way through day-to-day difficulties and tragedies. Bárbara's bookstore becomes both an island of peace, tolerance, and hope in a collapsing world and the target of attacks by extremists.

The young German woman's love for a Spanish Socialist parliamentarian binds her to a country sinking into a spiral of hatred and terror, two sides of the same coin. Hounded simultaneously by Stalinist *checas*, Francoist Fascists, and the German Gestapo, Bárbara struggles to keep her bookstore's flame of liberty from being snuffed out.

In our current turbulent times, the defense of common sense, tolerance, and respect for others has become a dangerous act. Books remain one of the few pillars upholding Western society, a society rendered feeble by its own contradictions and undermined by the Trojan horse of its culture that, like the Roman god Saturn, is willing to devour its own.

I invite you to join the club of readers who, from the trenches of books, hold out in the endless war against truth. Come, lose yourself in the beautiful story of Bárbara Spiel.

Prologue

New York
November 2022

Kerri Young was a keen hunter-gatherer when it came to old books, the ones that jumped out at you with their yellowed pages and begged you to open them even just once. She had studied philology at UC Berkeley with an eye to becoming an editor, though the desire coiled deepest inside her heart was to be a writer.

Kerri was making her way down Seventy-Second Street in Manhattan when she saw construction workers tossing old books into a dumpster. She froze, scrunched her upturned nose, and could not keep herself from calling for them to stop. Barely glancing at her, the workers tossed another box into the dumpster.

Kerri rolled up the sleeves of her cardigan, hoisted herself over the side of the dumpster, and started rifling through the books, hoping to rescue a few from demise. Her tiny Brooklyn apartment could not hold any more books, but she could donate them to the synagogue's library. Her fingers were caked with dust and globs of cement when they unearthed a dark green leather volume. Kerri wiped the front cover with her forearm and could just make out the tarnished gold leafing: *A Bookseller in Madrid*.

Kerri had been to Spain once but never to the capital. After a layover in Barcelona, she had flown to Majorca for a few glorious days of sunshine and relaxation on its beaches.

She flipped open the book and discovered it had been published in 1964 by a small publishing house in Boston. The first few lines sucked Kerri into what appeared to be the autobiography of a young German woman who had left the dangers of Berlin in the 1930s to open a bookshop in Madrid during the Second Spanish Republic. It smacked of Hemingway, the Woolfs, and the bygone generation that had tried to keep a second world war at bay.

She read the entire subway ride home. Back in her apartment, she threw herself onto the bed and lost herself in the incredible story of Bárbara Spiel until the first rays of dawn lightened the window.

After a quick shower, Kerri fixed a pot of coffee and hurried to the Manhattan publishing house where she worked. She took tiny sips from her thermos mug as she pushed her way across the street. She needed to get her newest discovery into the hands of her boss and friend, Alice Rossemberg, as soon as possible. The story of that marvelous woman had to line the stands of bookstores around the world. Kerri sensed its power to inspire the hundreds of thousands of people who understood that books were the key to changing reality and restoring a bit of sanity and heroism to this tumultuous, confusing world.

The two women spent that Friday morning reading, dreaming, and planning the future of *A Bookseller in Madrid*. The rest is history.

Part 1

From Berlin to Madrid

Chapter 1

My father was a writer. We had loads of books at home, our huge library bigger than anyone else's I knew except my grandfather Gábor's. He was a well-known playwright who passed away when I was young. I inherited another passion from my father: his love for the French language. We Germans have always had a somewhat ambivalent relationship with the French, swinging between deep admiration for their culture and literature and complete disdain for so many other things. Yet since Adolf Hitler's rise to power and relentless attempt to take over every aspect of German society, France had become just one more enemy to take down.

My other grandfather, Klaus, came from a much humbler background, and his family trade was woodworking, though he became a pastor. I was just a child when he built me a lovely little bookshelf for my room in our house on the outskirts of Berlin. From then on, I played at being a bookseller. I practiced all the time with my two sisters and my friends. When I finished my degree in French philology, it was the most natural thing in the world for me to start working at a highly acclaimed bookstore in downtown Berlin.

The store belonged to a well-known Jewish family. The owner was one of the women I admired most in the world. Ruth Friedman inherited the business from her father, who had inherited it in turn from his. Initially selling only books in Yiddish, the store evolved into a niche for foreign-language literature, especially French.

"That girl's a tough cookie," Mrs. Friedman said, flipping through the magazine for German booksellers. Hitler had threatened to do away with all non-Aryan cultures, but so far nothing had come of it. Mrs. Friedman believed his words were just a political maneuver to secure the support of all the racist Nationalist citizens.

"What girl?" I asked.

"Françoise Frenkel, the Polish woman who runs La Maison du Livre, the French bookshop. The Nazis have been giving her grief for a decade now, though I don't know if it's because she's a Jew or because she sells French books."

I had heard glowing reports about that meeting place for book-lovers but had never been able to visit. As soon as my workday ended, I would head straight there to continue my research. My goal was to finish my doctorate in French philology and then to open my own store. On top of all that, I was an editor for a few small publishing houses that translated books from French.

"Why don't the police do something to stop them?" I asked.

Ruth burst out laughing at my naivete. "The police? Hermann Göring is their boss! You think he'll lift a finger to protect the Jews or the Polish immigrants?"

My father, a Social Democrat, had a seat in parliament and had already experienced the wrath of Adolf Hitler and his henchmen.

After the burning of the Reichstag a month prior, the Enabling Act passed in March granted dictatorial powers to Hitler. Communist and Socialist representatives were denied access to their seats in parliament, and many of them were locked up in jails or in Dachau, the fearful concentration camp outside of Munich. My father had friends in the Centre Party and among the non-Nazi ministers. For the moment, that had kept him out of jail. Everyone advised him to get out of the country, but he was not yet willing to leave our family home and all the memories, especially everything he had shared with my mother, Magda.

That day, when my shift was over, I removed the pink apron all the female employees wore to reveal a floral dress, which was a celebration of the long 1933 summer, and went to pay my first visit to the bookstore of Mrs. Frenkel. From the outside it looked like a little French hole-in-the-wall, but inside it was open and welcoming, the kind of place you never wanted to leave. There was a poster on the door about an upcoming lecture by a famous French author. Several French newspapers lined a front table. Many Berliners bought French papers because censorship had already stifled most of the German periodicals.

A man with round glasses looked up as I entered. Besides us, the place was oddly empty for that time of day, when people were generally out and about doing their shopping. My presence clearly surprised the man.

"May I help you with anything, young lady?" he asked.

"Oh, I'm just having a look."

The man nodded and went back to his book. I wandered between tables and mahogany bookshelves, carefully opening the cover or running my fingers down the spine of one volume after another. I loved the smell of books and wood, of ink and paper—the aroma of libraries and bookstores. For me that smell was the gateway to paradise lost, where nothing bad could happen to me.

After a while, a handsome man in a double-breasted pin-striped suit walked in. He had a thin mustache, and his black hair was combed back, revealing dark eyes that devoured everything in his path. I observed him discreetly as he greeted the man at the counter and began looking through German and French titles.

I had lost my concentration. Every few seconds I glanced up cautiously at the stranger. I wondered where he was from and what he was doing in a store that so few Germans dared to enter anymore. Then an attractive, slender woman emerged from the back room emanating simple, natural elegance. She introduced herself to me as the owner, Françoise Frenkel, and asked if she could help me find anything.

"Good afternoon, my name is Barbara. I'm looking through your French collection. I'm finishing my doctoral thesis about Honoré de Balzac. Well, in fact . . . it's about why he became one of the greatest authors in French literature despite being rejected by scholars and other famous authors."

A smile played at Françoise's lips.

"Ah, Balzac's importance cannot be understated—one of the greatest writers of all time," she replied. "Not every book will go down in history, of course, but he painted a precise portrait of society in his day. No other author has hit the nail so squarely on the head. I think people were miffed at how easily storytelling came to him. Balzac could churn out a masterpiece in a matter of weeks." With a click of her tongue and a sigh, she continued, "The envy of his contemporaries was bound to come. The main difference between the genius and the artist is that the first does not need the effort and tenacity of the second."

I nodded in agreement.

"Have you read Stefan Zweig's essay on Balzac?" Françoise asked.

"Yes, of course; it was fascinating. That's where I learned the sad story behind the great writer. In fact, that's what convinced me to research him."

"One book leads to another. That's the magic of reading. Balzac, like all the great hearts, had to be forged in pain. There is no real art without suffering. It's the price the gods demand." Françoise lit a cigarette while she talked.

I longed to become a writer, and I knew Françoise was correct. A brief glance at the biography of nearly any famous author proved that literature was no bed of roses.

"At least they've managed to turn their frustration and pain into something good." I immediately regretted saying something that sounded so frivolous. At the time I did not realize that insecurity is one of the virtues of youth: the ability to question everything and believe that there is always a better way of doing things. Later, life batters away until you cede to harsh reality, or at least that is the excuse of those who become content to survive.

"Zweig published that piece with two other biographical essays, one on Dickens and the other on Dostoevsky. We can only hope that Zweig doesn't have to flee the country like other intellectuals have."

She named the fear that defined what was occurring around us. Just as things had started to stabilize after years of political tension and economic difficulties, the world as we had always known it was disappearing. How ironic.

The jingling of the bell at the front door announced the entry of four men dressed in the brown uniforms of the SA. They reeked of sour beer and sweat. They glanced haughtily around the store, as if waiting to make sure we were all paying sufficient attention, before going into action. Their pathetic, vulgar existence was only justified in their eyes by the amount of terror they inflicted on their victims.

As if taking a stage cue, the oldest of the rabid Nazi dogs yelled, "Damned Communist Jews!" and cleared an entire shelf of books with his short nightstick. His puppy underlings followed suit.

Over and above the crash of books against the floor, the SA belted out patriotic songs proclaiming the irrational beliefs of National Socialism. The man at the counter, whom I'd learned was Françoise's husband, raised his arms and ran into the pack of wild dogs to stop them. "Gentlemen, please!" he cried.

One of the Nazis shoved him down and another began kicking him hard. The man groaned. Françoise made to run to her husband armed with nothing but her glasses and a pen, but before she got there, the dark-haired stranger cut her off. Without a word, he held her by the shoulders until she stopped trying to enter the fray. Then the stranger turned and stared at the four SA officers.

"You've had your fun, comrades. Now, if you'll please move along." He spoke in such a low voice that I could hardly distinguish his words from the shouts of the Nazis, the groans of Françoise's husband, and the noise of books flying off the shelves to carpet the floor.

The oldest Nazi, who was clearly starting to gray beneath the cap covering his close-cut hair, frowned. Waving his nightstick, he ambled toward the stranger.

"Are you one of these damned Jews? Looks like it from those dark eyes and that dark hair."

"My hair is as dark as the Führer's, it's true; to my knowledge that is no crime. I've asked you politely to please stop beating an innocent man. I will not be so polite next time."

The SA officer guffawed at the man's threat. The other three, having left off throwing books around and beating the man on the ground, howled with laughter in turn. The fat old assault guard did not see the blow coming. Nor did I. The stranger's fist slammed into his jaw and knocked him off-balance. The Nazi looked up in shock and made to swing with his nightstick, but he barely had time to raise his arm, which the stranger immediately twisted. He deftly swiped the nightstick and commenced to beat the SA guard senseless. The three lackeys threw themselves on him, two of them bearing hunting knives. They were not laughing anymore. Instead, their faces were swollen with an anger that made me step back farther in fear that they would turn on us next. I looked behind me for a way out, but my mind was frozen in terror.

The stranger dodged the SAs' blows and knives but landed several punches, which left the Nazis increasingly confused and scared. Five minutes later, they struggled up from the floor and hobbled out of the store in humiliation.

"Thank you," Françoise said to the stranger as she ran to tend to her husband.

I was horrified and paralyzed. Blood coated the leather covers of several books, and hundreds of volumes blanketed the floor, sprawled out at grotesque angles. I picked up a few and put them back in their places, grasping at the hope of order to relieve my distress. Then I found myself face-to-face with the stranger.

"Let me help you."

I did not know how to respond, but we both spent the next long while organizing the books and smoothing their twisted pages.

"I haven't introduced myself," he said after some time. "I'm Juan Delgado."

"Juan Delgado?" I asked, puzzled.

He nodded. "I'm from Spain."

I had never met anyone from Spain. In Germany, there were all sorts of negative stereotypes and prejudice against southern Europeans.

"Pleased to meet you. I'm Barbara," I said, feigning a calm I did not feel.

Françoise and her husband had joined the cleanup efforts, and everything was back in order within an hour.

"Thank you both for everything," Françoise said. "It's gotten late. The least we can do is invite you to dinner."

My locked-up state continued and I seemed unable to respond to the invitation, but Juan accepted eagerly. Then he turned to me. "Don't worry; I'll walk you home afterward. The streets of Berlin are crawling with swine like those guys, drunkards looking to wreak havoc."

The four of us went up to the apartment above the bookstore, where the couple had lived since opening the business a few years before. It was a simple abode with few luxuries but with so many books that it seemed like an extension of the shop below.

"Dinner is chicken breasts over artichokes. It's not much, but with a good French wine and a bit of bread, I think we'll make do," Françoise said.

While her husband set the table, Juan and I stood around, unsure of what to say or do. Françoise rescued us from the awkwardness by arriving with two trays and placing them on the round table.

"Please, do sit down," her husband said. "Now to formally introduce myself: I'm Simon Raichenstein. I'm Russian, and my wife is Polish. We opened this bookstore in 1921 in a smaller location. Back then, we never could have imagined that twelve years later we would be in a situation like what just happened."

We all took our seats, and Françoise served the food on delicate china plates.

Simon continued speaking. "I got out of Russia because of the revolution. At first I thought that my country, which I love dearly, would modernize and leave behind the era of the czars . . . but really, now it's just a new kind of czar—the Reds—governing the Kremlin. And they're even crueler than the real ones."

"Don't burden our new friends with your sad stories, Simon. Nobody has it easy in these times," Françoise snapped.

The tension could be cut with a knife. It seemed that they were one of those couples who loved each other but could no longer stand to be in the other's presence.

"Forgive me," Simon said with an apologetic shrug.

"What's happening in Russia is an enormous social experiment. It's to be expected that few people understand it," Juan said.

"Are you a Communist?" Simon asked.

Juan shook his head, a spoonful of the delicious food in his mouth.

"And what if he were?" Françoise reproached. "This man saved your life, and likely the entire store." She refilled the Bohemian crystal wineglasses.

"True, true, forgive me. It's just that my family and I have been through so much . . ."

"I'm so sorry about that. By no means did I intend to imply that I'm in favor of what is occurring in the Soviet Union, but society does need new paradigms, and the bourgeois democracies either cannot or will not offer them. Which is precisely why Adolf Hitler has ended up on top here."

At that, I looked straight into the Spaniard's eyes and asked in a very serious tone, "Are you comparing National Socialism with Communism? My father was a Social Democrat in parliament and was ousted from his seat. He's on the verge of fleeing the country out of fear. Friends have invited him to the Netherlands to get him out of this mess. Nazism and Socialism are antagonistic."

"Not for the masses," Juan answered. "I'm a member of the Spanish Socialist Workers' Party, and I know how the common people think. Many of the people who voted for leftist parties now support Hitler. It's a reality we can't avoid. I've come to Germany precisely to study this phenomenon, because a few Fascist movements have sprung up in Spain, and we want to understand what's happened in Germany and Italy to keep it from spreading to our young Republic."

"Well, to be frank, the ascent of the Nazis here is a result of people being afraid of the Communists," Simon said. "You know, after the war there were several attempts to apply the Soviet system here, and people are afraid."

Françoise raised her glass and said, "Let's change the subject with a toast. Here's to being alive today, since we don't know what tomorrow holds."

We all clinked our raised glasses and sipped the delicious Bordeaux wine.

The rest of the evening passed in a more relaxed atmosphere. Juan told us a lot about his country, and by the end of dinner I was fascinated by Spain. I recalled that an old friend worked in a bilingual school in Madrid. I began to think it might not be a bad idea to pay her a visit and get to know Spain firsthand.

Later, Juan accompanied me through the empty Berlin streets. Very few people ventured out at night anymore to dine at the fashionable restaurants or while away the hours at the cabarets the city was famous for. The country's new masters did not approve of respectable Germans enjoying those degenerate spectacles, as Nazi propaganda frequently reminded us.

"It's a pity you've had to get to know this aspect of Berlin. I promise you things were really different a few years ago," I said timidly.

"The whole world is changing, you know? The optimism from the turn of the century has given way to entrenched pessimism. But human beings always manage to rise above."

"You really think so?"

The young Spaniard smiled at me, and my heart skipped a beat. I had the feeling that I had found my soulmate that night: Juan was the perfect mixture of realism and idealism, he was handsome and chivalrous, and he treated me with great respect. When we got to my door, he paused with his hands in his pockets, pulled out a cigarette, and, before lighting it, asked, "Do you mind?"

"No, I like the smell. It reminds me of my dad."

We stayed in the island of light from the streetlamp. The end of the cigarette pulsed like an incandescent rock expelled from an erupting volcano.

"Would it be terribly brash of me to ask if we could see each other again?" he asked.

I laughed at the combination of his stuttering accent and impeccable grammar. For the first time that night, he was the one who seemed intimidated.

I pulled out a card for the bookstore where I worked and handed it to him. "This is where I work. My lunch break is at twelve thirty."

"I'll see you then," he said with a mischievous smile.

From my doorway I could hear him whistling all the way down the street. It was the theme song from a movie I loved, *À nous la liberté*, with Henri Marchand. I sang it quietly to myself as I climbed the stairs to my apartment, hoping the lyrics about beauty and freedom were a prophecy for my own life.

Chapter 2

The hope that things will not get any worse is so often denied. Hitler had been in power fewer than eight months, and the pressure against all who dared question his designs grew by the day.

My boss was debating whether or not to close the bookshop. She knew that sooner or later it would be the focus of Nazi attention: It was too close to the synagogue and in its early years had sold Jewish books exclusively. I was not far from finishing my thesis. Juan Delgado and I had developed an avid correspondence after his return to Spain, and we had promised to meet up someday in Madrid. Things were complicated in his country as well. Juan told me there was a possibility of early elections and that the right-wing parties would likely come out on top. There were uprisings in some parts of the country, and the initial euphoria of the Republic had turned into widespread tension.

I spent many afternoons in Françoise's bookshop. She refused to close it despite the increasing difficulty of importing foreign books, especially from France. Many readers continued buying foreign newspapers from her since the government still intervened in the German press. Freedom of press and of expression had ceased to exist in Germany, though the majority of my fellow citizens seemed not to mind.

Things in the university were no more hopeful. After the expulsion of Communist and Socialist professors, it was now the turn of Christians, many of whom resigned in protest. The only islands of peace were my long afternoons in La Maison du Livre and the short phone calls with Juan, despite the constant background noise that made it nearly impossible to hear each other.

"I'm learning Spanish," I told Françoise, who smiled sadly in reply.

"Love is a sweet flower that quickly withers." She bit her lip in regret as soon as the words were out of her mouth. I did not know what to say. "I'm sorry," she continued, taking my hand. "That's unkind of me. You know things with Simon aren't going well. When we met here in Berlin more than a decade ago, I thought he was a gift straight from heaven, the answer to my loneliness. I missed my mother and brothers and sisters so much. He was also alone, separated from a big family. We were like two wretches shipwrecked on the same island who finally found each other after years of painful solitude. And, of course, our love for books brought us together. We spent entire days talking, but at the core we had very different interests. He wanted a family; the only children I want to take care of are my books. Motherhood is wonderful, of course, but if you don't want to be a mother, then it's the worst thing that can happen to you."

Françoise grew quiet. She was not given to opening up like that, and her eyes were glassy with tears.

"No, I'm the one who's sorry; forgive me," I said. "With everything you've got going on, I've done nothing but go on and on about Juan."

She shook her head. "No, no, your happiness comforts me from what I've lost."

We hugged, but the intimate moment was broken by pounding at the door below.

We stared at each other, our breaths catching in our throats.

"Who could it be?" I asked.

"Given the time, it should be Simon. But I don't know what on earth could be going on."

We went down the stairs to the bookshop. In the dim light, the books crouched like ghosts longing to spill their secrets to us. The light from the street came through the shop window and showed the silhouette of a man.

"Françoise!"

"Simon!" she exclaimed, hurrying to open the door.

Her husband's face emerged from the shadows like something from a horror story: His frantic eyes were swollen, his forehead bloody, and his suit disheveled.

"What happened?" Françoise demanded.

Simon did not answer until he had shut and locked the door with Françoise's key.

"We have to get away, now," he whispered. Only then did he notice my presence. Startled, he said, "Girl, go home. They'll be here soon."

"Who?" Françoise's voice was choked with fear.

"The Gestapo."

Françoise and I both shivered visibly. The newly formed secret police was to be feared even more than the SA. Gestapo agents circled at night to catch their prey like a modern-day Inquisition, and no one ever saw the victims again.

"But why is the Gestapo after you?"

Her question went unanswered. Simon went upstairs and started packing a suitcase. We followed him.

"What have you done?" Françoise insisted.

"Nothing! Well . . . I may have passed along some information to the Russian embassy."

"You did what?!"

"We needed the money, and I didn't think they'd find out. Anyway, they would've come for me sooner or later, either for being a Jew or for selling books. Have you forgotten what happened in May? Those fanatics burned a lot of our books. They're purging the culture, Françoise, and Jews are being expelled from all trades and professions."

Françoise knew all of that but kept hoping the fanaticism was passing. Things had gone very badly for the Jews in Poland in the pogroms, but then the situation had calmed down.

"I'm not leaving." Françoise's voice was so calm and confident that her husband looked up in disbelief.

"Things will be better in France. People still breathe freely there."

"You know that this shop is my life, Simon. What good would another French bookstore do in France?"

Simon closed his suitcase and looked at Françoise for a long moment.

"I spied for us, to get the money we needed to be able to escape. Germany has become a prison, though most people still don't see it."

"I'm sorry," Françoise said, shaking her head and swallowing back tears.

Simon sighed, nodded, and gave Françoise one last lingering look. Then he disappeared down the stairs.

The next morning, Françoise called me at work, and I went over as soon as I could get free. I found her slumped cross-legged on the floor with her head down, surrounded by a sea of books scattered around the floor. The Gestapo had ransacked the store.

I threw myself down and hugged her.

"It was awful. They destroyed everything."

"I'll help you clean up. I've got to go back to work, but I'll ask for the rest of the day off and can be back here around twelve thirty."

With a heavy heart, I left Françoise in the middle of that desolation. But I arrived back at the bookstore where I worked to find that things had taken a dangerous turn. Two SA bullies were guarding the entrance and would not let anyone in or out of the store.

"Where do you think you're going, little lady? You don't look to be quite Aryan," one of them growled.

"I'm German, and I work here," I said. The assault guard looked barely fifteen years old.

"This is a Jewish store. Those pigs can't be allowed to keep doing whatever they fancy. You'd better find more respectable work."

"Yes, perhaps I should dress up like a little soldier to intimidate people." I regretted my remark immediately. Without another word, the young guard slapped me so hard that my bottom lip started bleeding. I had never been hit before. That first time hurt my pride more than my face.

My boss ran out of the bookstore. She gathered me into her arms and shouted at the Nazi, "You damned brute!"

The people on the street passed by indifferently, as if this matter were no concern of theirs. Dissenters against Hitler's regime were invisible to the rest of the population. I had always been proud of being German, but at that moment I was wholeheartedly ashamed of belonging to a nation that had disavowed its humanity.

"Are you all right?" Ruth asked, looking at my lip. But without waiting for my reply, she said, "You'll have to go home, Barbara. We're closing the store. I've got family in northern Italy . . . This seems to be the time to go, before things get even worse."

"But if we all flee . . ."

"Barbara, love, sometimes fleeing is the bravest way to face evil. If we stay in Berlin, there may not be any survivors left when it's time to rebuild Germany. Our country is hurtling into a very deep abyss, and only God can save it."

Her solemn pronouncement surprised me. I had never known Ruth to be religious. I hugged her tightly, a show of love being my best response to fear and suffering.

I went home with my head hung low. I forced myself to eat, but my lips hurt with every bite. Then I returned to Françoise's bookshop and helped her with the mess. We cleaned in silence, and she did not even notice my bruised face. Over tea after we were finished, I said aloud a thought that had been forming in my mind all day.

"I'm going to leave the country. And I think you should too."

She stared at me with a mixture of anger and sadness. "I have nowhere to go, Barbara." With a gesture that encompassed the store, she said, "This is my life's work. I'd rather stay for now."

"But . . ."

"I respect your decision, my friend. Where will you go? Your dad is still in the Netherlands, isn't he?"

My father had finally heeded his friends' advice and gone into exile.

"He is, but I'd rather go to Madrid. I've been talking with my friend Maria. She says I can teach German at the school where she works. It's called El Porvenir, 'The Future.' I like the way that sounds, though what I really want to do is open a bookstore. Until all this calms down, I'll be safe in Spain. They haven't gotten involved in Europe's problems in years. And the new Republic sounds very promising."

"As does Juan," she added in a gravelly voice and with a raised eyebrow. I started to smile, but it turned into a grimace at the pain in my lips.

"Oh, Barbara, have you treated that cut?"

"It's not that bad."

We kept chatting for some time, as always ending up talking about books and the power of literature to change the world. In Berlin or Madrid, we both hoped that our bookstores would serve as little paradises for people of goodwill to get their fill of the fruit of the tree of wisdom and heal a world bound for destruction.

Chapter 3

Paris
December 1933

I had always dreamed of going to Paris. The city's splendor seemed untarnished by the threats growing throughout Europe. The specter of Fascism loomed over the continent as Communism had a few years prior. But being alone while walking down the boulevards of Paris did take some of the shine off. My father should have been at my side. He and I had planned Paris trips time and time again, but after my mother's death five years before, his ability to dream had fallen flat in every realm except perhaps politics.

I checked off tourist sites with low spirits until I came to the fascinating world of the bouquinistes along the Seine. There were countless boxes of old books attached to the quayside, and I was thrilled to lose myself in the booksellers' stalls. My mind went back to Berlin and to the books thrown to the floors of the bookstores or burned in pyres in the city squares. It was ludicrous to imagine such barbarism ever touching France. I could not help myself from buying a few antique editions of Balzac. I had had to leave all my books in Berlin, adding them to my grandfather's library. I feared that the Nazis would ransack or requisition my father's properties since he was a Social Democrat and had fled the country. So my books would stay under my grandmother's protection until I returned.

As I put the two books I had bought in my backpack, the storm that had been brewing let loose. I hurried to the modest hotel where I was staying near the Luxembourg Gardens. The next day I was to leave for San Sebastián, where Juan Delgado would be waiting to escort me to Madrid. The lightning and thunder grew more intense, and the rain turned from a sprinkle to a shower and then, suddenly, to a downpour. I joined the throngs of people running wildly for cover.

When I reached rue de l'Odéon, my eyes landed on a sign that struck me as altogether mysterious, especially for being in the middle of Paris. It read SHAKESPEARE AND COMPANY. The façade was so plain that, if not for the books visible through the windows, it could have been any sort of business. The only feature that stood out was the image of the great British dramatist. Without thinking twice, I entered the shop.

It was empty of clients. A thin woman with short hair smiled and brought me a towel.

"You're German?"

"Is it that obvious?"

"Well, I'm used to seeing a lot of tourists. One ends up learning how to tell them apart."

"I'm Barbara Spiel."

"Pleased to meet you. I'm Sylvia Beach."

"Are you American or British?" I asked, trying to place her accent.

"It's hard to say where I'm from. I came to Paris when I was fourteen. My dad was a Presbyterian minister and came here to work at the American Church in Paris. I've also lived in Spain and—"

"Spain?" I interrupted. "I'm headed there now to open a bookstore in Madrid."

At that, the woman burst out laughing. "Though it may sound odd, the land of Quixote is not known for its reading public. I wish you luck—you're going to need it."

"Things are changing," I explained. "The Republic has opened schools all over the country. I want to help people get access to books from other regions."

"Let's hope you're right. Anyhow, bookstores are always necessary. True freedom is found between the doors of a bookstore, and the world has never needed freedom as much as it does now."

It finally dawned on me where I was. I had read a few articles about this bookstore, which had welcomed great writers like Ernest Hemingway and James Joyce.

"Wait a minute, you're the one who published *Ulysses* by Joyce, aren't you?"

Sylvia nodded. "Well, booksellers have a moral obligation with literature, and the literary world needed a good shake-up." She glanced out the window and added, "I think it'll be a while before this lets up. Would you like some coffee?"

"I can't imagine anything better at the moment!"

Once we were seated with steaming mugs in our hands, the conversation veered toward Sylvia's upbringing and personal life.

"Family can be a blessing and a curse. My parents never got along. They separated when I was about twenty. I traveled constantly around Europe with my mother and sisters, and my dad stayed in Princeton. Books became my refuge, and as you can see, they still are." Her tone was jovial but her face showed exhaustion.

I nodded. "Books are the only companions that will never betray you."

Eventually it stopped raining, and it was time to go. I stood and held out my hand. As I left the back room and headed for the shop door, Sylvia caught up with me and held out a book, an antique edition of Balzac's *Lost Illusions*.

"I wish you all the luck in the world. Being a bookseller is a bit like working a lighthouse: You try to keep the world from getting stuck in the shoals. It's a Herculean effort, and society is dead set on going belly-up. We're approaching one of those dark nights of the soul. I hope that literature lights up your way. Good luck!"

That book was my companion until the train station of San Sebastián. I entered Spain hand in hand with Honoré de Balzac, who was, as he would be so many times in the future, my refuge amid fear and uncertainty.

Chapter 4

San Sebastián
December 4, 1933

In October, the president of the Republic, Niceto Alcalá-Zamora, charged prime minister Diego Martínez Barrio with forming a center-left government, dissolving parliament, and holding new elections. The elections would be very close. For the first time, women were allowed to vote, and many people had predicted that this would lead to victory for the anti-Republican, right-wing parties that had come together in a coalition called CEDA. The left was more divided than ever. At least that was what Juan Delgado told me in the first conversation we had after months of exchanging letters. We were in a small restaurant in San Sebastián, not far from the border with France.

A few months before, I had read *Death in the Afternoon* by Ernest Hemingway, and I was expecting a Spain full of bullfighters, flamenco dancers, and wine. Yet the Basque city of San Sebastián looked more like Paris than Africa, with its neoclassical buildings and sensational seaside promenade where the high Spanish bourgeoisie were out on display.

"We're living through a truly unique time. The military was unsuccessful in its coup d'état last year. In the few years that we

Socialists have been at the helm, the country has changed more than it did in the last hundred years combined."

"So then why didn't your party win the elections?" My question was sincere, but Juan got huffy.

"It's the anarchists' fault. For fifty years or so they've been causing trouble with their revolutions and attacks. You've got to understand that, in Spain, the anarchists are more powerful than the Communists. They represent all too well the country's latent individualistic spirit. And the massacre at Casas Viejas has complicated things." Earlier that year, a small group of peasant workers from Cádiz took possession of some land, and the situation turned into a killing spree.

"Well, it seems like a typical pendulum swing then for the right wing to win now," I said, understanding very little of Spanish politics.

Juan shook his head. "No, this is a right wing that doesn't want the Republic to exist. It's a conglomeration of monarchists and Fascists. In a few days the new parliament session begins. The good news is that I've been elected as a member from the province of Madrid. I'm one of the youngest on the floor."

"Oh, Juan, congratulations! I'm so happy for you!" I put my hand on his shoulder, and for the first time my friend looked at me in a different way. We had not seen each other in months. We both knew it was something more than friendship, but neither of us dared to take a further step. We came from very different worlds and had very different plans for our lives. We both intuited that it would be best to wait and see how things played out.

"This evening our train leaves for Madrid. It's a sleeper car, but don't worry, our compartments are adjoining but separate."

"Thanks," I said, though in Germany it would not have been looked down on for us to share a compartment.

We walked along the sea. For being the beginning of December, the temperature was quite pleasant. The weather in Spain could not help but be better than in Germany.

"It's a beautiful country," I said, arm in arm with Juan.

People greeted one another as they passed, and the children running about in shorts looked so happy and healthy. Many of them were as blond as Bavarians.

"You'll soon see that Spain is a country of contrasts. We're an old and proud people, hospitable and passionate, capable of the highest values and the basest instincts."

Later, we made our way to the station. It was much smaller than the station in Paris but had a provincial charm like southern France. Soon we were leaving the Basque city behind and crossing the beautiful meadows and forests of the north. A few hours later, at nightfall, the groves turned into endless plains, the towns small and far between. We went to the restaurant car for dinner and were seated near a bourgeois family on one side and a newlywed couple on the other.

"What did you think of the food in San Sebastián? The food is one of the best parts about Spain!"

"Yes, it was delicious. I'm not very hungry right now, though, and it's pretty late for dinner."

In Spain, the hours for lunch and dinner were so different from Germany and the rest of Europe that my body was out of sync. I could not keep track of when I was hungry or tired.

"They say that Europe ends at the Pyrenees," Juan joked.

"You studied law at the Universidad Central, right?"

Juan nodded. "It's a beautiful campus, like something from the United States. The king donated the land, though I studied in the older buildings in Madrid. I like history a lot, but I studied law. My father is an old union man with the printing trade, and he told me that there I'd get trained to defend the working class."

While the second course was being brought out, I studied the newlyweds near us. They had eyes only for each other. On our other side, the bourgeois mother was scolding her children beside their passive father.

"I think it's best to stick with your vocation," I said.

"My vocation is to change the country," he answered dryly.

Juan reminded me so much of my father. My dad had sacrificed everything for politics and only now, with his wife gone and his children scattered, did he recognize that he had wasted half of his life for a pipe dream and that his home had ceased to exist.

"I believe in social justice, of course. But the foundation of the world is the family," I said.

"Mm-hmm, just look at that couple with their children," Juan joked. The couple was in a heated argument just then.

"I didn't say it was easy." I was a little miffed and disappointed. Juan had been rather cold and distant, only talking about politics and relying on irony in every comment. I was making every effort to speak in Spanish to get used to the language, and this stilted the free flow of conversation. He seemed like a different person from months ago in Berlin.

He must have been able to read my face. He placed his warm hand over mine and looked straight into my eyes. "I'm sorry. The past few months have been very demanding. The party is so divided, and I've been working more than twelve hours a day. Don't pay any attention to me. How was your trip to Paris? Tell me about that."

The conversation took an upward turn. I told him all about Sylvia Beach and about my hopes of opening a bookstore similar to hers in Madrid. "Where do you think a good location would be?" I asked.

"Probably near Ciudad Universitaria, where the university is, because hundreds of students would go by every day."

I nodded. "That sounds promising. First, though, I'll be working at a school called El Porvenir. It's on a street called Bravo Murillo, I think."

"Yes, right near the working-class neighborhood Cuatro Caminos," he answered. "It's run by some German Protestants. Spain doesn't take kindly to Lutherans, and they're generally considered heretics."

"Well, then I'll be a heretic!" I chuckled.

Despite my father being a Social Democrat, both sides of my family were full of ministers: Lutherans and French Calvinists.

Juan shrugged. "I don't really get religion. I was baptized as a baby but since then haven't entered a single church. In Spain, the Catholic Church has always been at the service of whoever holds power. The church is actually one of the biggest opponents of the Republic because it can't stand to lose its privileges."

"The church is strong in Germany, too, but probably not as much as here."

We spent the rest of the evening discussing books. My eye fell on a man dressed in a black suit at the back of the restaurant car. His pale face and little blue eyes barely stood out behind his thick glasses. I noticed he was constantly staring at me and Juan. It unnerved me. He reminded me of Gestapo agents.

We headed back to the sleeper car and stood chatting for a while in the hallway while Juan smoked a cigarette next to the window. Despite the warm air, I shivered with a chill, and Juan offered me his jacket.

"Thank you," I said.

"I'm very glad you've come to Spain, Barbara. You're my best friend. In politics, I can't trust anyone. They're comrades, not friends. My brothers are all tied up with the printing press, and I haven't seen my schoolmates in years. Talking about books with you is my favorite thing in the world." The longer he spoke, the more melodious his voice became, as if reciting an old love song.

We drew so close together that I could feel his breath.

"We'd better get some sleep. We'll be at Norte station within a few hours."

"Oh, right," I said, confused. For a moment I had thought he was going to kiss me.

Before shutting myself into my compartment, I glanced down the hall and saw the man from the restaurant. It was just for a flash, but I shivered again.

"Are you all right?" Juan asked.

"Yes," I said, looking back down the hall, but this time there was no one. I gave his jacket back. As I undressed in my compartment, I thought about Françoise and wondered how things were going for her in Berlin. I naively believed I would be safer than she was now that I was so far from the Reich.

Chapter 5

I was ecstatic upon arriving in the city. Besides Berlin, I had visited London, Amsterdam, Brussels, Vienna, and most recently, Paris, but Madrid was unlike any other capital I had seen. It was smaller and held something of the charm of a provincial city. Water carriers and street vendors roamed about, and at every corner there was a stand selling nuts or fruit or churros, a treat that did not exist in Germany. It felt like time stood still and like modernity and the old ways of the nineteenth century were at home together in Madrid.

Juan took me by taxi to El Porvenir. The building was clearly of German architecture, surrounded by a lovely yard on a wide street that led to a plaza with a fountain. The surrounding buildings were modest. Mixed in with the automobiles there were wagons pulled by horses or mules, bicycles, and a few motorcycles. The noise was intense but still not as loud as Berlin. I was surprised to find Spaniards so vivacious and loud. They stopped to talk with one another at a volume meant for all to hear, and they seemed to prefer being outdoors despite the cold of winter. At the first ray of sunshine, all the tables and chairs from the bars, pubs, and taverns came out, to be filled with groups complaining about the government or chatting among themselves over beer or wine.

Juan helped me with my heavy suitcases and pressed the bell. A porter dressed in a uniform eyed us cautiously but invited us in with a kind tone once I showed him my letter of recommendation.

We waited for María—she used the accent on her name now that she lived in Spain—only a short time in a wide, high-ceilinged hallway. The ambience was austere and functional, as if every German mark spent on the school's construction was carefully accounted for.

María came out from the secretary's office and ran to hug me. Her greeting took me off guard. In Germany she had never been effusive.

"Dear María! This is my friend, Juan Delgado. We met in Berlin last summer."

"I'm so pleased to meet you, Juan. Please, consider this your home for whatever you need."

Juan's expression was one of bemused curiosity. Though the school had been there for more than thirty years, most of Madrid still considered it an odd foreign incursion.

"Thank you, I'm delighted to meet you," Juan answered. Then he turned to me. "I'll pick you up for dinner tonight, if you'd like?"

There was no use in answering. I smiled, and he leaned forward and kissed my cheek. I stood there stunned. Once he had gone, I realized María had an impish smile on her face.

"It's completely normal for people to kiss one another on the cheek in Spain. Even men in the same family do it. So who is that heartthrob?"

I had not told my friend anything about Juan. She was so serious, always focused on helping others, and I knew she had no patience for frivolities. At times the Lutheran spirit was so rigid that it put decency and decorum before spontaneity. Yet I had the sense that living in Spain might have changed that for María.

She helped me carry my luggage to her room. We would share the room until I got settled in Madrid and could open the bookstore. My father and grandmother had given me quite a bit of money, and I had saved the majority of my salary from the past three years. After exchanging it, it would amount to a considerable sum in pesetas. Yet before I could look for a location and set up shop, I wanted to get a feel for the bookstores in the city and adapt to the language and customs. I had traveled enough to know that immersing myself in a new culture would not be easy.

"How was your trip?" María asked.

"Very interesting. I met a fascinating woman in Paris. She's an inspiration for the bookstore I want to start here in Madrid."

"Fabulous. A lot of people will try to dissuade you. They'll tell you people don't read much in Spain, but our mission has had a bookstore here in the city since the last century, and it's still open."

"I didn't know that!" I answered in surprise.

"Why don't you just leave your things, and we'll get settled later. The bookstore is in a central location. We can get there by trolley and then do some exploring."

I was thrilled to go out on my first excursion. We walked to the roundabout at Cuatro Caminos, where we hopped onto a trolley in motion like two college girls. Sitting next to my friend by the window, I was entranced by the city, completely new to me.

"Madrid is so different from Berlin," María explained. "There aren't a bunch of fussy buildings, and the city isn't obsessed with showing off its old imperial glory, but we'll see it all this weekend. I took today off so we could have lunch together and visit a few places downtown. I want you to see the Museo del Prado and the Biblioteca Nacional. The museum and the library are spectacular, and we've got time."

Just then a Romani woman dressed in rags got onto the trolley and started asking the passengers for spare change. The driver threw her out unceremoniously.

"Why did he do that?" I asked, indignant.

"Gypsies get a bad rap here. People think they're all liars and cheats. Spaniards are quite hospitable to foreigners but terribly racist toward the Gypsies and the Moors, which is what they call Muslims. It's all got to do with their history. More and more people are moving from the countryside to the city, which is growing by the day. Most are crowded together in wretched buildings in Lavapiés and other lower-class neighborhoods, or they build makeshift shelters in the vacant areas on the outskirts. The government, you'll come to see, is a wreck, though it was that way before the Republic too. The Spanish people don't obey their own rules and laws. In that sense they're very anarchic. But you'll get used to it."

Half an hour later, on a street off Gran Vía, we jumped off the trolley and looked at the architecture of a nearby church. Then we walked to the bookstore where an employee was sweeping up the glass of the broken front window. María greeted him and asked what had happened.

"Last night some kids from Acción Popular had themselves a party throwing rocks at the windows of the store and that church."

"Oh, it's been a while since we've had to deal with that," María said, as if trying to ease my potential fear. Surely she was unaware of the violence everyone in Berlin had been dealing with the past several years.

The man sighed. "It's just so tense now that CEDA won the elections. If it isn't the extreme right attacking us, it's the far left. There's one thing they agree on: The heretics should go."

"Forgive me, I haven't introduced you. Barbara, this is Joaquín Guzmán, the director of the Librería Nacional y Extranjera. Joaquín, this is my friend Barbara, and she'll be helping the mission this year teaching German."

"Pleased to meet you," he said, holding out his hand.

"Barbara wants to open a bookstore in Madrid, and I thought it would be good for her to talk with you. I need to go run an errand in the church. How about I'll see you back here in half an hour?" María said, looking at me.

"Yes, sure," I said, a bit intimidated to be left with a man I did not know in the least.

We went inside the bookstore, which had the same stripped-down austerity as El Porvenir. Most of the books were in German, joined by some in English and some in French. The Spanish holdings were primarily pamphlets and collections of the four gospels, as well as textbooks.

"Our catalog is none too broad," Joaquín explained. "We aren't a typical bookstore. We write most of the materials we print. The founder, Federico Fliedner, opened the store as a way to import books from Germany, publish textbooks for the schools he started, and translate a few important Protestant titles. Miguel de Unamuno himself has used some of our books."

"Miguel de . . . ? I'm not familiar with that name."

Joaquín's eyes bulged. "He's one of the greatest Spanish authors alive today!"

I shrugged in apology. "In Germany, there are very few books in Spanish available besides *Don Quixote*."

"Well, we're going to solve that at least for you. I recommend starting with Pío Baroja, who's practically a Spanish Dickens. His novels capture Madrid to a T. You've also got to read Miguel de Unamuno, especially *Saint Manuel Bueno, Martyr*. And the poetry of Antonio Machado, Clarín's novel *La Regenta*, and the plays of Valle-Inclán." As he spoke, Joaquín was pulling out books and piling them up in my arms. Then he arranged them carefully into a cloth bag. "Don't worry, I'll bring them to the school for you. It's too heavy to be carrying around."

"How kind of you," I said. "Would you tell me some about Spanish culture? What are the main bookstores?"

At that, he smiled. "I don't know how it is in Germany, but here, the writers meet together in cafés. That's where they hold their *tertulias*."

"Is *tertulia* a kind of food?"

Joaquín chuckled. "No, it's a talk, like an enlightened conversation among the masters of a craft—a literary discussion, if you will. The *tertulias* at Café Gijón are the most famous, but they also take place in Café Cibeles, in Cervecería de Correos, and in Café Lion. You've got to pay those places a visit, especially in the afternoon. That's where you'll find the great writers, philosophers, and poets."

"How interesting," I mused, jotting down the names in my notebook. Once I opened my bookshop, organizing events with local authors would be a great way to spread the word about it.

"Most of Spain's bookstores are in Madrid. In the whole country, there are maybe two or three hundred, and more than forty of those are right here in our city. On Alcalá Street you've got Romo Bookstore; on Puerta del Sol, there's San Martín; nearby, on Carrera de San Jerónimo, Fernando Fe's Bookstore is one of the busiest. The owner holds all sorts of art exhibits and literary forums. Francisco Beltrán's bookstore and publishing house is on Príncipe Street."

"Well, I think I've got my work cut out for me!" I joked.

"Oh, I'm not finished. Two of the most important are the Hernando Bookstore, on Arenal Street. It's also a publishing house. And then Casa del Libro on Gran Vía is the biggest. You cannot skip it."

"Do you think you could introduce me to an author?"

Joaquín scribbled an address on a piece of paper. "You need to visit the Palacio de la Novela, in Carabanchel. They call it a 'palace for novels,' but it's a paradise for books. There is no library or bookstore like it."

The name intrigued me, and I was determined to see this mysterious place.

Chapter 6

Madrid
December 5, 1933

That night Juan took me out to eat at a Basque restaurant called Jai Alai, which specialized in fish, soups, and stews. It had become a favorite of politicians in its ten years of operation.

"How was your first day in the city?" he asked after explaining that he was jittery about the upcoming ceremony in which he would officially take his seat in the Cortes, the Spanish parliament. He was both nervous and excited for the congressional session to begin and also about the second round of the elections. I gave him a summary of what I had discovered but was surprised to see him frown.

"Carabanchel is actually two zones," he explained. "There's Carabanchel Alto and Carabanchel Bajo. The one right outside of Madrid is Carabanchel Bajo, on the other side of the Manzanares River. The building you're talking about, the Palacio de la Novela, is almost smack in the middle. The problem is that it's a dangerous area for a woman on her own."

"Oh, I've worked in some of the roughest neighborhoods in Berlin. My mom helped out in a church that handed out food and clothing. I'm sure I can handle it."

Juan's brow was still furrowed. "I'm saying it for your own good. I can go with you if you'll wait a couple of days."

"I appreciate that, but since I don't start teaching till next week, I want to take advantage of the time I've got to visit several bookstores, including that one."

Juan leaned back against the seat as if conscientiously relaxing. "Madrid is full of thieves, pickpockets, and dangerous types. It's clear a mile away that you're a foreigner, Barbara. It really would be better . . ."

Now it was my turn to frown. I was a twentieth-century woman and did not need a knight in shining armor to rescue me.

"I'll be going tomorrow."

Juan raised his hands in sign of surrender. "All right, but please be careful. I brought you here tonight for a reason."

Just then a group of young men dressed in medieval garb with short capes and antiquated instruments waltzed into the reserved room where we were eating. I had no idea that it was a *tuna*, a popular kind of musical group made up of university students who traveled around singing and performing like minstrels.

After they played a few songs, Juan took a little box out of his jacket pocket. He opened it to reveal a shining diamond ring.

"But, Juan!" I gasped, my hands covering my mouth in shock.

Juan got down on his knee, held out the ring, and said, "I've never met anyone like you, Barbara. I want to spend the rest of my life with you. I would be honored if you would accept and become my wife."

I was speechless. Since I had been in Spain, he had seemed rather distant and irritated, very different from how he had been on the phone and in his romantic letters.

"Goodness gracious, yes, of course I will!" I said without another thought. My head was spinning. The reality was that he and I were barely more than strangers, but we had seen death come close. So much of the world was coming unraveled all around us, so I decided I had to live in the moment.

"It'll take us a few months to get everything organized. I'll introduce you to my family and help you open the bookstore."

He stood up, and we kissed for the first time as the *tuna* played in the background.

I thought of my mom and sisters, so far away. How I longed to tell them about this. I would have to be content to talk it all over with María when I got back to El Porvenir.

We returned to the school by taxi, though I was in a cloud. I could not stop looking at the ring shining on my hand. At the door, we said goodbye with another kiss. I hardly noticed the cold. I was floating on air as I opened the gate with my key and crossed the porch to the building. I was walking along the hallway when a voice startled me.

"Miss Spiel?"

I turned and saw light coming from an open door. It was the office of Teodoro Fliedner, the son of the founder of the school and current director of the entire Obra Fliedner, the mission of which El Porvenir was just one part.

"Good evening, Mr. Fliedner. I apologize for coming in late."

"Oh, not to worry. I simply wanted to meet you. I've just returned from one of our schools in La Mancha," he said from his spot on the couch.

I went in, and he stood and held out his hand. He looked German through and through, but his accent was native Madrid.

"I'm sorry we can't pay much for your services. It hasn't been a good year in that regard," he said with an apologetic smile.

"Don't worry about that."

"Things are all shaken up in Germany, as you know. It seems everyone has gone mad. Our denomination is bent on falling into the arms of an anti-Semitic fanatic. I traveled to several German cities last year and saw that lunacy has taken hold of our people."

"I'm sure things will get better," I said feebly.

"Would you like a cigarette?"

"No, thank you."

"It's a vile habit. I smoke just one and only at this time of night, when everything is calm. I've got to find funding for the children's homes and the schools, not to mention the churches. Protestants here in Spain are very poor, and they pay a very high price when they convert . . . Forgive me for going on and on. Surely you must be tired."

I sat on the other couch.

"My maternal grandfather was a Lutheran pastor, so I can understand a bit of what you're talking about," I answered.

"If the conservatives are in power, we'll have problems running our schools again. The Republic has been a breath of fresh air."

"I hadn't understood how difficult it was to do what your family has done."

"Well, I don't want to bore you any longer. I hope you have great success with your bookstore. If I can help you in any way, do let me know. Spaniards are crafty. Be careful, and don't sign any contracts without reviewing them with a lawyer. Many distributors are not to be trusted."

"Thank you for the advice."

Teodoro stood. "I love this country. I'm more Spanish than I am

German, but I still can't get used to the informality and chronic tardiness. Yet the Spanish know how to enjoy life more than we do, I can assure you of that. I just pray that the madness taking hold of Europe doesn't come here."

"I'm so glad to have met you," I said, heading to the door.

"Rest well. Tomorrow will be another day."

Climbing the stairs to the room I now shared with María, I thought back to all that had happened since I left Berlin. My life had changed more in those few days than in the past several years. I felt like I was starting over, far from the reach of the Nazis in their arrogant brown uniforms. In Spain, I could rekindle my joy for life and for books.

María was already asleep. I did not want to wake her for the sake of sharing my news. I undressed, stared at the moon reflected off the hushed streets of Madrid, and breathed in the fresh smell of night. I lay down eager to explore the Palacio de la Novela the next day.

Chapter 7

Madrid
December 6, 1933

Winter had come, though there was no snow yet and things warmed up when the sun came out. But that morning thick fog blanketed the streets. When I woke, I looked to the bed beside me, but María was already gone. In the dining room, I met the Spanish cook, and she brought me a cup of coffee with cream and toast with jam. I studied the map of Madrid and the surrounding areas as I ate. To get to Carabanchel Bajo, I could take either several trolleys or a taxi. It seemed worth the expense to pay for a taxi and save myself hours of public transportation.

The taxi driver who stopped for me at the Cuatro Caminos roundabout had a thick mustache. He hardly glanced at me before asking where to. But he turned to look when he heard my answer.

"Carabanchel Bajo? It's not a place I can recommend with all the lowlife that's arrived the past few years. Those country folk are more dangerous than they seem. Even children are thieves, and their girls will sleep with anyone for four cents."

"I'm headed to the Palacio de la Novela," I said.

He studied me in the rearview mirror. "It's the Castro publishing house, one of the biggest and most popular in Spain. I like a lot of their Westerns and detective stories."

"They publish popular fiction?" I struggled to ask in Spanish. His nod lowered my spirits a bit about the mysterious building awaiting me. At least I would learn more about books in Spain, I told myself.

The car made its way through a phantasmagoric Madrid to the Puerta de Toledo. After that gate, a bridge with the same name took us over the river. At first, the buildings were like those on the other side of the Manzanares, but as we entered Carabanchel proper, the houses were smaller and the streets dingier.

At the Oporto Plaza, the car stopped. The passersby hurried along with their faces covered and heads pushed down low against the cold. There were very few cars about, only a handful of wagons and a few bicycles.

"Do you want me to wait for you? You won't find many taxis coming by here."

"Thank you, but I'll be all right," I said, paying him. The cold cut deep into my bones as soon as I got out of the car. My coat was little help.

I walked along the dull plaza and found the street I was looking for. It was narrow and the buildings around looked abandoned, all except an enormous three-story edifice with a wide entry and huge sign overhead that announced PALACIO DE LA NOVELA. I stared at the structure but turned when I heard a noise. A man with his face half covered by a handkerchief was walking toward me.

"This way, ma'am," he insisted. He was short and his suit had seen better days.

"Pardon me?" I said.

In answer, he opened the door to the palace quickly and beckoned me inside to an open foyer. He closed the door and then met my eyes.

"This neighborhood is no place for a lady on her own," he added in a reproving tone.

"I'm German," I said stupidly, as if that explained my actions.

The short man took me in at a glance and then removed his hat. "Allow me to introduce myself. I'm Luis Fernández-Vior, and I'm a novelist. Or, rather, I'm a slave to the editor of this palace." His smile showed yellowing teeth. "What has brought you here?"

"I'm a bookseller," I said, not sure what else to offer.

"Then we're allies. Would you care to see the great Palacio de la Novela? I'll be your Virgil, guiding your steps through the inferno and paradise of books."

Then he broke out in Italian: "Lasciate ogni speranza, voi ch'entrate."*

---

* "Abandon all hope, ye who enter."

Chapter 8

I came to learn that Luis Fernández-Vior was one of the most widely read authors in Spain, though no one knew his real name and he would never win a Nobel Prize or even be admitted into the guardian institution of the Spanish language, the Real Academia Española. He was an intriguing fellow, with a common enough presence that he easily could be overlooked in any setting.

"This building is newer than it looks," Luis began in a tour guide tone. "Some say it was built over an ancient cemetery. Four years ago, the owner of the publishing house, Manuel Castro López, decided to sell all of his locations in Madrid and move to Carabanchel Bajo. Many think he made his fortune by publishing the classics, but that's a lie. He's amassed his wealth from the sweat of hundreds of writers who work twelve-hour days to churn out his little Westerns, romances, and war stories. I've been at it for the five years since I retired from police work."

His last comment really surprised me. "You were a policeman?"

"Well, I may look short, but I've always been strong. But the muscle I've used most has been my brain. In my book *Un crimen en barrios bajos* I describe some of the cases I investigated in my years as an officer. But the writer who's made the publisher the most money is Luis de Val. He wrote sensational society stories. You'll see that here in the Palacio there are all sorts of books— adventure, women's novels, and more salacious genres."

There was very little activity in the building at that hour. Luis paused before a green door.

"And now, allow me to show you the greatest library in Spain."

He pushed open the door and we entered a dark room. For a moment I regretted having followed him without measuring the potential risk. What if he were actually a lunatic? But then he flipped a switch, and several lightbulbs gave a loud pop as they flashed on. When the enormous room was all lit up, my eyes beheld tens of thousands of books.

"Here is where the masses of Madrid and Spain come to feed. You're looking at the true opium of the people. It's where Ortega y Gasset's 'mass-man' is formed, for you see, mass-man must first be emptied of his own story and history."

The perplexing words of my mysterious guide gave me pause.

He went on, "The role of the intellectual is the exact opposite of the politician. The politician wants to captivate the masses so thoroughly that the individual dissolves and disappears; the intellectual appeals to each individual so that none loses his identity."

"So why do you work here?"

"Because, like everyone else, I've got to eat. The pension of a retired policeman allows for few luxuries."

We walked through the bookshelves replete with thin books and collections, all of them cheaply bound.

"Look at this Dantean inferno. All human passions are found herein: lust, greed, pride, gluttony, rage, envy, and sloth—the anti-values that render human beings mere beasts. We writers feed the monster, turning the readers ever so slowly into brutes who have lost all sensitivity. We are the mercenaries of the lie."

Luis's words left me breathless. I had always known books to be and to do good. Of course I knew that Hitler had written *Mein Kampf*, a volume full of hateful lies; that the Russian secret services had published *The Protocols of the Elders of Zion* to incite anti-Semitism; and that the works of social Darwinism like *The Descent of Man* were destroying the foundation of humanism as we knew it. What I had not understood was that those renowned works and authors needed other publications to spread their vile messages.

"So it would be better if all of this burned to the ground, so that people wouldn't read them," I ventured.

"That has occurred to me many times, but we—at least many of my fellow writers—slip in messages of hope, justice, and mercy toward all people. It may be like a bottle thrown into the sea of indifference, but some—a few—will find it and understand. With all the venom circulating through the veins of society, hatred and disdain are destroying the world. Fascism, Nazism, Communism, and other radical ideologies will do away with us all."

We left the book inferno behind. On the second floor, Luis showed me a very different set of shelves. They held beautiful editions of the classics, the immortal works capable of transforming the heart.

"And here is where humanity can find redemption. These volumes make us more human and bring us closer to justice and to truth: Homer, Aristotle, Thomas More, Rousseau, Victor Hugo . . ."

That room was much smaller but was a delight to the eyes. From there we went to the top floor, the workshops where the books were printed and bound and the cubicles where the writers worked.

"I write from home, but many writers have to come here. One book a week to feed the masses hungry for blood, sex, and death. They say that movies will destroy the book industry; others say that the radio will. Who knows? When those in power find a new way of entertaining the masses, they'll try to do away with books. They're just too dangerous."

Luis led me past dozens of small tables to a large office with luxurious furniture trimmed in gold, leather chairs, and a display cabinet that held the jewels of the publishing house. A heavyset man with graying hair, a short beard, and dark glasses studied us as we crossed the threshold.

"What are you doing here, Luis? I told you not to come back until you'd finished your next book. You writers are a lazy lot. If I didn't crack the whip over your heads every day, you'd never finish a story."

The man's eyes turned to me, and I felt myself undressed before his disgusting leer.

"Who's the dame?" he asked Luis.

"Mr. Castro, this is Barbara Spiel, a German who wants to open a bookshop in Madrid."

"Oh, how daring! Especially in these times, what with no government and the Republican system going to hell."

I had no words to answer.

"Yes, well, I was just showing Miss Spiel the Palacio de la Novela," Luis said as the editor stood and came over to us. He was much taller than he had seemed when seated.

"A bookseller . . . Don Miguel de Cervantes said the pen is the tongue of the soul, which makes you a dealer in souls," he concluded, licking his lips.

"And makes publishers the devil," Luis said, knowing full well how his comment would affect his boss.

Castro rose up to his full height but kept smiling. "It's a risky profession. We never know if the books we print will sell. People eat bread and drink milk but don't have to read to survive. We deal in the intangible. Everyone accuses us of greed, but they haven't put their prestige or fortune on the line."

He walked over to the display case, opened it with a key hanging from a chain around his neck, and took out a beautiful volume.

"There are five books every publisher wants to own, because they're the most dangerous books in the world: the *Book of Thoth*, written in ancient Egypt; the *Book of Dzyan*, which explains the origin of all things; the Voynich manuscript, which the Habsburg Holy Roman Emperor Rudolf II discovered; the *Necronomicon*; and, no less important, *Malleus Maleficarum*, the *Hammer of Witches*. That last one was written by two monks to weed out witches in the Middle Ages. Because of it, tens of thousands of women throughout Europe were murdered. Books can be dangerous, so we editors have to take care of our readers."

Luis snuck a glance at Castro, who took no notice.

"I wish you well with your bookstore. We're at your disposal, but do take care with what you sell. My publishing house can provide you with what people really want to read."

As we walked out of his office, the words of that abhorrent man resounded in my ears. My hairs were standing on end. Luis walked with me back through the streets of Carabanchel, now full of people since the fog had cleared. We said goodbye when we found a taxi.

"I'm at Café Gijón every afternoon if you'd like to talk with more writers. It's been a pleasure getting to know you, Barbara," he said, taking off his hat.

As the taxi pulled away, I still felt shaken. I could not tell if the Palacio de la Novela was actually a reader's paradise or if its walls hid the very inferno Dante had described.

Chapter 9

Madrid
December 17, 1933

I had been in Madrid for almost two weeks, and time had flown by. In the mornings, I worked at the school before having lunch with María and other professors, most of whom were Spaniards. María and I spent the afternoons together, and after dinner with Juan I tried to make headway on my thesis. Yet every day it felt less likely that I could ever return to Germany to defend it.

A couple of Sundays before Christmas, María convinced me to go with her to the German Evangelical Lutheran church on Paseo de la Castellana. That Lutheran chapel was the epicenter of the German expatriate community in Madrid, but I had no desire to get close with my fellow Germans. If things were tense in Germany, the situation was sure to be similar in a microcosm of its society.

The entryway to the beautiful chapel would easily be overlooked from the street, nestled as it was between two mansions. It led to a small courtyard, where a covered walkway with columns and arches joined the two church buildings. Rose windows stood out from the white-and-yellowish façade. The surprise came after the courtyard, though: Inside, the church looked more Orthodox than Lutheran. An enormous mosaic in the apse presided over everything. The altar itself was modest, and the stone baptistery was the only adornment. An organ sounded from the back.

María greeted several people and introduced me formally. Everyone was very nice, but no one asked me anything about myself. When we found a spot in a pew, I tried not to think too much about my mother's family. The building made me recall a childhood that would never return.

The homily was short. The pastor spoke about needing to love our enemies, an appropriate subject for the times we were living in. When the service ended, we went to an adjacent room for tea and pastries.

"I hope the sermon didn't feel too long for you. I know it's hard for young people these days to appreciate liturgy from the last century," the pastor said. He was a bald man with glasses and an intellectual air.

"Don't worry, I grew up in the church of my mother's parents. My mom was very devout, though my father wasn't," I said.

"I understand. Faith is a very personal matter, but most people try to make it a public issue. In a few weeks, the theologian Dietrich Bonhoeffer will be coming to give a series of lectures. We know each other from his time as a curate in Barcelona. My superiors were none too pleased that I had invited him, given his recent call to pastors in Berlin for peaceful resistance to Nazism."

The minister's comment took me by surprise. For some reason I had presumed everyone at the service would be a Nazi sympathizer. Our conversation was cut short, however, when a man slowly approached. The minister paled visibly and said, "Excuse me, ladies. I need to tend to others in the flock."

The man who had caused the minister such discomfort kept

walking toward us. His round glasses were familiar to me, but I could not place him.

"Señoritas," he said in painful Spanish before switching to German. "I hope you are enjoying this lovely chapel. Kaiser William II had it built in 1909 right beside the German embassy. The emperor had a chapel built at that time in three important cities: Madrid, Rome, and Jerusalem. It was a display of the empire's strength. The architect, Richard Schulze, went for modesty, given that freedom of religion has always been a thorny subject in Spain. The building's design is highly symbolic, reflecting the three states of man. In the first two capitals, nature is protected by two angels; the following show the Word as the only way to reach God. Finally, two Cerberuses protect the door, keeping evil at bay. You may be wondering why I'm telling you all of this. I studied architecture in Germany, but now I am at the service of the Reich. We want Germany's glorious past to return. The government accepts no beating around the bush. You're either with us or against us."

The threat in the man's words turned us as pale as the minister had been. And just like that, the stranger sauntered away. María and I exchanged a glance.

"They've come to the school to threaten Teodoro too. They must be from the Gestapo," she said.

"I've had my run-ins with people like that, and they're dangerous," I answered before asking if we could leave.

We took a long walk back to El Porvenir. Juan and I had planned to have lunch together that Sunday. Since the new government would soon be named and a new session of the Cortes had begun, he had planned a meal at his parents' house for me to meet his family.

"When will the wedding be?" María asked.

I shrugged. "Probably in the summer. Before the school year is over, I hope to open the bookstore. But first I've got to find a place, negotiate with distributors, figure out imports, and hire an assistant. I'm not sure I can plan a wedding and open a bookstore at the same time."

"I can help; you know you can count on me for whatever you need," María said and took my arm.

Juan was waiting for us in his new car when we walked up to the school, elbows locked. He greeted María in German and then opened the car door for me.

"Are you all right? You look pale."

I told him about our encounter with the Gestapo agent in the Lutheran church, but he was not surprised in the least. "There are more British, German, Italian, and Russian spies than anyone can count these days. Madrid is a beehive of conspiracies. The military has calmed down a bit with CEDA's victory, but they're miffed that Alcalá-Zamora has turned the cabinet decisions over to Lerroux's radicals. With Hitler in power, Fascism keeps spreading in Europe. Many see Mussolini as a statesman, a viable alternative to the Soviet Union, and Hitler takes radicalism even further."

The car wound its way through the streets of Madrid toward a residential area at the end of O'Donnell Street. I spent the time trying to make sense of the endlessly complicated scene of Spanish politics.

"Wasn't Mussolini in the Italian Socialist Party?" I asked with true curiosity.

Juan shifted uncomfortably. "It's best not to say things like that in my house. My father is a union man, a defender of the working class. He won't tolerate comments like that."

"I'm sorry; I won't," I said, confused. "In my house, there were no taboo subjects or things we couldn't talk about."

Juan realized immediately that his comment had upset me.

"Forgive me. You can talk about whatever you want to with my parents. I'm just nervous, that's all. It's the first time for you to meet my parents, and I want everything to go well."

I stroked his shoulder. "Don't worry about that."

We parked in front of the house, small but aesthetically pleasing. There was something British about it, and the lush front lawn gave it a welcoming look. Juan opened the gate, and an old mastiff came up, wagging its tail.

"Good boy," Juan said, scratching its back.

My fiancé's mother came out the front door. Mrs. Leonor Delgado had a kind face, gray hair with specks of its earlier blond, and green eyes that were wide and bright despite her age. She wore a simple dress. Juan's father stood stiffly behind his wife. He was wearing a black vest over a white shirt and matching pants.

As Juan's mother gave him a hug, his dad shook my hand. "Marcelo Delgado Ponce; very pleased to meet you."

"I'm delighted," I got out before Mrs. Delgado turned her hugging energy to me.

"Come in, come in," she insisted. "Everything's ready."

I was comforted to see that, except for minor details, families are rather similar no matter where you go. Juan's two brothers were seated at the table and stood to greet us when we came in.

Mr. Delgado sat at the head of the table, served the wine, and passed the bread around. We ate a stew called *cocido*, which, they explained, was a popular dish in Madrid.

"Do you like Spain?" one of Juan's brothers asked to break the ice. They were both younger than Juan and still lived at home.

"Well, I haven't seen much of it, but what I have seen is delightful," I answered.

"Oh, it's an impoverished, backward country," Mr. Delgado said.

"Marcelo, let's not start in on politics. Sundays are family time."

"Spain is in trouble, and this young lady knows it very well." He nodded in my direction but kept his eyes on his wife. Then he turned to the rest of us. "The Fascists have taken over Germany, one of the most powerful countries in Europe. Austria's got a semi-Fascist government, and it won't be long until the plague spreads to more countries. The Nazis have copied our ideas about rallying the people, but they've given it a Nationalist coat of paint."

"Well," Juan jumped in between mouthfuls of soup, "here we've got the president of the Republic to make sure that public institutions are respected."

"That worthless Andalusian is a bourgeois we can't trust," his dad snapped.

"Sanjurjo is in jail, and the officers that rebelled have been transferred to other posts," Juan countered.

"That's not going to stop that pious clique of hypocrites. They're the same ones that supported Primo de Rivera's dictatorship and that accursed king."

"Well, Pablo Iglesias, our founder, came to an agreement with the dictator and managed to get the country to take a few social steps forward." Juan relentlessly sought equanimity. It was one of the things I liked most about him. In notable contrast to most politicians, he never acted sectarian.

Marcelo turned red and smacked the table with his fist. "What kind of Socialist deputy are you? Those kinds of comments give our enemies the advantage over us. Don't think for a second that you're going to change the world from your seat in parliament. We, the UGT unionists, we are the ones who've broken our backs for Spain."

Mrs. Delgado placed her hand gently on her husband's arm to calm him down.

"Please, Marcelo; we have a guest. I don't want her thinking we're a bunch of brutes."

Mr. Delgado took a deep breath and calmed down. When Mrs. Delgado brought out freshly made flan for dessert, the conversation topics turned gentler. We spoke about soccer and bulls, the two subjects it seemed most Spaniards could agree on.

Chapter 10

I wanted to go with Juan to the Cortes when the new cabinet was installed. The legislative session of parliament had begun more than a week ago, and the deputies took heated, contrary positions. They were constantly interrupting one another, and the chairman could barely keep order and ensure that each speaker's turn was respected.

The cold had come to stay. Despite my coat, my legs shivered as I sat there in the old building. María and I were watching Juan from the space reserved for visitors. He looked so handsome and put-together that morning.

The chairman recognized Lerroux, the new prime minister, who stood to deliver his speech.

"Mr. Chairman and my fellow parliamentarians: We are here on this cold December day for the Cortes to ratify the new cabinet. A few months ago, when the president of the Republic placed his trust in me, I promised to hold new elections so that the Spanish people could speak. Never before have elections in our country been so representative. For the first time in our history, women have been able to vote. In this, let my colleagues from the opposition recognize, Spain takes the lead among the advanced nations of our world. According to the parties on my left, we are considered too conservative, yet while my party defended women's right to vote, the supposed progressives fought against it. One interpretation is that we are making strides, but only when it is electorally convenient. Even one of the most influential female parliamentarians on the left, who has voice and voting power in this very assembly, sought to deny the vote to those of her own sex. But I am not here to bring reproach. I want to inspire. I want to help Spain be once again as great as it has been in the past."

The applause from radicals and representatives of the CEDA party competed with the boos and jeers of the Communists and Socialists. The whole scene smacked more of a work of drama than a legislative session.

The prime minister continued, "A few months ago, our tongue-in-cheek motto was, 'We who are about to die salute you.' The extremists want to destroy the Republic. Just a few hours from now in the Teatro de la Comedia, the Fascists—pureblood Spaniards but as dangerous as those in Italy and Germany—will hold a rally. Let us be reasonable. There is still time for negotiation and mediation instead of tension and conflict. Our people deserve peace, bread, and work.

"The economic crisis devastating the world has reached us. Let's get through it together, not leaving anyone behind. Let's not pit one class against another, Catholics against nonbelievers, the poor against the rich. Are we not all Spaniards? Heirs of a glorious past, of an empire on which the sun never set. Let us walk together down the constitutional path. May this Republic that the people declared some two years ago turn our land into the most advanced and prosperous nation in Europe and the world," he concluded.

The pro-government parties stood with long, fervent applause while the rest booed Lerroux from where they sat. After comments from a few representatives of other parties, it was Juan's turn. I could tell by the way he approached the stand how nervous he was. He took a sip of water, cleared his throat, and began.

"We have made a mistake, and our enemies have taken advantage of it. Our former prime minister, Mr. Azaña, made a mistake. The Nationalists and a few of our parliamentarians wanted to hasten changes that have taken centuries in other countries. We are all Spaniards, but there are many ways of feeling and expressing this. While José Antonio Primo de Rivera and the Fascists who support him critique the democracy of Rousseau and say that liberal democracy is dead, many of our own think the same."

People from every side of the floor were booing my beloved. I knew that Juan would try to bring opposing positions together, but the hatred and dissension were deeply entrenched.

He went on, "The Fascists say that putting little pieces of paper in a ballot box is a conspiracy. That's what they call it. I have traveled throughout several countries this year, including Germany, France, Austria, Great Britain, and the Soviet Union. With deep concern I have confirmed that totalitarian systems are quickly spreading on all sides. People want stability over safety, but we don't have to choose just one of those. In my own party there are many good-hearted servants, and we must come together before the radicals suppress all our freedoms. Let us not fall into the same trap as the Italians, Germans, and Russians.

My comrade Largo Caballero recently said that generosity is not a good thing and that we should not be as generous with the conservatives as we were in 1931. I say that without heartfelt generosity there can be no harmony. And without harmony, there is no peace. Let us not take Spain to the edge of an abyss from which no one and nothing can save us."

As Juan descended from the speaker's stand, all but two or three deputies booed him. María and I got to our feet in the visitors' gallery and applauded. I felt very proud of Juan. He was risking his political career for the good of his country, something that very few were willing to do.

Chapter 11

Madrid
January 15, 1934

Christmas had been rather bleak that year, especially the night of Christmas Eve. I thought a lot about my mom and the little presents she used to hang on the tree for us to open Christmas Day. Besides the presents that Santa Claus brought us, my mom would spend weeks preparing small surprises. Most of them were ordinary things, like underwear, colored pencils, or money. But we would get more excited about them than about what we had asked Santa Claus for in our letters. In Spain, they celebrated Three Kings Day the night of January 5. The Fliedners' schools had adopted both celebrations, to the joy of all the students.

Some students boarded at El Porvenir and remained separated from their parents throughout the school term. These children from Protestant families traveled back and forth to the capital with the hope of finishing the last two years of high school and then going to college, something far beyond the reach of most Spaniards, especially those from humble backgrounds. I had developed a soft spot for a student named Tomás Fuentes. Dark haired and rosy cheeked, he was from a minister's family in Cantabria and was quite shy. He did not have the mannerisms typical of kids from Madrid, and most of his classmates scorned him. He was quite intelligent, capable, and hardworking. He spent much of his time studying in the library, and German came easily to him. I loaned him books to help broaden his vocabulary.

That day I had plans to join Luis Fernández-Vior for his afternoon literary discussion at the Café Gijón. Luis and I had gotten together a few times since my visit to the Palacio de la Novela, and he had given me a list of Spanish authors who were required reading. His list was even longer than the one from Joaquín, the bookseller from the Librería Nacional y Extranjera.

On my way out the door, I noticed Tomás standing nearby. "How are you, Tomás?" I asked. He smiled at me, but then I caught sight of the bruise under his eye. "Oh, what happened? Was it Sergio again?" Tomás did not answer. Sergio was a bully known to beat up the weaker students. "When I get back, I'll speak to Mr. Fliedner about it. Go to the kitchen and get some ice to put on your eye." He nodded and went off in that direction.

Luis was already waiting for me on the street with a taxi.

"Good afternoon, Barbara. Some of my colleagues are eagerly awaiting you. I've told them about you and your plans to open a new bookshop in town."

"You didn't need to do that! I'm just a German philologist, not a writer. I hope they don't have the wrong impression!"

Luis smiled as he shut the back door of the taxi, then sat up front by the driver. He called back to me, "We'll be there in fifteen minutes if traffic cooperates."

Traffic was rather slow at that hour, especially at the Plaza de Colón and along Recoletos, but the driver got us right to the door of the restaurant.

Café Gijón looked plain enough on the outside, but it was

decidedly elegant within. The waiters wore white uniforms with gold buttons, like admirals in the navy.

As soon as we entered, a cluster of men sitting in one corner called out to us.

"Luis, over here!" called one man, waving his arm.

We went over, and the two men hugged.

"Allow me to introduce you two. Barbara Spiel, Ramón J. Sender," Luis said, pointing to us in turn. "Among our little group of friends, Ramón is our *tertulia* leader."

The rest of the group stood and shook my hand amiably.

"This isn't what it used to be, ma'am. These days the pubs are more popular. Twenty years ago, the greatest minds in the country would gather here, along with famous actors and even bullfighters. But now the students at the Institución Libre de Enseñanza have found other spots. There are just a few of us faithful booklovers left here," Eduardo Dieste Gonçalves explained.

"Don't bellyache like an old man," Ramón said. Then he turned to me and asked if there were literary cafés in my country.

"Not that I'm aware of, and certainly not now with the Nazis in power."

"In Spain, the custom of *tertulias* dates back to at least the seventeenth century. Starting in the 1820s, writers and intellectuals would gather at clubs and cafés for debates and discussions on a wide range of subjects, especially politics. But tensions have grown such that we no longer want politicians to participate, even though some like Azaña are old friends," Ramón explained.

"Some of us come here for inspiration and to write," Luis added.

"Oh, I could never concentrate somewhere this noisy," I confessed.

Luis began, "Our subject for today has been chosen in your honor." I smiled at his syntax. He had switched from addressing me with formal pronouns to the informal second-person pronoun in Spanish. It meant that they considered me one of them. Luis went on, "Here we're all informal with one another, grammatically speaking. It doesn't bother you?" I shook my head. Luis continued, "So our subject today is bookstores in Madrid. We're all bookworms, and I'm pretty sure we've been to every, or almost every, bookstore in the city. In my opinion, the best place to buy books is . . . Cuesta de Moyano! Barbara, that's a cobblestoned pedestrian street that takes you to Retiro Park. It's lined with bookseller stalls of mostly used books, and I've found a few really fantastic editions there for a very low price."

Eduardo went next. "Another famous street is Libreros—you can't get more literal than that." I nodded. *Librero* was the Spanish word for *bookseller*. "It's where university students buy their books, which are mostly used. Most of the stores there are run by women, the most famous being Doña Pepita's store and Casa de la Troya. The legend goes that two dragons lived inside the well on Libreros Street. That was how they used to scare kids away from the area because, besides bookstores, there were a number of houses of ill repute."

Another member of the group, Sebastián, piped up next. "Miss Spiel will soon learn that there aren't as many bookstores in Madrid as there are in Paris or Berlin. Our people aren't given to the written word. There's a historical reason behind that: For the Inquisition, anyone who could read and write was a potential heretic, since the Moors and Jews tended to read their sacred books. Christians from long ago and many nobles prided themselves on being illiterate. Well, some things don't change. In your Protestant world, it's common for there to be a bookstore in or near every church. It's not that way in Spain, or at least it wasn't until the Protestants came, people like Federico Fliedner, the founder of your school. After that, Catholic bookstores started popping up everywhere—"

Ramón cut in. "All right now, Don Sebastián, we don't need a history lesson. We're talking about important bookstores, remember."

Sebastián huffed at Ramón and finished, "Well, there's no debate that the best bookstores downtown are Hernando's bookstore and publishing house and then the Casa del Libro."

Luis nuanced the discussion for my sake. "Let's admit that Spanish booksellers could not be accused of being overly friendly. When you go into a store, they look at you askance, as if they don't actually want to give up any of their treasured volumes. They don't like amateur readers or people who just drop in for a gift. Our booksellers like odd ducks, adventurous types who want to submerge themselves in unexplored fields and undiscovered authors. That's when their eyes light up. They suddenly drop the apathy and their distrust in humanity to become the nicest people on earth."

"I think you're being too harsh on them, Luis," Ramón countered. "They've got to price their books at a figure that's unreachable for the vast majority of pockets, and even then they barely clear a profit. To make a few coppers they spend hours and hours breathing in bookshelf dust, fingers crossed that one book leaves so another can take its place."

"No one has mentioned the latest book phenomenon in Madrid," Eduardo said provocatively. We all turned to him.

"Which is?" I asked innocently.

"Rafael Giménez Siles's experiment. Barbara, he's a pharmacist from Málaga—now an editor—who expressed his protest to Primo de Rivera's dictatorship by founding a publishing house. Many foreign books have been translated into Spanish thanks to him. He's the motor behind the Madrid Book Fair."

Eduardo nodded. "The fair was held in April and was a smashing success. I'd never seen so many people interested in books before."

"Siles is a pure-breed editor, not like my publisher. He's the one who got John Dos Passos printed, as well as *All Quiet on the Western Front* by Remarque."

"True, but he's also a consummate Communist. His publishing house released *Das Kapital*," Eduardo said with a sniff.

"Freedom of press and all that?" Ramón quipped. I later learned he was a well-known anarchist.

"We're staying away from politics, remember?" Sebastián said, eyebrows raised. "But if Barbara opens a bookstore, she'll have to have a stand at next year's book fair, and then everyone will know about it. Forgive our rudeness; we've hardly let you get a word in." My ears picked up on the pronouns he used, which were the formal way of addressing a person.

I smiled at them all. "Do use the informal address with me, Mr. Sebastián. In Berlin I worked in a Jewish bookstore that sold books in several languages, especially English and French. I also have a friend who opened a shop in Berlin dedicated to selling French books. Mainly I just want people here to be able to read more French and German books."

The gentlemen around me shook their heads sadly.

"It's hard enough to sell books in Spanish. I can't envision people lining up to buy foreign titles. Most Spaniards have a hard time with other tongues," Eduardo explained.

"My friends, don't discourage Miss Spiel. We're looking for a spot near Ciudad Universitaria. If you know of any possibilities, do let us know. She's hoping to open shop in early spring."

"Well, that's my dream time frame," I clarified. But the dream seemed further and further away from becoming reality.

"Don't give up; my friends and I will help you," Luis said.

I left the café with a lightness in my step. Since I had arrived in Madrid, I had spent much less time working on the bookstore project than I had hoped. Teaching, worrying about German agents, and planning the wedding had taken up most of my time.

The taxi dropped me off at the front door of El Porvenir. Before bidding me farewell, Luis promised to go with me to look at options near Ciudad Universitaria that might work for the store. I opened the gate and went inside El Porvenir's campus. It had gotten late, and most of the lights were already out. I heard voices coming from Teodoro's office. The sound of a German accent I recognized all too well froze me in my tracks.

"This is a German school funded by German money. So you will teach German and Spanish children the values of the Reich."

"I've already explained that I do not hold those values," the calm voice of Teodoro said.

"Then I will ask your mission in Germany to replace you with someone who does; if they do not comply, I will see to it that no further donations arrive."

"You can't do that! Hundreds of children depend on those donations."

"Poor little Spaniard wretches don't concern me. Many of them will just end up Communists like Indalecio Prieto."

"We provide education in Christian values, but then each student takes his or her own path. I can assure you that the values of the politician Indalecio—"

The Gestapo agent interrupted with a loud outburst: "You're just a Socialist, a damned revolutionary!"

Teodoro took a deep breath and quietly spoke. "You had best move along before you wake the children."

The agent stormed out of the office. I remained hidden in my spot in the shadows.

Teodoro closed the gate to the street and, heading back to his office, ran smack into me.

"Miss Spiel, what are you doing here?"

"I overheard everything as I was coming in."

"I don't know what you heard, but you can forget about it. I've got my convictions. They aren't exactly leftist, but what those mobsters want is intolerable. What kind of scum is in charge of our country these days?!"

"You've hit the nail on the head. They're gangsters like Al Capone."

"Go on to bed now, Miss Spiel. Joaquín mentioned your bookstore project to me. We can help you get set up with several distributors if you'd like."

His unsolicited offer felt like confirmation that I needed to get to work as soon as possible.

"Thank you!" I said, throwing myself at him with a big hug. Teodoro received it with awkward stiffness, but he did not chastise me. I ran to my room and told María all about my day. That night I let my imagination roam freely about what it would be like to open a bookstore in Madrid. I did not want anyone to wake me from that dream, not even the ghosts of Nazism or the dark hour sneaking up on Spain.

Chapter 12

Madrid
January 25, 1934

My beloved Juan had faced problem after problem since his speech in parliament. Largo Caballero, Indalecio Prieto, and Fernando de los Ríos were all Socialist ministers in Azaña's cabinet but could not have been more antagonistic. Many had called for a revamping of the Socialist Party given their losses in the recent election, but party leaders refused, perhaps to avoid being ousted by more extremist leaders. Like Juan, Indalecio Prieto was a reformist, but Besteiro was a pure Marxist and Largo Caballero was a Stalinist. Many Socialists wanted to expel the right through strikes, marches, and revolutions, but Juan thought this would only deepen the country's economic crisis. While my fiancé waged his political battles, I plugged away at my project of opening the bookstore. Preparing for the wedding fell into the background.

Luis took me to visit a building in the Moncloa area, on Donoso Cortés Street. It was small but spacious enough to start out. I would have to paint, buy furniture, and apply for a business license. Luis offered to request it in my name to save me the hassles often faced by foreigners.

In our room at El Porvenir, while I drew up plans for distributors and how to decorate the bookstore, María came in. She was all dressed up as if going to a party, which was something she never did.

"Why aren't you ready yet?" she asked.

I scrunched up my brow trying to think of what she might be referring to.

"Barbara, you know, the lecture by Dietrich Bonhoeffer, the theologian."

"Oh!" I had entirely forgotten. "Oh, well, maybe I should stay home . . ."

It was bitterly cold outside and had already gotten dark. I knew I would much rather stay warm and cozy and keep making headway on my business plans.

"Come on, this is a once-in-a-lifetime opportunity. Bonhoeffer is one of the few people who's dared to speak out against Hitler. For that reason alone we should go."

I nodded and got dressed quickly, choosing the warmest clothes I had. Half an hour later, a taxi dropped us off in front of the Lutheran church. I had expected throngs, but there were only twenty-some odd people scattered about the chapel.

The pastor's face lit up when he saw us. He ushered us forward to introduce us to Bonhoeffer. He was a well-kept man in his twenties with fine blond hair and a pronounced chin. He was indeed the prototype Aryan.

"Dietrich, these young women, María von Hase and Barbara Spiel, are teachers at the Fliedner school, El Porvenir."

Bonhoeffer smiled and shook our hands. "The Fliedners have been a great inspiration to German Christians. They founded the deaconess movement and promote solid education every-where they go."

The minister leaned forward. "Half of the people here tonight are Nazi spies," he said in a low voice. "None of the Catholic leaders or renowned intellectuals have dared to come out. What a country!"

"Don't be grieved, my friend. I love Spain and her people. Once they're allowed access to education and they wake up, they'll rule the whole world!"

Bonhoeffer took a seat at the table at the front of the chapel, beside the minister. All other conversation quieted. María and I sat in the front row to avoid having to look at Nazi agents.

The pastor's opening words were brief. "Our guest needs no introduction, so I'll turn the night over to him."

Bonhoeffer cleared his throat and began. "It's been said that evil triumphs when good men do nothing. These proverbial words are applicable today as never before. The evil razing the Western world is not evil in its purest state; rather it is the lie that has us believe that our adversary is an enemy who is nothing but malignant. The powerful political movements, not unlike many religions, aspire to wipe out all dissident voices. Rousseau and Nietzsche have already commented on the dismantling of the paradigms that have governed society for some two thousand years.

"Most people are not malicious; they are simply stupid. The self-satisfaction of stupid people makes them more dangerous than wicked people. Stupidity is more pernicious for humanity than bad behavior. We can resist evil and fight against it at all costs, but we are powerless against humanity's stupidity. Stupidity cannot be contained by brute force or by protest. Human stupidity is deaf to reason: Fools do not listen to arguments and are un-moved by facts.

"Humanity lost the intrinsic values of Christianity, and philos-ophy has been adrift since then. Nazism, just like Communism, has replaced religious feeling and used it to its advantage. Thus, our struggle against Nazism is not against an ideology; we are actually facing a false religion, complete with false gods, priests, and even a sacred book.

"Nazism has taken root among the common people who do not understand the world we live in and who feel scared. Stupidity is not bound by social class nor level of education. There are stupid people with spry intellects, yet they are stupid because they do not think for themselves. They have delegated that crucial function to others. Man without God feels so alone that he joins the crowd in order to belong to something bigger, to fulfill a mission, to find purpose in life. Nazi power depends on the stupidity of the Ger-mans, but also on their loneliness, as they have lost the sense of community the church used to offer.

"The truly stupid people aren't the ones who don't reason but those without the critical thinking necessary to counteract the lunacy of their world. The problem is that any one of us can be-come an evildoer if our critical thinking is stunted. This is why, today more than ever, we must examine all things and cling to the good."

When he paused, a handful of people applauded while others quickly vacated the chapel.

"Are there any questions for Dr. Bonhoeffer?" the pastor of the church asked those of us remaining.

My hand shot up.

"Go ahead, Miss Spiel."

"But hasn't the church been at the service of the powerful?"

The theologian nodded. "Yes, when religion appropriates faith, it becomes an institution. The work of the church is not just to tend to the wounded, those crushed under the wheels of the cart, as it were; but to throw ourselves into the spokes of that wheel to stop it, though it cost our lives."

His words stunned me. His way of talking about religion had nothing to do with the rules and expectations I had been taught. That man was talking about pure love, the kind of love that leads to sacrificing oneself for others.

Chapter 13

Things were not going well in the country. There had been an anarchist insurrection in December 1933 before the new government had even come together. Among the insurrectionists, about seventy-five people died and at least a hundred were wounded, while the police forces lost fourteen, with at least sixty wounded. The government wanted to revise certain articles from the 1931 Constitution to appease the Holy See, since several Catholic schools had been closed, the Jesuits had been expelled, and many convents had been burned in the early months of the Second Republic. Basque Country and Catalonia rejected the centrist leaning of the new government and threatened to declare independence.

I wrote to Françoise Frenkel with the ridiculous hope that she might be able to come to my wedding, but her reply was dismal. Things in Germany had worsened in the months I had been gone. Besides political parties, now there was a ban against all unions, newspapers not controlled by the regime, and the self-governance of federal states. Françoise assured me that, far from making a dent in Hitler's popularity, these restrictive measures had increased it. Jews faced increasing pressure to get out of Germany, and life had become frankly unbearable. It was next to impossible to import books, and the store saw fewer and fewer clients. Françoise was set on staying, though, until she could stand it no longer.

Some of the most influential left-wing leaders were invited to our wedding. For security reasons, it was held on an estate outside of Madrid. Juan feared some sort of attack by the extreme right.

My mother-in-law helped me into my dress. None of my family members had been able to come, and I was sad. Besides María and Luis, the few friends I had in Madrid were Teodoro and his wife, Joaquín, and some of the teachers from El Porvenir, including Teodoro's sister, Catalina. One of the problems we had faced in planning the wedding was whether or not to have a religious ceremony. Juan was agnostic, but his mother wanted a Catholic wedding; I was Protestant, but I did not care what kind of ceremony it was. Juan's father wanted a justice of the peace to perform the ceremony. Like most engaged couples, Juan and I felt like the only ones without a choice in the matter.

Eventually it was settled that we would have a civil service but that Teodoro would speak.

That morning the sun shone brightly in Madrid. The blue sky was our church dome and the trees of the lovely lawn beckoned us to paradise lost. Juan was waiting at the front while the judge turned a disapproving eye to the extravagance of flowers and wedding decorations. Spaniard austerity, especially that of the Republican era, contrasted with that red Socialist wedding. Dressed in tailcoat and top hat, Luis escorted me.

As I walked toward the podium that served as an altar, a few tears escaped and ran down my cheeks to my exposed neck. Luis winked as he handed me over, and the sparkle in his eyes made me smile.

The judge was brief. After Juan and I exchanged rings, we were invited to kiss. Everyone clapped and cheered, and Juan and I took a seat. Teodoro stood up and looked around at those gathered. Most were Juan's friends, the majority atheists or agnostics, not counting Indalecio Prieto, who always implied that he believed in God.

"We are here to celebrate the union between Juan and Barbara," Teodoro began. "Marriage is not a sacrament, at least not for us Protestants. We believe that the union between a man and a woman is always recognized by God. The book of Genesis says, 'Therefore shall a man leave his father and his mother, and shall cleave unto his wife: and they shall be one flesh.' 'One flesh' means so much more than sexual union. Above all, it is a mystery how those who were once two are made one. Certainly we continue living as two people externally"—here his exaggerated gestures indicating me and Juan solicited some laughter from the attendees—"yet God sees only one. These two, if they want their union to last, must come to see themselves as one. Getting married is so much more than a commercial transaction, a bringing together of two households; likewise it is so much more than mere emotions. Love must turn into deep friendship to prosper. Those who today dream of being together forever will soon enough be longing for their former life. Self-abdication, self-sacrifice, and putting the other first are the instruments of true love. The apostle Paul describes love masterfully in his first letter to the Corinthians: 'Charity suffereth long, and is kind; charity envieth not; charity vaunteth not itself, is not puffed up, Doth not behave itself unseemly, seeketh not her own, is not easily provoked, thinketh no evil . . . Beareth all

things, believeth all things, hopeth all things, endureth all things.'
That is true love.

"Juan and Barbara, I hope that the love you profess today in
public leads you down the path of life and stays with you till your
dying breath."

Juan and I stood at the sound of the wedding march, and people
began to clap, whistle, and whoop. We processed out of the seating
area, and while we took wedding photos, the guests enjoyed the
appetizers. By the time we returned, the guests were already seated at
their places under a large white tent. Joining us at the head table
were our closest friends: Luis, Teodoro, and his wife were on our
right. Juan's parents were on our left. At a nearby table sat Teodoro
Jr., who also worked with all the projects of the Fliedner family.

Indalecio Prieto came up to congratulate us. He was a smiling,
friendly man.

"Congratulations to you both! You're crazy to be getting married
in times like these, but the Republic needs new sons and daughters.
And so, cheers!" he joked, raising his wineglass.

Prieto turned to Teodoro. "I've got to say, I enjoyed your sermon. You're aware that I grew up at the missionary school in Bilbao
run by José Marqués. My parents sent me because it was what they
could afford, but I learned quite a lot from those men of God. I wish
it really were love that ruled the world, as you exhort, but I'm afraid
that's just not the case."

"Yet we've always got to give it a chance, don't we?" Teodoro
replied.

"Our enemies aren't going to come give us a big hug. We all
thought that the Republic would unite us as brothers. It hasn't. It's
the same old story: Those with privileges are loath to give them up."

"Would you give up yours?" Teodoro asked.

Prieto sighed and stroked his chin. "I suppose not."

"These things are solved through dialogue, but it's hard for us Spaniards to listen to one another."

Teodoro's inclusivity surprised the Socialist politician. Prieto asked, "You consider yourself a Spaniard?"

Teodoro nodded. "My family has been here for two generations. For us, Germany is a place to get resources and rest up every once in a while, but I'm afraid that nothing remains of the country my ancestors knew."

"That's a pity. I hope we don't get ourselves in a similar situation here."

Teodoro shrugged. "The future of the country truly is in your hands, Indalecio."

The politician looked at him with an ironic smile. "You see that lot over there? They've got the majority in the party. Extremism is always more attractive than dialogue. Pray for us—we're going to need it."

As Indalecio Prieto walked away from our table, the worry on Teodoro's face startled me. Despite the excitement over our wedding and the upcoming opening of my bookstore, a dark shadow hung over me. It was as if the hatred I had tried to leave behind had taken root in Spain as well and was itching to consume everything.

Chapter 14

We decided not to take an official honeymoon. We had planned a road trip to the northern coast later in the summer. In the meantime, we were happy with a night at the Hotel Nacional and another in Toledo. Juan wanted to show me that thousand-year-old city. Yet I was distracted with all the details about the bookstore. It had taken more time than I thought to get the space ready, to turn it into a place where people could feel welcome and at ease. I had set up a children's corner, which was cutting-edge for bookstores in Spain at the time. They were generally geared toward middle-aged men in liberal professions. I had also set up a juvenile literature section and a corner for events like lectures and recitals.

As we headed back to Madrid from Toledo, my head was spinning. There were only a few hours before the inauguration, but there was so much to do.

"What's on your mind, love?" Juan asked. He had shown his affection freely since the wedding.

"I'm worried we won't get back in time. I was hoping to make sandwiches and pick up some extra drinks."

"It'll all work out, don't worry," he said, resting his hand on my leg.

The two nights since our wedding had been marvelous. I had never been with a man and had hardly even kissed my first and only boyfriend, Juan. I was very nervous the first night, but Juan was so tender. Half an hour later, we were both enjoying our new-found freedom with each other. The next day, in Toledo, we were more interested in getting back to the hotel than in seeing the city.

I shook my head and came back to the present moment. "I hope so. Luis said he'd bring some friends to make sure everything was ready. Maybe I should've pushed the opening back a week."

As soon as the city skyline came into view, my heartbeat quickened. We had stopped at a restaurant on the way, but I had hardly touched my food. There was a sizable knot in my throat. The day held a strange undercurrent of loneliness, and I longed for my father or one of my sisters to be there with me.

Juan parked half a block from the bookstore. There was only an hour until the grand opening. We walked up, and I saw that the door was already unlocked. "What . . . ?" I looked nervously at Juan, but he just pushed the door open. I was shocked to see ten or so people waiting inside to surprise me. One of them was my father. I flew into his arms and burst into tears like a little girl. I breathed in the scent of his cologne and the unique smell of his suit.

"Dad!"

"My darling, I'm so sorry I couldn't make it for the wedding. All the countries in Europe are on high alert. They held me up at the border of France an entire day. But at least I made it in time for the opening. The place is magnificent, Barbara!"

Not letting go of him, I showed him all around. Luis came up and showed me the food table with platters of neatly arranged canapés and sandwiches.

"Does it meet the lady's approval?" he asked with mock deference.

I grinned. "The only thing missing is the people." I had very low expectations. It was a gray, rainy day—normal for Berlin, but guaranteed failure for an event in Madrid.

"They'll be here, have faith," he said, signaling to two young women to move the glasses and wine to another table.

An hour later, all the chairs were placed. Ramón J. Sender had agreed to say a few words, and I knew that Teodoro and others from the German expatriate community would be there.

Ten minutes before Ramón was to begin, half of the chairs were still empty. I checked the clock incessantly in my anxiety. Juan wrapped his arms around me and, after giving me a kiss, said, "Relax. Some dreams are slow to come true. There will be other days."

"Yes, but this is a beginning with bad luck."

"You don't believe in luck," he chided.

Just then Ramón showed up with several friends. He introduced them to me, and they took their seats. Then came Teodoro and his wife, several of their grown children, some of El Porvenir's teachers, and quite a number of my students. By this point the room was getting full. Then some of Juan's friends from the party, including Indalecio Prieto himself, walked in. A few minutes later, everyone was crowded into the back of the bookstore.

I stood to address them all. "Thank you so much for coming to the opening night of Madrid's newest bookstore, the Librería de Madrid. The name may not sound very original, but with it I pay homage to the city that has given so much to me. My father and my husband are both here, as are my in-laws and so many friends. Welcome to you all."

The crowd applauded, and I sat down between Luis and Ramón. Luis took my place in front to introduce the night's speaker.

"Books—our eternal companions. Tonight we inaugurate a new home for culture to find a place to flourish in this Spain full of caciques, uneducated people, fanatics, and sectarians. Opening a bookshop is always a way of staring down the impossible: Why would people come and buy books? Of course they'll buy meat or fish, milk or bread, but books? It never ceases to amaze that a handful of paper turns into something of value due to a bit of printed ink. So the great Ramón J. Sender is here to explain exactly what it is in books that makes us fall in love with them."

Ramón stood ceremoniously, milking the drama as if he were going to deliver a sermon.

"This, ladies and gentlemen, is not a store. It's a temple. What you see on the shelves and on the tables or what's showcased in the front windows are not objects or even symbols. They are windows and doors to other worlds. You may think I'm exaggerating, and perhaps that's the case. I am an author, after all, and so histrionics come naturally to me. We writers are the prophets of today. Begging the pardon of the political leaders here with us tonight, I hazard to say that politics and ideology have devoured everything. Man is no longer free; he is a slave to modernity. It has taken his time, his dreams, and even his soul. Yet when we open a book, the world is re-created, as if we were back in the paradise we lost.

"From antiquity, books have been one depository for the sacred, a gift the gods used to communicate with humankind. That is why this bookstore is a gift for the city of Madrid.

"Thank you, Barbara, for this wonderful gift. And now, there's food and drink for all!"

The audience stood and applauded over their laughter. María and several of her friends served drinks. A few writers came up to congratulate me, and others came to try to sell me their books.

I felt so loved and cared for in this place that was not *my* city. I decided that from then on I would write my name with the accent: Bárbara.

The night was better than my wildest dreams. Then a rock came soaring through the front display window with a crash. It was wrapped in a piece of paper that I hurried to smooth out. I read the handwritten note aloud: "We won't let you get away with poisoning the minds of Spain's youth. Defenders of the Nation."

I looked at Juan, and he shrugged. Then I looked at all the silent faces gathered around me in the store. I raised my glass and said, "They won't get us down. Let the party continue!"

Part 2

Of Books and Children

Chapter 15

Madrid
March 12, 1936

Time had flown by. The bookstore had developed a reputation among the students coming and going in Ciudad Universitaria. I held a book club and organized activities for children on Saturdays, as well as presentations and small classical music concerts. I loved the hours I spent in the store, a haven from the swirl of violence and danger all around.

Françoise Frenkel and I continued to write letters. She kept me up-to-date on what was going on in Germany. Foreign currency was hard to come by, and the Nazi regime was working hard to improve its image before the upcoming Olympic Games in Berlin. I was also having a difficult time importing books. It seemed that industries worldwide were slowly preparing for war. Full-blown censorship had hit German bookstores, and the police confiscated books by authors like Voltaire. Clients had learned to get to the bookstores first thing in the morning after a new shipment to buy the books they wanted before the authorities removed them.

Things were not like that in Spain, though political violence was on the rise. It had affected me as well.

The Falange, an extreme right-wing Fascist party, had many supporters among university students, especially those in the law school. From time to time they painted their symbol, the yoke and arrows, onto the front window, egged the store, or filled the lock with glue.

Luis and I had become very good friends. He helped out in the store in the afternoons, which were the busiest hours. Juan spent most of the day at party headquarters or in congress. Throughout 1934 and most of 1935, the political climate was very turbulent. There had been an attempted revolution in Asturias that required the army's involvement, an attempt at independence in Catalonia, and street fighting between parties.

The general elections in February 1936 did little to calm the country. The Popular Front was a conglomerate of leftist parties, and right-wing groups accused them of electoral fraud. The election results were so close in most districts that the winning of a seat came down to a handful of votes.

Deputies from the right and the left had been tossing threats around freely on the parliament floor. That day some of the threats moved from words to reality. Juan showed up at the bookstore in the afternoon with terror on his face. He was about to faint. I led him to a chair and Luis went for water.

"What's going on?" I whispered. My first thought was that something had happened to his parents.

"They've tried to kill Luis."

"Which Luis?" I asked gently.

"Luis Jiménez de Asúa."

Juan was very close with Luis Jiménez, a professor who spoke out against the Primo de Rivera dictatorship and had a big role in drafting the 1931 constitution.

Luis handed Juan the water and asked, "How did it happen?"

Juan gulped down the water, loosened his tie, and lifted his clear, open eyes. I was so grateful he had not lost that transparent look amid everything going on in the country.

"We think it was revenge from the Falange for Juan José Olano's death yesterday. He was the university student attacked supposedly by leftist activists."

"Oh dear God," I said, shaking my head, though the worst was yet to come.

"This morning I was going to meet up with Luis to go together to a student rally at the university. I was walking up as he was coming out the door with his bodyguard, Jesús Gisbert. I waved at them, crossed the street, and got into Luis's car. We'd gone only a few yards when three men opened fire on us point-blank. The bullets hit the bodyguard and grazed my arm but didn't even touch Luis."

That was when I first noticed the bloodstain on his jacket at the shoulder. I helped him get it off and saw the torn shirt.

"They already treated it at the hospital. It's a superficial wound, but this complicates everything. After the doctor cleared us, we went to the Ministry of the Interior, and the minister told us he'll order the arrest of all the high-ranking Falange leaders."

It would be one step closer to the abyss. Gil Robles of the right-wing CEDA party had not recognized the Popular Front's victory in the elections, and the right was extremely displeased with the amnesty law. Yet a good part of the left also ignored the laws. One wondered who still supported the idea of the Republic.

We heard a ruckus in the street. A right-wing student group was marching, and as they went along, they broke the store windows of businesses owned by supposed leftists.

"I'd better go lock up," Luis said, heading for the door. He was lowering the roll-up metal door when two Falange students pushed him down, kicked him away, and hoisted the metal door back up.

Juan jumped to his feet and pulled out his gun from his jacket. He was authorized to carry it due to the risk factor of being attacked.

"Don't do anything!" I yelled, following him out to the street. The students were about to break the window with a metal rod when they saw Juan with the gun.

"Go on, you son of a bitch, shoot us!" they yelled, swinging the rod threateningly close to Luis.

"Move along and you won't get hurt."

"We're not afraid of you. We'll be back and burn this nest of red shit to the ground!" one of them screamed. He could not have been older than eighteen. But they did run off.

I helped Luis up, and Juan offered to take him home by car. I closed the store for the day and, still shaking, got into the car. Luis was lying down in the back.

"We'll take you to the hospital," Juan said.

"No, for the love of God, don't. I'm fine; nothing is broken. A nice grappa then straight to bed, and I'll be like new in the morning."

Juan helped Luis get up the stairs to his flat and then we headed home. I could not stop shaking.

"Don't worry, those pigs will pay for what they've done," he said, resting his hand on my leg.

I shook my head and, through tears, said, "I don't want any more violence. That's why I left Germany."

At home, Juan opened the car door for me as well as the building door. We took the elevator and went inside our apartment.

The heat was on high. I collapsed into a chair in the living room and dissolved into tears again.

"Do you want us to leave, to get away from Madrid?" Juan asked gently.

I shook my head and looked at him with vision blurred by tears. "Where would we go? It's like this everywhere. We can't get away from the craziness."

He took me into his arms. The comfort of his body against mine and the sweetness in his voice as he spoke managed to relax me. "I'll take care of you. Nothing's going to happen to you. Things will calm down soon. It's just the aftereffects of violence from faraway places. Spaniards are a peaceful people. I truly don't think we'll have another civil war. The last century was a mess, but we've learned our lesson."

I wanted to and tried to believe my husband's words. He knew the situation better than I did, as I was still a foreigner in this land. I listened to the sound of the rain against the windows and thought of how the world would keep turning despite us—we human beings who thought we were so important but were no more than fleeting shadows, the traces of which would be gone within a few short years.

Chapter 16

Madrid
May 24, 1936

That Sunday morning the weather was perfect. The political scene was still bleak, but I felt so happy that it seemed nothing could ruin the opening of the fourth year of the Madrid Book Fair. The stands along Paseo de Recoletos sparkled as we booksellers raised the roll-up doors to greet the thousands of readers waiting impatiently.

The trees provided welcome protection from the almost-summer sun. Magnolias, lindens, acacias, and planes lined the long strip while the recently planted flowers showed off their bright colors to passersby. Over the noise of the nearby traffic, birdsong added more melody to the calm Sunday morning already ringing with the city band's rehearsal of the "Himno de riego," which had become the new national anthem.

Despite increasing street violence and the endless security issues, Juan Bautista Bergua, together with Rafael Giménez Siles, had managed to pull off another year of the book fair.

Posters on the trolleys advertised the fair with quotes from famous authors like Cicero, Roger Bacon, and Pliny the Elder. The success of the publicity was seen in the throngs filling the street. Most people were waiting by the information booth since the fair itself was off-limits until the opening ceremony.

Juan came by with a few government officials, including the director general of security, José Alonso Mallol. A few minutes later they were joined by the vice president of parliament, Luis Jiménez de Asúa; the prime minister, Santiago Casares Quiroga; the mayor of Madrid, Pedro Rico; and several others.

Then President Manuel Azaña Díaz arrived with the highest level of authorities all dressed in cutaway coats. They cut the ribbon, and the fair officially began.

The writers all around me were exultant on this, their special day. My hands were sweating. Beside me, Luis waited calmly for our illustrious clients to approach. The government officials were making the rounds to each stall. Azaña spoke briefly with each bookseller, shook his or her hand, and continued his tour.

The president stopped at the Bible Society stand to speak with Adolfo Araujo García.

"How marvelous that colporteurs are no longer persecuted for selling Bibles as they were in the days of Borrow," Azaña said.

"We're thankful for that and hope those times never return," Araujo responded, handing the president a pocket edition of the Bible.

"Thank you," he said, nodding and looking at the leather-bound book. "I'm not sure if Spain needs more Bibles or more schools."

"Well, those aren't incompatible, Mr. President."

The entourage reached the stand of the Ruiz brothers, which was next to mine. Azaña paused to leaf through several books.

Juan was a few paces behind the higher-ranking authorities, but our eyes met for a moment. Then the president was standing before me.

"I've never been to this bookstore. Is it new, ma'am?" he asked me.

"I'm Mrs. Spiel de Delgado. We opened shop two years ago near Ciudad Universitaria. We primarily sell novels and all sorts of books in French and German."

Luis Jiménez de Asúa stepped in. "She's Juan Delgado's wife."

"Ah, of course, the German. It's a pleasure to meet you."

"Thank you," I responded, smiling as they moved along.

The thirty-seven stands of that year's fair were soon packed with visitors. Juan returned to mine and blew me a kiss.

"See you tonight. Hope it all goes well!" he called.

I still had butterflies in my stomach anytime I saw him. True love only grows with time. He was the most important person in my life, and his mere presence filled me with joy.

Luis whistled and rolled his eyes at us. "Oh, you lovebirds," he said with a wink.

Three hours later, when I was about to take a lunch break, I heard a familiar voice. "Mrs. Spiel?"

I looked up to find the pastor of the Lutheran church on Paseo de la Castellana.

"Good afternoon, I'm so happy to see you. Would you like to see any of our books? We have several German theolog . . ." I trailed off as I saw him shaking his head.

"No, but I'd like it if you would join me for coffee. I have something important to discuss."

His tone and tight face startled me and told me I should acquiesce.

Café Gijón was nearby. At that hour it was full of people having lunch, but there were a few tables reserved for the fair's booksellers. We sat at one of these. After looking carefully around him, the minister blurted out, "Things are about to get really bad in Spain."

"I know there's a lot of political tension, but once it's summertime, everyone will go on vacation and kick the problems down the line to September." I spoke with deliberate levity to counteract his weightiness.

"No, Hitler's tentacles reach farther and farther. They're sending me back to Germany. The denomination is controlled by the Nazis, and they want only pastors who espouse their beliefs to represent in other important countries. Thanks to one of my parishioners, I've learned some disturbing news."

"Why are you telling me?"

The waiter brought two cups of coffee and a plate of pastries. The pastor waited until he left.

"Spain has had secret agreements with Germany since 1928, but the government doesn't even know about them. General Bazán signed an agreement with Wilhelm Canaris about the exchange of information between the secret services of the German army and the Spanish army. An agent has been asking about you."

"Me?" I was floored.

"They know you're the daughter of an important Social Democrat leader and deputy."

"My father is living in exile."

"For them, once an enemy, always an enemy. Watch yourself."

I tried not to take the warning seriously.

"The left runs the government right now, and they won't deport me. Plus, my husband is a Spaniard."

"I'm not talking about deportation. The Gestapo doesn't use legal means."

"Oh, I see."

"Be very careful. The Nazis are planning something. The ambassador bought a copy of *El Sol*, one of the few newspapers that doesn't cow to the Reich. They're in contact with Gil Robles and the Falange. And a German businessman living in Spanish Morocco, Johannes Bernhardt, is trying to get Hitler to support the Spanish military."

"Support them for what?" I asked innocently.

"For a coup d'état. The military has never aligned with the Republic. Sanjurjo is in exile, but he hasn't been idle."

"The people support the Republic," I argued.

"In the big cities, yes. But in small towns and the countryside, Republican ideas haven't taken hold. This is a country of uprisings and coups. You need to be very careful and, at the first sign of danger, get out of the country."

I shrugged. "Where could we go?"

"To Great Britain or Mexico. Anywhere far away. One last thing . . ." Without realizing it, I had been digging my nails into the palms of my hands. He leaned even closer to me and continued, "Warn your friend Mr. Fliedner as well. The Nazis want to shut down or take over his schools."

The minister stood and looked all around, his black hat a wrinkled mess in his tight fists.

"Will you stay in Germany?" I asked.

"No, I've got family in Austria. I'll be safer there."

The beating of my heart quickened as I watched him walk away. If the pastor was right, Spain might become a military dictatorship like in Portugal or, even worse, a Fascist regime like in Italy. I had to get to Juan as soon as I could and tell him what I knew.

Chapter 17

Madrid
May 24, 1936

Back at the fair, I told Luis that I needed to run some errands and asked him to stay and close up the stall that afternoon. He cocked his head at me but did not ask any questions.

"You look pale," was all he said.

I shook my head. "I'm fine."

I took the trolley toward the congressional building. I got off at the Plaza de Neptuno and walked up Carrerra de San Jerónimo. I remembered Juan saying something about having lunch at the Palace Hotel. Two porters dressed in livery jackets opened the doors for me. I had hardly stepped inside the foyer when a thin man with very short hair approached me.

"Mrs. Spiel."

It took me aback that he knew who I was.

"Forgive me for startling you like this. My name is Alan Hill-garth, attaché to the embassy of the British crown."

"Do I know you?"

"No, but we've been watching you. You're well connected in the German community in Madrid. You sell books to the German school, to the embassy, and to many members of your community.

Today you were approached by the Lutheran pastor of the church on Paseo de la Castellana."

I was speechless. The man went on, "I don't know what the minister told you, but be very careful. German spies and the Gestapo are watching you. No one followed you here, which is why I've risked speaking with you directly. Yet there are spies in the hotel too. Would you come with me to a private room for a brief conversation?"

Without waiting for a reply, Hillgarth took me by the arm and led me to a small adjacent room. Two waiters were changing the tablecloth, but they left when they saw us enter.

"We have something in common, you and I. I write novels, which is why I could go to your bookshop without raising suspicions. My country needs a spy."

"I'm not a spy. Are you being serious?"

Hillgarth crossed his arms and answered, "Do I look like I'm joking? Your father has requested asylum in Great Britain. He no longer feels safe in the Netherlands. It's up to you whether his request is accepted or denied. War in Europe is unavoidable. We don't know just how far the Nazis will go, but we suspect that they will get a long war started in Spain as a trial run for their weapons and strategy and as a show of force."

"Will that happen soon?"

"It's likely a matter of weeks. The Nazis are trying to get the high-profile Germans out of Madrid in case the coup is unsuccessful in the capital. The four branches of secret services in operation here are on alert: Canaris's Abwehr, Ribbentrop's Office of Foreign Affairs, Himmler's SD, and a few private informants."

I tried to control my shaking, but my body was reacting to the stress the only way it knew how.

"Your mission will be very simple. We'll see each other in your bookstore once a week. You'll inform me of what you're hearing, seeing, and discovering at the church, the German school, and anywhere else you visit under the auspices of your work. In exchange, we will offer you an escape route should things turn ugly. And the visa for your father."

"Can I think it over?"

Hillgarth shook his head.

"Very well, though I have no idea how I'm going to do it."

Hillgarth brought several things out of his pocket: a miniature pistol, a tiny camera, a pass for entry into the British embassy, and a key.

"The key opens a safety deposit box at the Banco de España, the national bank. Inside it you'll find enough money in pounds to flee the country if you're in danger, but you must alert us first."

The spy put his hands on my shoulders and smiled. "War makes strange bedfellows. Don't forget what's at stake. Spain is a powder keg. We aren't sure which is better: a government in the hands of the extreme left or a right-wing military regime. For now, orders from London are to support the Republic and keep the Nazis from achieving their goal. Good luck."

He left me alone in the room. I did not know whether to go home, run to the hotel dining room and throw myself into Juan's arms, or go back to the bookstore and pretend that nothing since my lunch break had actually happened.

Chapter 18

Madrid
May 24, 1936

In the end, I went back home. I paced back and forth in front of the window and peered out the lace curtains a thousand times. I was obsessed with the thought that someone might have followed me home, but everything looked normal. I called María to ask if I could pay her a visit the next day. That would give me a chance to talk with Teodoro Jr., who had taken over directing the Fliedner projects after his father retired at the end of the previous year. I still did not know him very well, nor did I have a read on whether or not he squarely opposed the Nazi regime. But from what the Lutheran minister had told me, I gathered that Teodoro Jr. was not a rabid fan of Hitler.

I had fixed a light supper of chicken soup and cod fillets cooked the way Juan liked. He had called to tell me he would be home soon, but it was already past nine o'clock. When finally I heard the key turn in the lock, I ran to the door and jumped into his arms before he had even gotten inside.

"Are you all right? This isn't an everyday greeting," he said.

I tried to smile but could not get my face to work. Instead, I broke down weeping with the day's stored-up tension.

"What happened? Have you had news from back home?"

"No. Let's talk over dinner. It's probably all cold by now."

I served the soup, and while Juan scarfed it down, I told him about my run-in with the minister. He gave no reaction, as if reserving all judgment until the end. Then I described what happened in the Palace Hotel. That did provoke a reaction.

"They asked the wife of a deputy in the Spanish parliament to be a spy? Those English pirates have no respect."

"You aren't surprised about the military coup?"

Juan started on the cod. I had hardly touched my plate, my nerves having quelled any appetite.

"We're not fools. The secret service has been keeping an eye on the generals and several politicians, not to mention the party's internal spy network. On March 8 some of the most important generals met together: Mola, Orgaz, Franco, and some others. They agreed to stage a coup and set up a provisional military junta headed by General Sanjurjo."

"I thought he was in Portugal."

"He is for now, but that doesn't stop him from conspiring. It was a mistake to pardon his earlier coup attempt. We know that the ringleader here inside Spain is General Mola, who's in Pamplona and is trying to get the Carlists to join. We also know that the attempt will occur in July, using some planned military maneuvers as pretext."

"So what is the government going to do?"

Juan shook his head.

"Nothing?" I was aghast.

"They already tried something like this in thirty-four, but they don't have the balls for it. They were conspiring back in February as well. I'm telling you they won't be able to pull it off. They know that the people are on our side."

"But they have the support of the Nazis and the Italian Fascists. That English spy told me he doesn't know who his country will support if the military rebels. That's why the right keeps trying to stir up trouble. They want it to look like war is inevitable. Plus, the left is committing its own share of crimes," I said.

Juan frowned at my last comment. He was a just man but, at the end of the day, belonged wholeheartedly to a left-wing party.

"The opposition will never come together in agreement. We know all their movements thanks to General Juan García Gómez-Caminero, who is loyal to the Republic, and thanks to the UMRA, the Republican Anti-Fascist Military Union. Their informants keep us up-to-date. Also, the director general of security has bugged several phone lines to keep tabs on the generals."

Just then I grimaced. There were shooting pains in my abdomen.

"Are you all right?" Juan asked.

"Yes, I think—" Another stab of pain kept me from finishing.

Then I felt something wet between my legs. I looked down and saw that it was blood.

"What's going on?" Juan asked, now visibly afraid.

I looked up but could not speak. Then I passed out. When I opened my eyes, I found myself in a hospital room.

Chapter 19

Madrid
May 25, 1936

My stomach hurt terribly and I felt nauseous. I started when I saw a nun dressed in white taking something away from the room. Juan jumped up from his chair and took my hand.

"It's okay, sweetie, I'm here."

"What happened?" I croaked out. I was very thirsty.

"The doctor gave us some good news," he said. His eyes were shining. "You're pregnant!"

"What?"

"But you have to be on bed rest for a few weeks. It seems it's something of a high-risk pregnancy."

Though I had known that I could get pregnant anytime, the news bowled me over.

"Wow, that's . . . that's wonderful!" I tried to sit up, but a new shock of pain forced me back down.

"Don't move. You need to stay here tonight. Tomorrow I'll bring you home, but you have to promise me you really will stay in bed."

"But there's so much work right now. We're in the middle of the book fair. I can't just . . ."

Right then Luis and several of our writer friends appeared at the door. They surrounded the bed and Luis explained things to me.

"The fair is a smashing success, and everything's going fine. I found an assistant. You don't need to worry about a thing."

"But it's too much work for you," I countered.

"I'll be at the bookstore in the mornings and at the fair in the afternoons. The assistant will cover the rest of the hours. She's a French bookworm and I'm sure you'll get along famously. So now you have no excuse not to rest."

The rest of the group blew me kisses and filed out. Once we were alone again, Juan said, "I'll stay here in the hospital with you tonight."

"No, you've got to work tomorrow, and I'm totally fine here. Go home and get some rest."

Juan, who had already spent the previous night and the entire day in the hospital waiting for me to wake up, gave me a look of something between relief and guilt. He got his hat, kissed my forehead, and, before leaving, said, "I'll be back tomorrow at noon to pick you up. Get some sleep."

I was exhausted. As soon as the lights were off, I drifted into a very deep sleep that turned into a nightmare. In my delirium, someone was chasing me through the streets of Madrid in torrential rain. There were men with scary black dogs. I woke up right as they were about to get me.

I opened my eyes, but it was very dark. The quiet of the hospital was interrupted only by an occasional moan from a far-off room. I groped for the glass of water on the bedside table, but it was just out of reach.

"Here's the water," I heard from the darkness. I nearly jumped out of my skin. "Have I frightened you?"

The voice was terrifyingly familiar. It was the same Gestapo agent I had seen on the train I took to Madrid and who had threatened me and María in the Lutheran church. It had been a long time since I had seen him. He had not been at any of the important events held at the German embassy.

"Why are you here?" I croaked.

The man drew close enough for me to see his face among the shadows.

"I came to warn you. I believe that the Lutheran pastor troubled you yesterday at the fair. Don't worry about him anymore. He now rests in peace."

My heart was racing. "What did you do to him?" I eked out.

"He's gone to meet his maker. You should know that for several years we've been inclining public opinion in Spain in our favor. Our press attaché has done a fabulous job, and we spare no expense for this endeavor."

"Why are you telling me these things?"

"Because with the snap of my fingers I can have you kidnapped and whisked off to Berlin. The only thing that keeps me from doing so, which is a little problem we can surely overcome, is that you have many contacts and friends, and your husband is a Socialist parliamentarian. If you came to work for us, you would be safe from harm."

I could not believe my ears. "Be a Nazi spy? That's what you're suggesting?"

"A patriot. You are German, are you not?"

"I left the country and have no plans to return."

The man stared at me. In the dim streetlight coming through the window, his pupils looked like two empty saucers, but something like a little flame sparked in them.

"It seems to me you haven't quite understood. We are going to win this war and will rule the world. The Aryan race is superior to all others. The Third Reich will last for a thousand years, and whoever's not on our side will die. If you refuse to collaborate, once our allies take control of Spain, I'll come back for you and take you back to Germany. Is it clear now?"

My mouth was drier than ever, and I was struggling for breath. Compounding my fear of this man was the new fear that my panic would make me lose the baby.

I nodded. It was all I could do in that moment.

"In the chapel of the church there is a door that leads to the embassy. Here is the key to that door. I'll expect a report from you every two or three weeks. Understood?"

"But I don't know anything," I pleaded.

"Spy on your husband and his colleagues and on other members of the German community. Find out who's on our side. All information is useful at present."

Without a sound, he slipped out of the room, but his disgusting cologne lingered for hours, reminding me of his threats. I had no choice but to be a double agent. If either side discovered me, the consequences would be unthinkable. I vowed within myself to do everything I could to trick the Nazis and spoil their plans in Spain, even if it cost me my life.

Chapter 20

Madrid
July 17, 1936

I stayed home for several weeks, not just in the effort to avoid a miscarriage. I was afraid of running into the Gestapo agent. I knew it was ridiculous to think that hiding inside the apartment would keep me safe, but my room became my castle.

I spent most mornings reading, and Juan would try to come home for lunch. He found a girl to cook and clean for us. María often came by in the afternoons since classes were on break. Through her I got word to Teodor Fliedner Jr. to watch his step and to keep from openly speaking out against the regime in Berlin. The lives of hundreds of children depended on German donations. María was also at risk, but her faith in God was a shield that warded off fear and kept her calm.

Luis came by every now and then and kept me up-to-date with the goings-on at the bookstore. Though the fair had been a success, sales dropped in the summer when people flocked to the coast to avoid the heat of the city. That was in fact how the deputy José Calvo Sotelo ended up dead. His cadaver showed up one morning in the Este cemetery. José María Gil Robles had been the intended target of the attack, but he was on vacation in Biarritz with his family, so the attackers found someone else. One of the worst aspects of the story was that agents from the national police force, the Civil Guard, were involved. Along with four Socialist activists, they took the politician from his house and murdered him in cold blood.

Aware that the event could be the perfect excuse for an armed uprising, Juan complained to the director who had ordered the killing. He returned home furious, blaming Largo Caballero for the execution of an anti-Republican politician.

The day before had been hotter than usual. People in Madrid dealt with the dog days of summer by living on the patios of the bars and cafés. I had been going back to work the past few days and had turned in a largely made-up report at the German embassy so that they would leave me alone. I had also visited Alan Hillgarth once at the Palace Hotel, but I had no relevant information to share given my prolonged bed rest.

That afternoon after we closed up the bookstore, Luis escorted me home in the taxi, saying that the streets of Madrid had become too unsafe. A good part of the army had indeed joined an uprising in the protectorate of Morocco. Though the government did not seem to take it very seriously, the tension was palpable.

Many working-class activists had started hunting down Fascists, which, in those tense moments, could mean anyone in a suit or driving a nice car. Members of the National Confederation of Labor, and of the General Union of Workers, had asked Santiago Casares Quiroga to arm them, but so far the prime minister had refused. Very early that morning Juan had gone to party head-quarters, and I did not expect him home that night.

"The government is falling apart. As soon as a new prime minister is named, they'll arm all the workers."

"Wouldn't that be a good thing?" I asked Luis as we rode.

"Well, you know what happened in Russia. The military scares me, but so does the militia running around armed in Madrid. This isn't going to end well."

"Let's hope it all comes to nothing," I said, but I was aware of the many interests hiding behind our conflict. The hatred accumulated over the past several years was the perfect raw material for a long, bloody war.

The taxi left me right at our building's front door. Before going in, I checked our mail and found a note. It read, "Come to the Edelweiss immediately. For your own good." I had not been to that German restaurant much, but I knew it was a favorite among the expatriates.

After the taxi with Luis in it drove away, I hailed a different one to Jardines Street. The restaurant was run by a Mr. Rothfritz. Though I did not know who had written the note, I went in expecting to find the Gestapo agent. It had been several weeks since I had seen him.

"Mrs. Spiel," said a man I did not recognize. "Your contact has left for Berlin, but until things calm down I'm in charge. I'm Mr. Meyer."

The name sounded familiar, but I could not recall where I had heard it.

"I run a nightclub on Gran Vía and know many members of the leftist parties. I know that for the moment, no one will come after me, but my boss has told me you should seek refuge in the German embassy. Every citizen of our nation is a potential target for the militia."

"But I'm married to a Socialist politician," I said.

"I'm aware of that, but things are going to get ugly. They'll shoot first and then ask questions."

"And I'm pregnant."

The man shrugged. "My boss expected you to respond that way. Then you should continue providing us with information. But don't turn in your reports at the embassy or at the church. By tomorrow morning they'll no longer be safe places. I'll come by your bookstore. However, I would advise you to store away all of your German titles, at least until things calm down a bit."

Just then we heard a loud noise. Someone had thrown a smoke bomb into the restaurant. Then several Molotov cocktails went off, and fire broke out. We could not get out the front door. The restaurant owner screamed in German for the diners to escape through the kitchen.

In the alley behind the restaurant, we all coughed and rubbed our eyes, stinging from the smoke. A band of militia members surrounded us. They beat several of the men. One of the militia women charged toward me, but when she saw I was pregnant, she barked at her comrades to take me in for questioning. They grabbed three other people and gruffly crammed us into the back of a van. As the vehicle bounced over the cobbled streets of Madrid, the only thing I begged God for was to keep my baby safe.

Chapter 21

Madrid
July 17, 1936

$\mathbb{W}$e were driven to the Legazpi neighborhood, to a huge warehouse that must have served as a bus depot but was currently empty. They put me in a side office, and I do not know what happened to the others. After five hours with no food or water, my hands tied behind my back, and having wet myself, a woman came in dressed in workers' overalls, the outfit that became the uniform of many militia fighters. She was very pretty, with huge dark eyes set off by makeup and very pale skin that contrasted starkly with her black hair. She smiled at me as if were friends and plopped down on the other side of the table.

"Why am I here?" I asked. "I'm married to Juan Delgado, a Socialist activist and deputy in the Cortes."

"We're not Socialists," was her only explanation.

"I'm pregnant, I've wet myself, and I need to eat something before my baby starts to be at risk."

"What were you doing in that restaurant? Don't you know it's a beehive of Nazis?"

"I'm from Germany. A friend invited me to eat, that's all."

The woman leaned forward. "Tell me the truth and you can go."

"Who are you people to detain me?"

"We're the authority now. The Fascist military has pulled off a coup, and we don't know who's with us and who's with them. The Germans are on their side; there's no doubt about that."

"My father was a Social Democrat deputy in Germany until he had to go into exile."

The woman lit a cigarette and took a long drag.

"Everything that's happened is the Social Democrats' fault. They always believed that revolution wasn't the answer, that the businessmen and the bourgeoisie would behave themselves and share their wealth. And they have the audacity to call us naive. The only solution for Spain's problems is a Communist revolution. Our enemies are everywhere, even in the left."

"That's insane," I said.

She hopped to her feet and slapped me across the face a few times. I felt dizzy, and there was a buzzing in my ears.

"You'll speak when I tell you to. Where are the rest of the Nazi rats hiding? In the German embassy? In that school on Bravo Murillo that the Germans started?"

"No." I shook my head. "Those are good people helping poor children. The school has been in Madrid since the last century."

The woman threw back her head with a grating laugh.

"Some of the bourgeoisie think their alms and pity are enough for the working poor, but we're going to put a stop to that once and for all. Those military pigs have served them up to us on a platter. The time for revolution has come. They stopped us in thirty-four, but they won't stop us now."

"I can take you to their hideout." I said it in a confidential tone so she would untie me and I would have a chance to escape.

She glowered at me. "I thought you said you didn't know anything and that you weren't a Nazi."

"I don't, and I'm not, but the man I was eating dinner with is. He told me where they would be hiding."

She frowned.

"And why did he tell you?"

"Because he thinks I'm on their side."

She took out a knife and came up to me. I held my breath, not sure of her intentions. She bent over and cut the cord from my wrists. My shoulders popped when I brought my arms forward. I rubbed my wrists together.

"Take us there."

"Okay," I said, not even trying to mask the fear in my voice.

The woman called over two men, and they loaded me into a Renault that they had painted red initials on. I directed them to the Lutheran church. The gate was locked.

"Here?" she asked. It was past midnight by then, and we could not see anything inside the church.

One of the militiamen broke the lock, and we went through the courtyard. The same man yanked open the door to the chapel with one tug. That telltale smell of candle wax and wood always brought me back to my childhood and the feeling of being safe as I sat between my mother and grandparents at church. But I did not feel safe right then.

"There's no one here," she said flatly.

"Wait, you'll see."

I went to the back of the chapel and opened the door that covered the door that led to the embassy itself. Before they could catch up, I unlocked that second door, which was metal, then shut and relocked it. Running down the passageway, I heard several gunshots. I knocked at the door at the far end of the passage, and a man opened. He gave me a questioning look.

"How did you get here?" he asked, his gun trained on me.

Seeing that I was pregnant, he ushered me inside, then shut and locked the door. As he led me downstairs, another man came out to meet us. It was Meyer, who had somehow made it to the embassy.

"So you managed to get away. I hope now you see what your leftist friends are capable of."

I was so weary I did not even respond. A nurse led me to a bed, helped me into a change of clean clothes, and brought me a light supper. After that, I fell fast asleep.

Chapter 22

I slept the entire next day and part of the following day, but on my second night in the embassy, sleep eluded me. I was sore and humiliated. Plus, I was scared I would lose the baby. I had been spotting some, and the embassy doctor told me to continue my bed rest. We had no phone line and no way of leaving the embassy. A group of militia fighters was watching the door. Even though the coup had failed in the big cities, the rebels were gaining ground in the rural areas and in Spanish Morocco. The Germans and other citizens of foreign nationality were sure that things would be wrapped up soon and that they would be able to get back to their daily activities. We never miss routines as much as when we lose them. I missed having coffee in the morning in my kitchen, Juan's goodbye kisses, the mornings at the bookstore, meals together with my husband, and snuggling in bed together. I knew that all our routines would change when the baby came, but we were lucky to have held on to our love for each other amid so much hatred. The lack of peace in this world was directly related to the lack of peace in people's hearts. Many philosophers blame society, lack of education, or various environmental factors, but what really makes the difference is a family that raises a child in the basic values of respect for others, honesty, dignity, and love.

Despite not sleeping well, I felt rested enough when morning came. I was determined to leave that building and go home. I had done nothing wrong and there was no reason I needed to be hiding from anyone. I got out of bed and put on my clothes, which someone had kindly washed and folded for me. As I headed out, Meyer stopped me.

"Have you lost your mind? Don't you know what's happening in Barcelona? Germans are being arrested by the dozens and their businesses ransacked, and probably some have been killed. I told you you'd have to choose between the chaos and your country."

I eyed him with disgust. My husband was a Spaniard, as was the child in my womb. I wanted nothing to do with Hitler's Germany of freely roaming anti-Semitism, racism, and the persecution of anyone considered different.

Meyer went on, "We're the only answer for this kind of chaos. That's why so many people follow us. These out-of-control militias are worse than brute animals."

"I've seen how things go in Germany. The Brownshirts are no different."

"Those stupid drunkards were wiped out in the summer of thirty-four. Order now reigns in Germany."

I knew he was lying. Françoise had kept me up-to-date.

"There's even greater tolerance toward the Jews now, though of course they're still under close watch," Meyer added. "Give them an inch and those rats will take more than a mile. If you'd like, I can get a message to your husband. If you must leave, it would be better that he come pick you up."

An apparently helpful offer from such a despicable man surprised me, but I accepted. Though it had probably saved my life, I did not want to spend any more time in the embassy.

Juan came immediately. Within the hour he was waiting for me at the front door with his car and bodyguard. He had me in a tight embrace as soon as I crossed the threshold. But then we were surrounded by the militia.

"Comrade, we have to question any German who exits the embassy," the one who seemed to be the head honcho said.

"I'm a deputy and a trusted friend of the prime minister," Juan answered evenly.

The militiaman frowned in disgust. "We're not bound by the government's orders but by our own party. Who's leading the assault on the Montaña Barracks? We are, because the repressive instruments of the state are on the side of the rebels, and many of those who call themselves the left don't want a real working-class revolution. Look here," the man spat out, "what makes you different from the bourgeoisie? You'd better take that tie off before someone does it for you."

His comment sounded like the sansculottes of the French Revolution, the bitter radicals who claimed that their looting and revenge were revolution and social change.

Juan's bodyguard pulled out his gun, and the militia fighters, unarmed, took a step back.

"We're leaving, whether nicely or not. You choose, comrade," Juan said. His voice indicated that his patience was over.

"All right, all right, it's nothing to get ruffled up about. Your wife is with child, and we respect that, but she shouldn't be out on her own. Being married to you doesn't keep her from being a German."

We got in the car with the energy of fear still coursing through our bodies.

"What's going on, Juan?"

He did not answer. He was watching out the rearview mirror. The militia leader had written down the license plate number.

"Why did you hide in the embassy? That wasn't smart."

"I was getting away from other militia fighters who had taken me."

"At home I'll tell you everything," he said.

We arrived home without delay. I made sure the door was locked tight and then went to the kitchen to fix tea.

We sat in front of the window. It was very hot, but at least there was a breeze.

"There have been a lot of changes in the government. Martínez Barrio tried to form a cabinet yesterday, but people wouldn't have it. Azaña gave the order to dissolve the army, and we've lost some loyal troops. Meanwhile, there are rebel uprisings in more and more cities."

"So it's complete chaos." Anxiety turned my question into a statement.

"For the moment, there's a lot of confusion. But the coup will be put down soon and then order will return."

For the first time since I had known him, I did not believe my husband.

"Who's the prime minister right now?"

"José Giral."

I raised my eyebrows. Giral was a straw man with no support and no leadership skills. The situation would remain very dangerous until we had some form of stable government.

"I asked Luis to close the bookstore for the time being. Foreign-owned businesses are the target of a lot of the looting and violence. So are churches and convents."

"That was smart; thank you. How is El Porvenir?"

"I'm not sure," Juan answered.

I was worried that the fanatics would have attacked the school in Madrid and the children's homes outside the city. "We've got to go check on them."

"Largo Caballero is trying to get Azaña to form a cabinet made up of leftist leaders. Until then, I've got no authority. You saw what happened in the embassy."

"But I can't leave my friends at a time like this."

Seeing my determination, Juan offered to go with me. Everything seemed calm when we drove up. But the porter was clearly afraid when he opened the gate for us. The day before, extremists had tried to enter the school grounds, but the parents of some of the students and a few friends of the Fliedner family had stopped them.

Teodoro Jr. was meeting with the teachers in the dining hall. He smiled when he saw us enter but did not interrupt his talk. ". . . is quite trying. Yesterday my brother Juan barely managed to hold services at the Iglesia de Jesús. Outside, on Calatrava Street, there were shots ringing all around. So I'm asking you all to stay in the building for now and not let anyone out."

"Shouldn't we go to the embassy?" one of the professors from Germany asked. Other expatriates voiced the same concern.

"You are more than welcome to go. My family will make that decision when the time comes."

Once the meeting was over, I went up to Teodoro, and he thanked us for coming by.

"Can we be of any assistance?" Juan asked.

"For the time being, we're all right. We just need things to calm down soon."

"Where's María?" I asked, surprised not to have seen her with the other teachers.

Teodoro's face fell. "She went to the Baptist church on Sunday, and we haven't seen her since."

That worried me. I would have seen her if she had gone to the embassy. I was afraid she might have been detained like me.

"We'll go now, but I'll ask the prefect to step in if you need it," Juan said, knowing full well it would be nearly impossible to stop the militias, armed by the government itself, if they decided to attack the school.

Back at home, I went straight to bed. I was exhausted, and the pains in my abdomen had returned. I was so scared of losing the baby. That night, for the first time in years, I asked God for something. I asked him to keep my friends and my baby safe. The world was falling apart so fast it seemed like the only hope was a miracle.

Chapter 23

Madrid
October 1, 1936

The hope that the government would be more stable with Largo Caballero as prime minister vanished within weeks. At the beginning of September, the rebel troops on the mainland had come as close to Madrid as Talavera de la Reina. The early euphoria over the war had given way to fear. The people of Madrid had lived the first few weeks of the uprising like it was a party, in a mix of fanaticism and naivete. But the government had failed to reestablish order in the streets, and the *checas*—the extralegal jails and torture chambers of the various political parties—were still in operation.

Many everyday prisoners had been set free during the early days of the conflict. They found a ready home among the various paramilitary groups just like war veterans in my country did among the SA. There was widespread repression of the middle classes in Madrid fueled largely by a declaration of the Nationalist rebel general Quiepo de Llano. In a famous speech he claimed that Madrid would easily fall to the rebels thanks to the "fifth column"— his term for citizens living in Republican-held territories but working clandestinely in favor of the Nationalists.

Francisco Franco was named the head of the Nationalist government. At his inauguration, he promised that he would not stop until he had freed Spain of the reds. More and more refugees fleeing Franco's advance flocked to Madrid. They shared their terrifying stories with us. Prisoners were executed with no trial, women were raped, and anyone belonging to a political party or a union was locked up.

The basement of the building of the phone company Telefónica was outfitted as temporary shelter for these refugees. I joined Teodoro Jr. and several teachers from El Porvenir to drop off blankets and food.

As we handed out the supplies, a woman hugged me and started crying. "Thank you so much for everything, especially in your state."

My pregnancy was obvious from a mile away by then.

"We've got to give one another a hand," I said, pulling back to look at her and smile. "What's your name?"

"Olga, my name is Olga." Two young children were clinging to her skirt.

"Is your husband here with you?"

A new wave of tears overtook her. "We're from Ciempozuelos. When the military came, they rounded up a lot of men, including my husband. They strung up the prisoners by ropes over the corral where the fighting bulls are kept. They goaded the bulls to charge, then lowered the prisoners to be gored. My Julián was one of them. The bull's horns ripped his intestines out. They forced us women to watch our husbands die. After that, a group of Moors raped me. But I didn't feel it at all. They've destroyed my heart. If it weren't for them"—she nodded to her children—"I don't know what I'd do."

I hugged her again. It was all I could do for her.

Sobbing into my shoulder, she asked, "Why is there so much hatred?" I had no answer.

When I was ready to go, Teodoro Jr. offered to drive me. The militias had taken possession of many private vehicles, and gas was rationed. But Teodoro had managed to avoid having his car requisitioned.

"Any word from María?" I asked with mixed dread and hope.

"No." His voice was heavy. It had been more than two months, and we feared the worst.

"Juan has asked among the Rearguard Vigilance Militias and the Special State Department of Information on O'Donnell Street, but no one knows anything. Indalecio Prieto is also asking around. He's trying to get the information services organized and do away with the chaos of the *checas* and their arbitrary practices."

Teodoro left me at the bookstore, where Luis and I were going to meet and make a decision about reopening. Teodoro and I said goodbye, and I promised him I would keep up the search for María. Her family deserved to know what had happened to her, and I was determined to find her. The German embassy had relocated to Alicante in August. Since Hitler had ordered all Germans to leave Republican-held territories, few of my compatriots remained in Madrid.

Luis was waiting for me with a feather duster in hand. "My dear Bárbara, it's like time has stood still here in the bookstore. What a pity, this unexpected war. I could never have dreamed we'd be in this situation."

I nodded. "Times are turbulent and dangerous, and standing up for the truth can cost you your life."

Luis sighed and pointed to the piles of books. "They're the only things that can save us. There's hope and comfort in their pages. They help us understand the world and ourselves."

I looked around the bookstore and wanted to cry.

Luis continued, "Anything written by Fascists or supporters of the coup has been banned. Miguel de Unamuno spoke out in favor of the uprising, so we've got to put him away and several other authors."

I had no idea about the prohibitions. I could not believe a democratic government would allow that. Seeing my shock, Luis said, "But it's even worse on the other side." He held out a copy of *Arriba España*, a publication of the Falange.

"How did you come across that?" I gasped.

"I know people."

I read the paragraph he was pointing to. It was a disgusting rallying call to burn the newspapers, books, and magazines of all Jews, Marxists, and Masons, and it was cloaked in patriotic religious language.

"I hear that in Baleares and other places, as soon as the rebels took the party headquarters, they brought all the books out to the street and burned them in big pyres," Luis added. "The Fascists have banned authors like Sabino Arana, Rousseau, Marx, Voltaire, Lamartine, Remarque, Gorky, and Freud. Not even primary school libraries are safe. It's a new Inquisition all over the country."

His description of the lunacy kicked the legs out from under me. The book burning in Germany in 1933 had been only a foretaste of what was to come.

"So should we even think about reopening the store?" My timid question hung in the air. Luis looked around at the shelves and tables covered in books that had lain untouched for too long.

"Will that belly of yours let you?" he asked.

I nodded.

"Then tomorrow morning, let's start sowing hope in this desolate world."

That was one of the few bright spots of the early months of the war. It would be several more weeks before any others came.

Chapter 24

Madrid
November 6, 1936

We kept the bookstore open despite pressure from some of the militia groups who did not approve of a German-run shop. The closer the rebel troops got to the capital, the more nervous and violent the fanatics inside Madrid became. There were rumors that Largo Caballero's government would relocate to Valencia and that some of the artistic treasures held in the capital would be evacuated. Those rumors were like alarm bells ringing from house to house.

Some radio transmissions announced the imminent fall of the capital. We knew that if Madrid surrendered, we would have to flee. Juan would be executed without a second thought, and I would end up jailed for being his wife.

That morning Juan left home very early. The night before, we had gotten everything ready in case we had to leave. Over the past few days, the bombing had been relentless, and it was a mercy no bombs had fallen near us yet. Juan's parents had already gone to Valencia and were setting up a place for us as well.

Luis sauntered into the bookstore in a jolly enough mood. I was packing up books to take them to the basement in the hope that we would eventually return to the city.

He eyed the boxes. "What are you doing?"

"We're leaving, Luis, and I think you should too."

"I've never been a member of any party."

"But you tried to organize the writers' union."

At that, he burst out laughing. "Frogs will grow hair first. Plus, the publishing world has gone to seed. The Palacio de la Novela is now just the people's library project. The owner found a way to channel Republican fervor into his pocket by cranking out the cheapest serial slop one could imagine. But then he headed for the hills, and the workers have rebranded as the Trabajadores de Editorial Castro. Can you believe that name? The 'Workers of the Castro Publishing House,' ha!"

"It sounds like something you would support, though."

His forehead wrinkled. He was not exactly a Communist. "You know I was a policeman. For decades I chased after not only ne'er-do-wells but also anarchist terrorists. I don't trust fanatics of any stripe. I can just imagine the kind of sectarian rubbish they're going to publish. When you and I met, I told you the powerful had always wielded culture to impose their ideas. Those supposed revolutionaries are no different. It's the same dog with a different collar."

The bomb siren went off, so we closed up the shop and headed for the nearest shelter. During the first few weeks of the war, people had paid little attention to the warnings, but the death toll kept rising, and now everyone fled before every bombing attempt. And now, besides air raids, there was cannon fire from the front just outside the city.

We were still some distance from the shelter. As pregnant as I was, I could no longer run well, and Luis's legs were perhaps less agile than his mind. We heard the dreaded sound of plane motors overhead and, within seconds, the whistle of bombs falling from the sky.

Some three hundred yards away, the first projectile landed right on a trolley car that was, fortunately, empty. Riders tended to flee their vehicles as soon as a siren sounded.

Luis and I threw ourselves down and covered our heads, but a second shell fell much closer, and some of the fragments flew too near for comfort.

For half an hour we dared not move from our frozen spot. When the danger passed, we dragged ourselves up and started walking again, horrified to see that the bombs had hit an elementary school nearby. Many people were crowded around the ruins trying to get the children out while mothers were still running up and screaming the names of their sons and daughters. We joined those who were clearing the rubble. Firemen and other brave souls dared to enter the building looking for survivors.

Soon enough, the first bodies were brought out: five- and six-year-old children mangled by shrapnel. Others were wounded or missing limbs but alive. I wiped my tears with my sleeves and kept moving rubble.

The mothers paced the rows of cadavers looking for their children. Some sighed with relief that their babies were not there; others, at recognizing their own, let out howls of grief as if their insides were being ripped out.

Luis could see that I was queasy and weak. He took me home. When Juan arrived, I was in the kitchen trying to scrounge together a meal from the little we got from our ration cards. It was meager even though our allowance, thanks to Juan's position in the government, was greater than the rest of the population's.

"They're leaving," he said, taking off his coat and shoes.

"The cabinet? Doesn't that seem cowardly?"

Juan still defended his colleagues. The prime minister had made valiant but unsuccessful attempts to reestablish order in the capital, and the Republic had splintered into a thousand sectarian groups incapable of working together. The Francoists were winning every battle.

"Well, the government has to be protected," he said.

"What will we do?"

"They've ordered me to stay here with General Miaja. There's fear that the Communists will leverage the situation to take control of the city and set up a Stalinist regime."

I crossed my arms and left dinner on the burner.

"How are they any different from Largo Caballero? He's said dozens of times that a Soviet-like regime is the way to go."

Juan gave me an annoyed look. "It's politics, and we have to make everybody happy. The Soviets are apparently the only ones interested in helping us, which is why the Communists are key right now. The prime minister doesn't want them to become our intermediaries."

Juan's explanations did little to convince me. The war was becoming an international conflict. The Germans and Italians, as well as the Soviets, saw Spain as a chance to test out their weapons and practice for a European war that seemed closer and closer. The hatred sown over the years was growing daily. Whoever won, the repression afterward would be vicious. The crimes committed in the rear guard were scandalous, truly crimes of war, and most of them either with the approval of or ordered by the authorities.

"What will happen if the Francoists enter Madrid?" I asked, unable to mask my fear.

"Well, if they get in, it's all over for us."

Chapter 25

Madrid
February 8, 1937

Franco had not managed to take Madrid, but he had completely surrounded it in siege. People said he was not actually determined to take the capital and that a long war was in his best interests. Premature surrender would not allow him to reach his true goal: eradicating everything and everyone he considered to be an enemy of Spain and gaining complete control over the rebel elements, which were a conglomerate of diverse parties, ideologies, and interests. The execution of José Antonio Primo de Rivera in Alicante left the door wide open for Franco to assume political control of the Nationalists. No other politicians among the rebels could touch him.

No one wanted to say it out loud, but the Republic was losing the war. Madrid was not safe. Largo Caballero's government was still in Valencia. Plus, there was an internal war of vengeance going on within the Republican side, especially since the arrival of Soviet support in the form of weapons and advisers. Things were even worse in Catalonia and Basque Country, where the Nationalists had their way in the war.

We had closed the bookstore for good. I divided my time between El Porvenir and our apartment. It had been so long since I had seen Meyer that I had allowed myself the illusion of being free of him. But then one day there he was, walking up right as I was heading into the school. I froze. Though he had actually been helpful the last time I saw him, I knew that his presence was not a good sign.

"Mrs. Spiel, how nice to see you again. I was worried something might have happened to you, though a woman as astute as you are will surely survive a war like this and many others."

"I can't say the same for seeing you," I replied. I saw no reason to pretend.

"Well, I come bearing good news, though it will cost you. Don't worry, it won't be too pricey."

"Don't you see my condition? I could go into labor at any moment. My due date is just a few days from now."

He gave a cynical smile. "This won't require much effort. We need a report with the maps of Madrid's defense systems and troop placement. In exchange, we'll tell you where your friend María is."

His request was so bizarre I was speechless. I had all but given up hope of finding María. There had been a massacre in the Modelo Prison in Madrid, and in November and December there were systematic executions in Paracuellos—a result of the government having hightailed it out of the city and what had seemed the imminent fall of the capital to the Francoists.

"I have no way of getting you that information."

"Your friend is in danger. I don't know how much longer they'll keep her, but these reds are hard to predict, and they know they're losing the war."

Meyer licked his lips, enjoying my defeat. I could not allow María to be killed.

"My husband doesn't bring those kinds of papers home."

"Of course he doesn't. That's why you'll have to go to the government offices with some excuse and take some pictures." He handed me a piece of paper with an address. It was an apartment in Carabanchel. "You've got two weeks, and not a day more." With that, he walked off.

I stayed glued to my spot in front of the school gate. I did not know if I already would have gone into labor by the following week, but I had to try to save María. I was more and more convinced that the Republic was going to lose. And things were getting worse in Europe with the aggressive politics of a German dictator who rose to power on the incompatible promises of peace and the restoration of Germany's former glory.

Chapter 26

Madrid
February 9, 1937

I found myself in the predicament of betraying my husband and the government he represented or saving the life of my friend. Meyer knew he had found my weak spot. It was the last week of my pregnancy, I was hardly sleeping, all my movements were sluggish, and as a first-time mother, I was terrified.

I did not sleep a wink the night after my encounter with Meyer. I kept stewing over the decision. I would have to come up with some excuse to go into the headquarters of Madrid's defense forces and get the information that would doom the city I loved and lead to a decisive victory for the Francoists.

I knew what would happen if Francisco Franco took complete control of the country. I had heard what the Nationalist army did upon capturing a city: summary trials, mass executions, and the widespread raping of women.

Dawn was breaking when another option occurred to me. I had not been to the Palace Hotel since the last time I had seen Alan Hillgarth. Perhaps he could help me.

As soon as I got to the hotel, I asked for him at the front desk.

The employee gave me a distrustful look but pointed to an armchair where I could wait. Sitting was exactly what I wanted to do.

Fifteen minutes later, Hillgarth appeared, took me by the arm, and gently led me to a private room.

"I thought you'd never make up your mind, but it seems you've changed your tune," he said.

I told him briefly what had happened with Meyer. He showed no surprise but only murmured that he had expected as much.

"Now that Meyer trusts you, we have an opportunity to trick the Nazis. The Republicans are losing the war. Their improvised army can, at best, hold out against the Nationalists, but they can hardly make an offensive move. If the war drags on and war in Europe starts, then they just might have a chance."

"Things are that bad?"

"In France and Great Britain, public opinion is against a war, and the United States sees old Europe as incorrigible, but Hitler will keep pressing until armed conflict is unavoidable. It's just a matter of time. That's why the Führer asked Franco to go ahead and wrap up this war. He doesn't want to have to busy himself with Spain as well. Yet the general has chosen a war of extermination. He thinks the only way to win is to completely wipe out the adversary. Otherwise, in his opinion, the country will be back in the same old mess fifteen or twenty years from now."

My head sank low to my chest. "It's all terrible."

"Tomorrow I'll get you a false report, but it'll be so good that Meyer will swallow it whole. He'll get you the information about where your friend is being held, and I myself will go and get her out."

"I don't know how to thank you," I said.

Hillgarth smiled and, shaking my hand, said, "Just sell a lot of my novels."

I breathed easier on my way home from the hotel. I would not have to betray my husband and the cause he believed in, even though the Republic was taking turns that neither he nor I agreed with. María was on my mind the whole ride home. She did not deserve to die in a secret jail. She was the kindest, most selfless person I had ever known. I was willing to do anything to rescue her.

Chapter 27

Alan Hillgarth got the report to me. It was so detailed that, if I had not known it was false, I would have thought it came directly from the Republican high command. I got in touch with Meyer and headed for the apartment in Carabanchel.

That day my labor pains began. I was nervous that labor would start before I was able to get the information I needed to save María.

A ball of nerves, I knocked at the door and waited. Meyer himself opened. There were two people I had never seen before there with him, a man and a woman.

"Leave us," Meyer told them.

I handed him the report and asked for the information about where María was being held.

"Not so fast," he said.

"As you can see," I said, pointing to my enormous belly, "I don't have a lot of time left."

He ignored me and studied the documents. "Where did you find this?" he demanded.

"I got lucky. We hosted a dinner and some of the high-ranking government officials came. They left their briefcases with their coats. While everyone was busy with cocktails before dinner, I found this report, took photographs, and asked a friend to develop them for me."

"Incredible. In a few days you've achieved what we've been trying for weeks."

He handed me a signed card. "When our people enter the city, hand this card to an officer, and nothing will happen to you."

I took it but was losing patience. I just wanted to know María's whereabouts.

"Here's the address. She's in the Buenavista *checa*, headed up by a piece of trash named Luis Omaña. He and his men tend to have their way with the female prisoners and the families of the detainees."

I was horrified imagining what my friend had been put through. I took the piece of paper and turned to go, but he called out, "We'll need you for other jobs—after the baby comes, of course."

I waddled out of the building as fast as I could and took a taxi toward the Palace Hotel. To make sure no one was following me, I got out in front of the Prado.

Enormous bags now covered the monuments of the beautiful city of Madrid. Many buildings had been destroyed by bombs, and the streets were nearly impassable with holes from bombs and from trenches that had been dug.

At the hotel, I asked for Hillgarth to be called. He was surprised to read the address.

"Dear God, it's a police commissary headed by a well-known Socialist. How is it that your husband couldn't find her?"

"Maybe she isn't officially registered. How do we get her out?"

"Don't worry, I've got contacts. You go home and rest. Now you can just focus on the baby."

I followed the British agent's advice. The pains had grown stronger and stronger, and by the time I was home, I knew they were contractions. I called Juan, and within an hour of arriving at the hospital, I was bringing our son Jaime into the world. Despite all the scarcity and fatigue of the past several weeks, he was healthy and whole. I returned home after two days in the hospital. Time slowed to a stop, and the rest of the world disappeared. The only thing that mattered was my little boy. The greatest miracle that a woman is capable of had come about through me: the bringing forth of new life. Nothing could separate us as long as I was breathing.

Chapter 28

Madrid
May 17, 1937

Motherhood was not the bed of roses I had naively thought it might be. My mother was not there to help me, and I could not even call her for advice. My in-laws had decided to stay in Valencia. And my closest friend, María, was an empty shipwreck of her former self. The Fliedners had nursed her body back to health after the months in the *checa*. When she was physically strong enough, one of them took María back to her family in Germany. Though it was no easy place to convalesce, at least she would be away from groups that persecuted people just for being German.

The early weeks of motherhood were marked by the frustration of not producing enough milk. Jaime nursed for hours on end but never seemed satisfied, and he cried constantly. The nurse at El Porvenir recommended I find a wet nurse for him, but I had not wanted to try that. I intuitively knew how special the bond was that formed when nursing a baby. Only after several wearisome weeks did my persistence win out and our bodies get into sync with each other.

The frustrations of being a first-time mother had a positive result: I found myself scheming for a way to reopen the bookstore.

Things were as tense as ever politically. Largo Caballero resigned due to pressure from the Communist Party, with which he had long been in dispute regarding managing relations with the Soviet Union. The prime minister had sent the vast majority of the country's gold reserves to Moscow to get the Soviets to arm the Republic. Republicans within and beyond Largo Cabellero's party critiqued that move, but that was not the straw that broke the camel's back. The fighting between factions, especially in Catalonia, had gotten worse. The fighting between Communists and anarchists further destabilized those who supported the Republic. The fall of Málaga to the Francoists is what led to the Socialist leader's resignation.

Juan had not been a close confidant of Largo Caballero's. When we were invited to a dinner held that night with Juan Negrín, I came to understand that my husband was about to occupy a distinguished position in the new cabinet. He had long been a pupil of Indalecio Prieto, always on the more moderate side of the party, and he was now receiving the fruit of his restraint.

Juan Negrín was a cheerful man from the Canary Islands and skilled at conversation. He was neither a unionist nor a career politician. He had dedicated most of his life to medical research and teaching physiology at the Universidad Central. As one of the most cultured men in the PSOE, the Spanish Socialist Workers' Party, he spoke several languages. Negrín came from a conservative, religious family, had studied in several European universities, and was fluent in German. His wife, María, was from a well-off Jewish family and was a professional pianist. Juan had told me that Negrín and his wife had grown estranged after the loss of two children, but they kept up the marriage for the sake of appearances.

Indalecio Prieto was Negrín's political mentor and the one who brought him into the party. He knew that the PSOE was light on intellectuals and that the much more revolutionary leaders of the UGT, the General Union of Workers, held more sway in the PSOE. Thus, this physician from the Canary Islands was something of a rare bird in the party.

Negrín had reorganized the customs guard and was constantly at the front encouraging the troops. He had served as minister of finance while Largo Caballero was prime minister, though the two men were as different from each other as could be. Largo Caballero was a worker who wanted a Stalinist revolution; Negrín was a bourgeois who admired French politics. Western democracies had distanced themselves from the Republic, and with the change in cabinet from Largo Caballero to Negrín, President Azaña wanted to show them a more moderate executive branch, since there were three Communist ministers acting in the name of the Soviet Union.

Some thought that Negrín would try to negotiate peace with the Francoists right away.

"Peace is only possible if Franco accepts a few minimum requirements. If we backpedal from the advances made by the Republic, all this bloodshed will have been in vain," Indalecio said, seated beside Negrín.

Machismo was even stronger in Spain than in Germany, and it was uncommon for men to discuss politics when women were present, but in those days people hardly spoke of anything else.

"The insurrectionists will accept only unconditional surrender," Juan said, well aware of the ethical outlook of several of the generals. Some had initially supported the Republic but then sold their ideals so as not to be marginalized in the army, as was the case with Queipo de Llano.

That night was the first time I had left Jaime with a babysitter. I had hoped to get home early, but the night was dragging on.

"The main thing is to get the democracies to support us. We can't trust the Russians," Indalecio said. He knew the spurious intentions of the Communists and how they squandered their resources.

"What do you think, Bárbara? I'm curious how someone from the outside sees this conflict." An uncomfortable silence followed Negrín's question. Excepting Juan, he displayed the least amount of machismo among the group.

"I haven't been in Spain long, just three and a half years, and part of that time has been during war. Spanish society seemed happy to me despite the problems. Things were changing little by little, but extremist parties and a few politicians have pushed the country to the edge of a cliff."

"So you think the politicians are to blame?" he asked with true curiosity.

"Most people just want bread and peace, and they couldn't care less about anything else. Ideologies sow hatred and arguments. My father dedicated his life to politics in Germany. He was a Social Democrat, as you all know, but he realized that the extremists took advantage of the crisis to inoculate the people with fear. I think it was one of your philosophers, Ortega y Gasset, who talked about this in *The Revolt of the Masses*. He said that Bolshevism and Fascism are sterile revolutions; they don't bring forth anything new or good. I think he was on to something. At the core, they are modern religions."

Everyone stared at me, and Indalecio's brow was furrowed.

"That's how Hitler's on the verge of dominating Europe. That Bohemian corporal has gotten pretty far," he said.

"Well, the masses do what the propaganda tells them to now. The Republic put forth great effort to educate people, and I think that the elites did not like it. Educated peasants are dangerous and much harder to manipulate. The same is true for workers and the proletariat in general. What I don't understand is why the Communists don't want to educate people, at least not enough for them to think for themselves."

Negrín smiled at me. Apparently he agreed with my take on things. "I would add only one thing to what Bárbara has said. I think that most people are highly influenceable—that is, manipulatable. Sometimes the game is not who governs best but rather who manipulates best, as Machiavelli noted. People like me are at a disadvantage in comparison with people like Franco, Hitler, Mussolini, or Stalin. I want to convince people, not manipulate them."

I gave Negrín a pained smile. Perhaps if he had been named prime minister in July 1936, things would have turned out differently. But by now a diplomatic end to the war would be difficult at best.

As we headed home, Juan slipped his arm around my lower back. It had been a long time since he had seemed relaxed to any degree. "I had almost forgotten why I married you. This damned war has created distance between us. Sometimes it feels like we've been together all our lives, but we barely get to see each other a couple of hours a day. I only see Jaime at night. I'm afraid that, at the core, I'm too much like your father."

He was correct, but I did not want to add to his burdens any more right then.

"Circumstances put us human beings to the test so often that we forget what even the humblest fisherman knows. Problems are like water around a boat: They're not a problem while the boat stays afloat, but if we let the water get inside, it'll sink the boat. Don't let all these problems end up drowning you. You'll always have me by your side. I'll never judge you or throw anything in your face. Love isn't just a feeling, nor is it an easy decision. But I've decided to love you with my entire soul."

That night was magical. We made love and felt like our minds and bodies were one once more. It felt like nothing and nobody could ever take that from us, but like we might lose it any moment if we forgot who we were and why we had decided to spend our lives together.

Chapter 29

Human beings cannot handle too much truth. Therefore, we lie to ourselves or accept other people's lies. A few thirst after truth, and we call them philosophers or mystics, but soon enough they are sidelined and rejected by the majority that does not want to ask questions and, above all, does not want to know the answers. Throughout history, many writers, true visionaries, have been classified as lunatics despite being the ones who were actually sane.

We had all been warned about the tidal wave of hatred and violence that had started in places like Russia and then Spain and was about to crash over the world. But most people did not want to admit that the war was lost. They held on to the idea that ideals are more powerful than weapons. Yet reality has a way of imposing itself.

The Republicans had suffered defeat on the Aragon front, and the fall of Catalonia seemed inevitable. Madrid was increasingly isolated. Indalecio Prieto tried to convince Azaña and Negrín that it was best to avoid an even greater bloodbath, but his voice went unheeded. He was removed from his position as head of the Department of Defense, and the prime minister assumed control of it.

Despite the ups and downs of politics, our life had changed little. The German spies had left me alone since Jaime was born. Hillgarth had come into the bookstore one day, but his visit was uneventful. He asked that I immediately communicate with him if I gained any information that would allow his country to help at the end of the conflict. International politics were incredibly tense, and the Allies were heading for war against Germany and its allies.

Book sales were few and far between, but at least working in the bookstore gave us something to do. Luis came every afternoon. He no longer wrote novels. Paper supplies had nearly run out, and what was left was used for propaganda.

"Some of my friends have been detained and others murdered in cold blood simply for wearing a tie and looking like little gentlemen. Terrible, isn't it? Madrid has become a pathetic mirror of the Soviet Union. I say pathetic because here there hasn't even been any real revolution: While young idealists die on the front, in the rear guard the cowards and assassins just run around threatening and killing innocent people."

I knew that everything Luis was saying was true, but it made me feel responsible. After all, Juan was part of the government.

Luis continued, "This isn't going to end well. I'm afraid that everything's going to blow up and that even more innocent people will die."

"If the war in Europe starts, we have a chance," I said, parroting the same narrow-minded drivel as the rest.

Luis pursed his lips. "Look, Bárbara, Spain is completely destroyed. Do you think that another couple of years of us killing one another would be good for the country?"

Just then we heard the chime ring and turned eagerly to the door. A beautiful, dark-haired woman entered. She wore elegant clothes with a matching purse. That was a rare sight in those days.

"Good afternoon. May I help you find something?" I asked, walking up to her.

She smiled at me, but something in her eyes sent a chill up my spine.

"Do you have any Agustín de Foxá?" she asked.

I cocked my head in confusion. Foxá was a well-known Falange writer. I had heard about his book, published by a Francoist press. It was a novel called *Madrid, de Corte a checa*, and in it the main character describes his life from the proclamation of the Republic to his escape from the capital to seek safety in Salamanca.

"I'm sorry, we don't carry anything by Foxá. His books have been banned by the Republic."

"Oh, I didn't know," she said, still smiling. I looked more carefully at her eyes. They were the only part I felt like I recognized in the face with so much makeup framed by a highly stylized hairdo.

"Do we know each other?" I asked innocently.

She turned and made a gesture I did not catch. Right away several militia fighters stormed into the store and began ransacking the place, throwing books all over the floor.

"Ah, yes, we know each other. You tricked me once, but I've found you. I see you're no longer pregnant."

I started trembling. It was the militiawoman who had interrogated me after the attack at Edelweiss restaurant.

"I don't know what you want from me."

"We know you're a Nazi spy. For now, your husband's job is protecting you, but that won't last much longer. All the traitors are being punished. I want you to know we're watching you. I want you to feel me breathing down your neck."

The militia took several armfuls of books out to the street and set them on fire. Luis and I stood motionless, paralyzed by fear. The pyre soon lit up the front windows. The scene reminded me once again of Germany. For all that time I had managed to deceive myself to avoid reality: I would never be safe. Violence does not halt before any border. It is everywhere, and nothing can stop it.

Chapter 30

The Republic's last hope was dissolving like a sugar cube. The Battle of the Ebro became attrition warfare, and our side had far more to lose. The offensive had started well in July, so well that Azaña thought the tide might be turning in favor of the Republic. But the Francoist counterattack was once again decimating our hopes. There was another cabinet shake-up, and this time Juan was affected. Many government leaders appreciated that my husband had stayed in Madrid throughout the most difficult days, and he had managed to keep his position despite all the upheaval. However, government headquarters never returned to the capital, and the militias wielded more power by the day.

Madrid was poised for a bloodbath. We had kept the bookstore open despite multiple threats, but now that Juan no longer officially worked for the government, we feared the worst.

For Juan, it was endlessly ironic that the Republican army suffered such a terrible defeat now that it had finally gotten itself organized. The government had channeled nearly all its remaining resources to the Battle of the Ebro. The hope was to keep the Republican zone from being split in two. If it were divided, everyone knew that the end of the war would not be far off. The reds managed to hold their position, but the losses of military resources and human life were devastating.

The only good part about Juan being fired was that now we could spend our days together. We had become near strangers due to his work and then the stress of the war. Now we could eat our meals together, take Jaime out for walks, or stay in bed talking and dreaming about the end of the war and the return to regular life.

I was more cautious after the militiawoman's threat. Juan went with me to open the store and then stayed home with Jaime. He came to get me at lunchtime, and then in the afternoons I was with Luis.

That day Luis and I were taking stock. He was now thinner than I had ever seen him.

Trying not to sound overly worried, I asked, "Do you have enough to eat?" His rolled-up sleeves put on display the veins bulging out of his stick arms.

"Of course! Every day it's a feast at my apartment: veal, sea bass, hake, cod . . ."

"I'm being serious."

"Princess, Madrid is starving to death. Yours is one of the privileged families. I can't even remember what a fried egg tastes like, or a baked potato. I'd happily eat a plate of chard right now if I had the chance, and I've always hated greens."

For several reasons the flow of food into the capital was practically nonexistent. The rebel troops controlled most of the country's agricultural lands, and there were no able-bodied men available to work the fields. Drought took care of crushing what remained of our hopes for food.

"I can bring you some eggs and rice," I offered.

"Well, sometimes I go by Café Gijón. The union workers run it now. They don't know a thing about cooking, but at least I can afford it. Besides, at my age, fasting is better than gorging."

I was worried he would catch one of the diseases going around the city. The general weakness of the population rendered most people highly vulnerable to illness and epidemics.

Luis changed the subject. "We're nearly out of stock. How many months has it been since we got a new shipment—a full year? The bright side of absolute desperation is that people buy up all our books!"

I stayed quiet, an idea dawning. Hesitantly, I asked, "Do you think there might be anything decent left in the Palacio de la Novela?"

Luis shrugged. "The workers running the revamped publishing house have raided part of the collection just for the sake of the paper, so they have something to print their leaflets and Communist novels on. But we could always go and take a look around."

I had not been back to that book paradise—or book inferno, depending on one's perspective—in a very long time, and I was antsy to see it again.

Gas was rationed, and very few taxis circled the city anymore, so we took public transportation: the subway and then a trolley. For a long time now the subway stations had become more than just shelters from the air raids. People who had lost their homes were living in the stations. We had to weave around mattresses and all sorts of belongings to reach the platform. To my surprise, the noisy subway car, with its telltale scorching odor, came on time. Since trains that broke down were no longer able to be fixed due to the lack of materials, the cars that did circulate were always stuffed to the brim.

Once we came back up to street level on the other side of the river, a trolley took us to the Palacio de la Novela. The neighborhood had changed quite a bit since my last visit, now marked primarily by collapsed buildings, rubble, trash, and weeds. The façade of the Palacio also reflected the devastation of war. The workers who took over the publishing house had removed the bars from the balconies and all exterior decorations, and the sign was gone. We knocked at the heavy door, but there was no response. It opened at the slightest bit of pressure from Luis's hand. We exchanged a coconspirator's look of excitement and fear, like two children about to enter a forbidden room.

Luis knew the building by heart, but he pulled out the flashlight he carried at all times in his backpack. The electricity was constantly shutting off for unpredictable lengths of time in the city.

"Is anyone here?" he bellowed.

To all appearances, the building had been abandoned. The apocalyptic air of no workers in such a huge building that had once been a beehive of activity made us feel like we were witnessing the end of the world.

"Let's go to the basement. That's where most of the inventory is," he said.

We took the stairs. Several basement rooms had flooded, the tubes and plumbing having burst from disuse. We were descending into a state more primitive than civilization.

Two of the largest rooms were in good shape, but they were unattractive, soulless shells of what they had been on my first visit to the Palacio.

We flipped through several volumes of nineteenth-century classics. Luis put them in the makeshift cart he had grabbed on the way in. In the next room, we helped ourselves to some Greco-

Roman texts and detective novels. Luis, like all authors, was pleased to see his works in print. I have never known an author who was not.

On the second floor, we bagged several more books, including some in French, but on the top floor we beheld the desolation of the abandoned writers' tables.

"This building always seemed to me like a galleon with writers forced to row, but it's sad to see it empty," Luis said. I rested my hand on his shoulder.

"Better times are coming."

"Surely, my dear, but my eyes won't see them. The war has taken my health and vigor, and I doubt I'll live to see a peace agreement. However, I'm not so sure I want to survive this war. I foresee all too clearly the Spain these pious hypocrites want to enforce and how they'll set us back at least a hundred years, if not all the way back to the Inquisition."

"But if the war in Europe starts, the Republic still might have a chance," I said meekly.

Luis gave me a skeptical smile.

We went into the office of Mr. Castro, the editor himself. It had, of course, been looted. Luis went up to the display case where the most valuable books were kept, but it was empty. He sighed. "I had hoped to rescue a couple of the boss's treasures. I've always had a weak spot for dangerous banned books."

"Well, looks like you aren't the only one." I shrugged.

Just then Luis smacked his forehead as if remembering something. "Wait, maybe they're still here. I was one of the writers that the boss trusted the most . . . Don't ask why—I have no idea—but on more than one occasion I saw him move the display case and . . ."

I helped Luis push the piece of furniture, and a trapdoor appeared.

"Eureka!" he exclaimed. We pried it open and found a small room full of books. Many of them were of inestimable worth, but Luis only had eyes for those stored on shelves trimmed in brass.

"They're here!" he exclaimed.

We leafed through them and confirmed Luis's hunch: Many were custom editions! Luis pulled down one of the volumes Castro had shown me on my first visit. It had a mysterious, dangerous look.

"*Malleus Maleficarum*, the *Hammer of Witches.*" His voice was low with awe as he stroked the spine.

"Of all of these, is that the only one that calls your name?" I asked.

"It's a unique work that sent shockwaves throughout Europe. Think about it: Some books are written to theoretically help the world but end up destroying it."

"Like Marx's *Das Kapital*?"

He nodded. We added a few more of Castro's prized volumes to our pile. As we closed the trapdoor and replaced the display case, we heard a noise from downstairs. Luis and I stood stock-still.

Then we heard a woman's voice we both recognized: "You're sure they came in this building?"

I stared at Luis in terror. "What are we going to do?" I mouthed.

"The back stairs." His voice was barely audible as he pointed down the hall.

We crept out of the office and opened a metal door to metal stairs that led to the building's back door. We moved as fast as the need for silence allowed, but just before we got to the street, we heard them above us.

"Stop!" the woman barked at us.

We ran down the empty street. A trolley car had just paused to let passengers off, and we sped up to catch it. The militiawoman and two men were running after us, but the trolley pulled away before they could reach us.

"We've got to get these books to the store," Luis said. My eyes were nearly unseeing with fear. Luis changed the plan. He handed me *Malleus Maleficarum* and said, "Actually, I'll take all these to the store. You take this one and go home."

After we were back across the river, we parted ways, and half an hour later I was in the safety of our apartment. Juan was giving Jaime a bath. I fixed dinner.

As we ate, Juan asked me how I was doing.

"I'm all right. Could you sing to Jaime tonight? There's something I want to read."

While Juan went through the bedtime routine with our son, I went to the little room we called the office. It was the modest library I had pulled together over the years. I sank into the chair whose cushions had by now conformed to the shape of my body, opened the cover of *Malleus Maleficarum*, and started reading.

Chapter 31

The power of books has always been underestimated, perhaps because the humans who wield power are so busy amassing their fortunes and masterminding the puppet strings of politics that they have no time to read. Yet a book is capable of changing the course of world events. That must have been what drew me in so deeply to *Malleus Maleficarum*, the *Hammer of Witches*. It was published at the end of the fifteenth century, when the printing press had started to change society. Until then, books were luxury items owned by very, very few people.

After *Malleus Maleficarum* was published in 1486, some theologians advised against its illegal and unethical prosecution tactics. Yet the authors, two Dominican friars named Heinrich Kramer and Jacob Sprenger, were following Pope Innocent VIII's orders.

It was a fascinating read both for its exaggerated tone and repetitive comments and for its subject matter. It began by endeavoring to prove the existence of witchcraft and sorcery. My father had told me about many of the esoteric practices of the Nazis that grew out of Theosophy and the Aryan legends that were behind some of their policies. The spiritism so popular in the nineteenth century was an outlet for the darker sides of society that usually stay under wraps. The second part of the book described specific practices of witchcraft, specifically pacts with the devil and details about spells, sacrifices, and sexual relations with demons. The last part addressed how to detect, arrest, try, and execute witches.

I devoured it in one prolonged sitting. There were too many similarities between what I was reading and what was occurring in the world around me.

Evil took care of itself and, though it adapted its shape and expression according to the times, had always been present in human history. There had always been inquisitors representing one ideology or another. Under the guise of obtaining information from their victims, executioners took pleasure in torture and violence. It would not be long until I myself would become one such victim of a modern inquisitor.

Chapter 32

Winter is an entrenched enemy of joy. Madrid's inhabitants were already so constantly hungry that we could hardly think of anything but food, and now it was freezing cold. People burned everything they could: furniture, the trees growing along the streets, shipping crates, and even doors. Anything burnable was worth sacrificing to fight the bitter cold of that winter. And we knew it was even worse for our compatriots in Catalonia. Franco's troops already held most of the region and were about to make their final attack on the city. We could not explain how or why Madrid managed to hold out. Many people tried to escape to Valencia. There were rumors flying about the war being over soon and the brutal repression that would follow when the Nationalists ruled the country. That inspired many people to try their luck escaping by boat to Africa, Italy, Portugal, or the Americas. The ships were jam-packed with people and some were intercepted by Francoists before they reached safe waters, but attempting to escape still seemed like a more desirable option than standing still and waiting to be caught like a rabbit.

"We've got to get out of here," I pleaded with Juan, sensing that he would be the last man in Madrid to surrender.

"I've asked for transportation out of the city, but they say nothing is available till after Christmas."

"What it we just started walking? At least we'd be getting away from this horror."

"The roads are overrun with people, and there's no food to be found along the way. Plus, Jaime . . ."

I knew he was right, but I did not want to wait around and see what Franco's men would do to Juan. That was why I had gotten out of Germany before it was too late. And now I was trapped in Spain.

"I'm going to go ask at El Porvenir. I don't know what the Fliedners and the other workers are going to do, but if they've got transportation of some kind, we could go with them."

I had to walk through the bitter cold since public transportation was no longer working and there were hardly any private vehicles left. I was stiff when I reached the gate an hour later. The porter opened it quickly and ushered me into the chapel to get warm. It was the only room they kept heated, thanks to the careful rationing of wood from the trees they had cut down. I had arrived about an hour before the children would be celebrating Christmas.

I got so close to the heater that I worried about injuring my hands. They were painfully numb from the cold and it took quite some time before I regained sensation.

"Ah, Bárbara, how nice to see you, though I would not have expected you to venture out in this cold." Teodoro Jr. smiled and sat down beside me on the pew. "It'll be the leanest Christmas since the war started. We have almost nothing to give the children."

I sighed and shook my head. "I'm so sorry."

"The Swiss nurses did manage to bring some chocolate on their last visit." He handed me a bar. I scarfed down a couple of pieces and put the rest away for Juan and Jaime.

"What are your plans? Will you, your family, and the workers stay here when Franco's troops arrive?"

Teodoro looked up to the ceiling and then gestured to the entire building. "My grandfather built all of this. He didn't do it for his family; we would've had an easier life in Germany. Spain was deep in his heart, and he dedicated himself to the country heart and soul. Did you know that he went through the last two years of high school here so he could go to college in Spain? He really wanted to understand the people. We've grown up here and inherited his love for the Spaniards. Where would we go? Germany is on the brink of war, with a fanatic in charge who's destroying all that was ever good and beautiful about our nation." He let out a long sigh.

"I feel the same, but for the Francoists, we're Lutherans, or heretics, as they say. I heard that they killed a few Spanish Protestant pastors and even a missionary."

Teodoro stood and went to the piano, stroking its cover while his gaze wandered out the large windows. "No one's born to live this life forever. I love my family, the schoolchildren, and the older people we take care of, but I'm ready to accept God's will. His strength is made perfect in my weakness."

"I wish I had your faith."

"Faith isn't something one *has*, my dear friend. It's something one *practices*. It's believing that the impossible thing is possible and not giving up hope. Will you stay for the meeting?"

I nodded and stood to help some of the teachers finish putting up decorations. The children came in and sat down. My heart hurt seeing how pale and skinny they were, with dark circles under their eyes. Many of them were orphans and others had been sent by their parents to Madrid to have a better future.

Elfriede Fliedner, Teodoro's cousin, sat at the piano. We all stood and sang one of the most well-known songs.

A mighty fortress is our God,
a bulwark never failing;
our helper he, amid the flood
of mortal ills prevailing.
For still our ancient foe
does seek to work us woe;
his craft and power are great,
and armed with cruel hate,
on earth is not his equal.

Did we in our own strength confide,
our striving would be losing,
were not the right Man on our side,
the Man of God's own choosing.
You ask who that may be?
Christ Jesus, it is he;
Lord Sabaoth his name,
from age to age the same;
and he must win the battle.

And though this world, with devils filled,
should threaten to undo us,
we will not fear, for God has willed

his truth to triumph through us.
The prince of darkness grim,
we tremble not for him;
his rage we can endure,
for lo! his doom is sure;
one little word shall fell him.

When the hymn ended and the last note of the piano rang out, my eyes were full of tears, but my heart felt stronger. I was going to need all the strength I could get.

Chapter 33

Teodoro Jr. made sure I was driven home. I do not know if I would have made it walking by myself. I was missing my family in Germany terribly. I had a new family, but the family-sized hole in my heart was hard to fill. I mused on an idea that had occurred to me. If I were able to understand the reason why each particular circumstance happened, I might be able to find the beauty in everything that occurred. The hymn in the chapel at El Porvenir had filled me with an energy I could not explain. I went up the frigid stairwell to our apartment but stopped short when I found the front door open. Inside, everything was in complete disarray: the plates and cups smashed, clothing ripped apart, the pages of books scattered all around. My heart pounding, I ran to Jaime's room. He was not there and neither was Juan. I sank to the floor and started sobbing. I do not know how long I lay there on the freezing hardwood floor, but I finally dragged myself up. I had to go find them.

Outside my door, I heard a voice call to me from the landing. It was our neighbor, Aurora.

"They were taken, Bárbara. It was the gang from the *checa*. They came a couple of hours ago."

"They took Jaime too?"

"Yes. There was a woman screaming things I can't repeat. She was asking for you."

I burst out crying again. Aurora hugged me, and it took me some time to calm down and breathe normally again.

I did not know where to go or what to do. The only person I trusted in Madrid besides the Fliedners was Luis. He would be up. He hardly slept anymore and was more ghost than man these days with how thin he was. He answered at the first ring of the telephone.

"I'll come right away," he said. And then, "No, you'd better meet me here. They might come back."

Luis did not live far from us, just a twenty-minute walk, but the chill stabbed into me and took my breath away as soon as I stepped outside. The streets were empty. I did not meet a single soul, as if the world had suddenly been emptied of all inhabitants. I wondered if I were having a nightmare, but unfortunately everything was all too real.

The night watchman opened the door of Luis's building to me, and I climbed the five flights of stairs to his tiny loft apartment. He opened the door before I even knocked. It was even colder inside his apartment than in the stairwell. I had been to his place only once before, and that had been in nice weather. With the drafts and the cold, I understood now why he was sick.

"I'm so sorry, Bárbara. This damned country has lost its mind."

I collapsed into the only chair in the room, and he sat on the edge of the bed. There was no electricity, and two candles provided the only light.

"What should I do?"

He gave me the pained look of someone with no answers.

"These people don't even respect Christmas Eve. They're a bunch of damned pagans. We can't do anything for the time being. If we spend all night walking around looking for them, we'll freeze to death. Is there anyone who can help us?" he asked.

I shrugged helplessly. "Indalecio Prieto went to Mexico. He's been traveling throughout the Americas as a Spanish ambassador since he lost his post here. Juan Negrín is in Barcelona. The rest of the government hates him for being too moderate. The war here inside Madrid between the factions just keeps going. The Communists are wiping out the anarchists, like what happened in Barcelona, and the government of the Republic is mainly symbolic now."

Madrid had become complete chaos. Juan was on the side of those pushing for negotiating a peace agreement with Franco, as were Indalecio and Azaña, but Negrín leaned on the radical wing of the Socialist Workers' Party and on the Communists. On the other hand, the Nationalists would not negotiate. Franco demanded unconditional surrender. The French were already holding secret conversations about recognizing Franco's regime as legitimate, as were the British.

"So who can help us?" Luis repeated, but I had no answer. Only a miracle could rescue my family.

Then a faint idea occurred to me. "Well, Juan does have one Communist friend. He might be able to help. His name is Manuel Azcárate, and his father, Pablo Azcárate, was close with Indalecio."

We grabbed onto that shred of hope and, as soon as dawn came, started walking to Communist headquarters.

The city was desolate. People in threadbare clothing walked with their heads low, venturing out with the desperate hope of having luck with their ration cards. When we walked up to the building occupied by the Communists, two militiamen stopped us at the door. I explained that I was there to see Manuel Azcárate, the leader of the Communist Youth. They allowed us to enter.

Manuel was very young. We had met only once, at a local government meeting, but he remembered me. His eyes rose in surprise as I told him what had happened.

"I have a good guess where they might have taken Juan, but the child . . . that concerns me. What you've described sounds like a group from the infamous Buenavista *checa*. It seems to draw the worst of every group. We'll have to get an order from Colonel Segismundo Casado and show up with militiamen to get them to pay attention to us."

Manuel made several calls. The order arrived within a couple of hours, and he gathered a group of ten men he trusted. Armed to the teeth, they went in a small truck, and we followed in another.

"You two had better wait out here. This is likely going to be dangerous," Manuel warned.

"I'm sorry, but I have to go inside with you," I answered.

Manuel nodded. "Brave women like you are what this Republic needs."

We left the cars parked in front of the police commissary that had turned into a *checa*. The guards out front looked nervous. Manuel walked up with the poise of authority, and no one stopped him until a sergeant stepped forward.

"You can't come in here armed," the sergeant said.

"We've got orders," Manuel replied, holding out the piece of paper.

They took us to García Imperial, second-in-command to Luis Omaña. The thug had his feet propped up on a table and was smoking a pipe. I knew exactly what his lewd gaze was doing to me.

"Juan Delgado? Yep, I think they brought him in early this morning for conspiring against the Republic."

"Who accuses him?"

"Ah, that's classified information. They were also after his wife, the German spy, Bárbara Something or Other. I don't suppose that would be you, little missy?" he said, devouring me with his eyes. I tried to hide my fear.

"Bring Juan Delgado here immediately," Manuel stated.

"I'm no Communist, and your party doesn't interest me."

"It's an order from the colonel."

"Want to know where you can put that order from your little colonel?" García Imperial snarled.

Manuel's men pulled out their guns, and the policemen followed suit.

"Hold on now, everybody. Let's have this little party in peace." García Imperial's tone had moderated to jovial placation.

Just then Luis Omaña walked in, a thug as despicable as his underling, though more astute. He knew that if he plugged the leader of the Communist Youth, the retaliation would likely be the end of the Buenavista commissary. For years Omaña had enjoyed impunity for kidnapping, robbing, torturing, and then murdering his victims. His plans for making himself scarce before Franco's troops entered the city were secure. He was not going to put all of that at risk just for a second-rate politician.

"Bring the prisoner," Omaña ordered one of his men.

Manuel tried his question a second time. "Who denounced him?"

"Ana Ortiz, the militiawoman; surely you know of her. She's

chased down more fifth-column double agents than anyone. Those traitors are coming out of hiding now. They've got snipers posted throughout the city and have infiltrated the Republican army and the militias."

I knew exactly which woman he was talking about. She had been trying to accuse me of espionage for years. Now that the city was in chaos, she had seized her chance.

"Where's the child?" Manuel asked, taking advantage of Omaña's apparent willingness to cooperate.

"We don't keep kids here," the police commissioner said flatly.

After a few minutes of awkward silence, Juan appeared at the door. His face was bloodied and swollen to almost unrecognizable, but at least he was alive. He could barely stand upright, and two of Manuel's men stepped up to support him.

As we were leaving, the porter leaned over and whispered into my ear, "The child is at San Rafael's Asylum. That's where some of the women from Ventas women's prison are being held, to make more room for men in the prisons."

We kept our eyes on the assault guards and militiamen as we walked out of the *checa*. We did not breathe easy until we were driving away.

Finally, Juan spoke. "I'm so sorry, honey. I couldn't do anything to protect Jaime." He leaned into me and sobbed on my shoulder, a wreck from grief and nearly twenty-four hours of beatings and interrogation. I gently stroked his abused face and kissed his wounds as lightly as I could. But all I could think about now was finding Jaime.

Chapter 34

Madrid
December 25, 1938

Manuel drove Juan straight to a doctor. A thorough examination showed that his wounds were all superficial and would heal in time. But emotionally he was nearly unresponsive.

Then I told Manuel what the Buenavista porter had told me.

"The San Rafael Asylum? It used to be a Catholic hospital and orphanage. But in thirty-six they transferred all the female prisoners from Ventas to San Rafael. Most of them were political prisoners since the jails had already been emptied of the common prisoners at the beginning of the war."

"So Jaime could be there."

"If the militiawoman took him there, he might be. Her group hunts down and imprisons fifth-column spies. She's renowned for her cruelty, but I'm guessing this is a trap to get at you," Manuel said.

I did not care. I just wanted to get to Jaime.

"We've got to be smarter than she is. I'll send someone to ask a few questions and then—"

"I'll go," Luis interrupted. We all turned to him in surprise. "You're forgetting I used to be a policeman. I know a few former agents who had easy assignments, like the women's prison. I'll ask around and then we'll see how to get the boy back."

I had to admit that it was better for Luis to go than me. If I were arrested, we would have two problems instead of one. That woman seemed like the reincarnation of the devil himself.

Manuel arranged for a car to take us to the asylum, which was in the northern outskirts of the city. I asked to go along just to the gate and wait outside with the car.

Juan stayed at Communist headquarters to start recovering from the beatings he had endured.

Before Luis walked through the gate, he turned and waved. I tried to ignore the ominous feeling I had.

An hour later, Luis had not returned.

Manuel was sitting up front beside the driver. He looked calm enough but was toying with his cigarette lighter constantly.

"We've got to go in," I said.

"I'm not sure that's a good idea."

"I'll put on a nurse's uniform or whatever I have to do to get in."

Manuel turned and studied me. "Very well." He pulled out his gun and checked to make sure it was loaded. Then he handed me a pistol. "Be careful; the trigger is very sensitive."

We got out of the car and walked to the building. Two guards let us pass when Manuel showed his credentials. An officer met us at the door.

"A friend of ours went in over an hour ago, Luis Fernández-Vior," Manuel explained.

The officer looked at the list in front of him.

"Yes, he's on here. Agent Vázquez saw him. I'll call for him."

The policeman asked one of his subordinates to get Vázquez, who appeared not long after.

"Vázquez," the officer asked, "have you seen a Mr. Luis . . ."

"Luis Fernández-Vior," Manuel supplied.

"Yes," Vázquez answered. "He was here about an hour ago asking about a young boy. He believed that Ana Ortiz, the militiawoman, had brought the child in."

"Is Mr. Fernández-Vior still here?"

"No, sir. I told him that Ana Ortiz had not brought in any children in the past few days. I gave him her address. She's in a house on Gran Vía, one requisitioned from an actor who escaped to the Francoists."

Manuel looked as surprised as I felt.

"Is there another exit?" I asked.

"Yes, ma'am, right out the back. I walked him there myself. I love Mr. Fernández-Vior's detective stories."

Manuel and I thanked the officer and raced back to the car.

The address was off the Plaza de Callao, near the Palacio de la Prensa movie theater. The driver screeched up, heedless of the parking, and Manuel and I ran inside the building. The porter confirmed that Ana Ortiz lived on the top floor in a large apartment that looked over the plaza. Since the elevator was out of order, we took the stairs.

Panting, we got to the fifth floor and found the door open. An expansive living room led to a large deck. The apartment looked empty, but as we approached the deck, we saw a body on the floor.

"Luis!" I screamed, running up to him.

He was bleeding from his stomach, and his shirt was stained red. I lifted his head gently, and he opened his eyes.

"She took him," he gasped out. "That damned . . ." The pain would not allow him to finish.

"Where? Where did she take him?"

"I don't know. She was all sweet and friendly when she opened the door to me, saying there must have been some mistake, that I could leave but she hoped I found the boy I was looking for. But then Jaime cried. She pulled out a dagger and . . ."

While I spoke with Luis, Manuel searched the house for a clue.

"We'll call a doctor," I told him.

"Don't bother. This is a dignified way to exit the scene. Old age has never become me," Luis said in barely more than a whisper. "I'd rather go now, like this, while my head and legs still work."

Tears were streaming down my face. Luis had been my Virgil all this time, guiding me through the twists and turns of a world I did not know. I was going to be so lonely without him.

The world is such a strange place. We have no idea why we are born, and we bear the mark of Cain on our foreheads. Death waits patiently for us and then robs us of the only thing we actually ever had.

Luis died a death worthy of a writer, putting a dramatic full stop to his story. I let go of his lifeless body. My friend was no longer there.

"Bárbara, we haven't found much, but she may have fled to a town en route to Valencia. It seems she has family in that area."

I was speechless. Grief was ransacking my insides, but the only thing pushing me forward was rage and the need to rescue my son as soon as possible. The city's days were numbered, and a militiawoman could not simply waltz through the battle lines surrounding Madrid. I had to get my little boy back.

On the deck, I looked up. The sky had reddened, as if Spain were no longer capable of dealing with any more blood and suffering. The purple clouds reflected the cold of that Christmas Day that would be the worst and saddest one of my life.

"We'll take you back to your husband. You two will be staying in one of our safe houses for a while," Manuel said.

Manuel had been so good to us, but he did not understand that a mother without her child is a walking dead woman. The only thing on my mind and in my heart was the need to get Jaime back no matter what it cost.

Part 3

One, Great, and Free

Chapter 35

Madrid
January 1, 1939

The grief in my heart was debilitating. All that mattered to me was finding Jaime. I knew that the Republic was falling apart and that our lives were in danger, but none of that mattered since Jaime was not with us. Luis had died because of me, and Juan was done in by everything that had happened since his arrest and subsequent torture. Manuel tried to help me, but the damned militiawoman had disappeared. We had even gone to her hometown and questioned her family members, but no one knew her whereabouts. After six days of constant searching, I was beginning to lose hope.

That morning I was pacing the house Manuel had arranged for us to stay in, feeling sadder and more frustrated than ever. Juan's lack of energy for anything at all kept him depressed in bed.

"Honey, we have to do something," I said, sitting down beside him.

"I'm a coward," he groaned for the thousandth time. "I didn't protect you or Jaime."

"Juan, it's not your fault; you have to believe me. You were attacked by people with guns, and then they tortured you."

"I wish they had just killed me instead of taking Jaime."

I swallowed hard. "We're going to get him back. You have to believe."

"Believe? In what and in who? That crazy woman is capable of anything."

And for the thousandth time I said, "I just don't understand why she hates us so much."

Something in my question hit Juan differently that time, and he opened up in a way I never saw coming.

"Bárbara, this really is all my fault." He broke down with great heaving sobs. This was different from his now frequent bouts of weeping.

"What do you mean?" My voice had grown small and hesitant. I could tell there was something there.

"I . . . I had an affair with Ana. I was so lonely. You and I had grown distant, both of us focused on our own things. I met her at a political meeting. We slept together, but it was a one-night stand, and I didn't think it was worth telling you about. The next time I saw her, I told her it was over. That's when she arrested you. I didn't think I'd ever see her again."

Nausea roiled in my stomach, despite the fact that I had hardly eaten for days. He had known all this time and had not said a word about it.

I shoved all my various feelings and reactions aside and focused on what counted right then. "What do you know about her? Surely she mentioned something about her future plans to you."

Dots were connecting in Juan's head. He sat up.

To encourage him, I said, "Forget what you did. Now we just need to save Jaime."

"Yes, I remember now. She wanted to flee Spain and go to Venezuela. I think she has family there, an aunt maybe. I bet she's trying to get on a boat to the Americas from the port at Valencia."

I jumped to my feet. It was still very early in the morning, and there was not a second to lose.

"Where are we going?" Juan asked.

"Manuel can help us."

We managed to get ahold of him despite the early hour. As soon as I told him what was going on, he arranged a car for us and letters of safe passage to get us through the checkpoints. Juan drove. I could do nothing but pray to God that Jaime was still in Spain.

Two hours into driving, we came to a checkpoint. The guards looked very rough and their uniforms were little more than rags. They hounded us for money. We did not have much, but I gave them my gold earrings. Other than that run-in, we reached Valencia without incident.

Juan drove straight to the port. Manuel had given us the name of the colonel in charge who would know which boats had recently set sail and which were about to launch for the Americas. Time for finding Jaime was running out, but at least we felt like we were finally on the right path.

Chapter 36

Bombs and shells had wreaked havoc on Valencia. Of all Spanish territory, Valencia, Madrid, and Barcelona had suffered the worst of Nationalist air raids. Colonel Ramírez, Manuel's friend, told us that people no longer went into hiding during the attacks. Instead, they ran to the coast to gather the dead fish that floated up after the bombs hit the water. The port was one of the hardest-hit areas, since the rebels wanted to render it useless and stop the few ships that managed to get out.

"The bombers are Italian planes. They've killed countless people, not to mention those left homeless, mutilated, or driven literally insane. Just four years ago this was one of the happiest cities in the country. I can't make sense of everything that's happened," Colonel Ramírez said.

I listened but was growing impatient. Fortunately, Juan was back to himself. The weight on his conscience had been worse for him than the actual beatings from the militia. He nodded at the colonel and confidently steered the conversation.

"Are the names of all travelers on board the ships known?"

The colonel shook his head. "It's impossible to keep records anymore. We're doing well to keep track of the ship names and their final destinations."

"How many have left for the Americas in the past few days?"

Ramírez looked up to the sky, thinking. "None. And I'm sure of that. Two set sail for France, one went to Algeria, and another I think was bound for French Morocco."

His answer did not fill me with hope.

"When does the next one crossing the Atlantic leave?" I asked.

He looked down at the lists in front of him and answered, "In one hour there's a boat leaving for Cuba. It stops in Venezuela before its final destination of Argentina."

"That's got to be it!" My cry was a strangled mixture of excitement and terror.

"They'll pull up the gangplank in thirty minutes. You've got to get on board before that if you're going to find him."

"You can't delay the departure?"

"No, I'm sorry; that's impossible."

Ramírez told us the berth number, and we raced out. To our dismay, it was on the opposite end of the port, and it took us twelve eternal minutes to get there. We would have so little time to get on board, search the boat, and find our son.

Two sailors stopped us on the gangplank.

"Where do you think you're going? Do you have tickets?"

We explained what was going on, but they eyed us with suspicion. Juan held out the authorization that Colonel Ramírez had given us, and they accepted it reluctantly.

"All right, we'll help you, but we've got to remove the gangplank in fifteen minutes to prepare to push off."

We ran the rest of the way to the boat but saw no sign of Ana on the main deck. There was no luck on the upper two decks either.

"Five minutes left," one of the sailors informed us.

Juan and I were willing to set sail with the boat if we had to, but the sailors would not have allowed it.

"How do we get to the third-class deck?" Juan asked.

One sailor pointed to a set of stairs, but the other said, "You don't have time. You've got to get off the boat now."

We ran to the stairway. A narrow hallway led to a large room filled with chairs and surrounded by windows that looked out to the sea. We looked all around, but Ana Ortiz was not there.

"They've got to be here," I said.

"Yes, but where?" Juan replied.

The sailors were making their way toward us when I glimpsed the silhouette of a woman down a hallway. Her back was to me.

"Ana!" I screamed. She turned, and Jaime was in her arms.

I dashed toward her, and she ran up the stairs to the main deck. Juan overtook me, but just as he was about to reach Ana, she leaned over the edge of the boat and held Jaime out over the sea. Juan came to a dead stop and raised his arms.

A mangled cry erupted from deep within him. "Please, no, don't do it!"

Ana bored into him with her cold eyes and, just like that, let go of my two-year-old darling.

Chapter 37

Valencia
January 1, 1939

Without a second thought, Juan threw himself overboard in the same spot. Ana tried to slip away amid the uproar and confusion, but I tackled her. I pinned her to the ground with the full weight of my body. She kicked and writhed. At any other time, she would have been stronger than me, but I was fueled by maternal rage and nailed her hands to the deck with my own. She turned. I looked straight into her bloodshot eyes.

"Get off me, bitch!" she screamed. "That asshole stood me up. You both deserve what you got and more!"

Ana's fate was of no concern to me. I just wanted my son to be okay. She stopped fighting when the two sailors replaced me in holding her down. Soon enough several of the ship's officers and the captain arrived. Other passengers and crew members had also jumped into the water after Jaime.

I stood and looked over the rail. Juan was holding a small bundle. Sailors swam up with a life jacket for Juan and soon a rowboat approached.

I got off the ship and ran to the ladder that led down from the dock. The rowboat had arrived, and Juan put Jaime on the ground and tried to revive him. I crumpled beside them, unable to stop crying.

"Oh God, oh God, please!" I said it over and over and over.

Juan kept blowing hard into Jaime's little mouth to force air into his lungs. Finally, Jaime coughed and then spat out a gush of water.

"He's okay!" Juan screamed.

I grabbed Jaime and pressed him to me. He was shivering with cold, but he was alive and in my arms.

Two sailors escorted Ana to the port authorities, but she no longer mattered to me. Now we could go back home, forget everything that had happened, and try to start over.

Chapter 38

There was nothing to eat. We were no longer under Manuel's protection. Teodoro Jr. thought it would be best for us to relocate to El Porvenir.

Things in the city kept getting worse. Negrín had fled, and the short-lived government of Besteiro, Casado, and Miaja was now in direct conflict with the Communists. People already talked about it like the "little civil war" in Madrid.

Juan knew the Communists had gathered at Ciudad Lineal to face the part of the Republican military that had led the recent coup. Supposedly, the Communists wanted to keep Casado from handing over the city to Franco. But right then, after a long and bitter winter, the rest of Madrid just wanted the war to be over, whatever Franco's peace terms were.

The Communist troops were coming from El Pardo with the goal of invading the rest of the city. We heeded Teodoro's advice and moved into the school. We were under no illusion that it would be safer there—nowhere was safe in Madrid—but at least we would be among friends.

Word spread that the Communists had successfully taken control of the capital, but they did not have the numbers to control any of the other Republic bastions still holding out against the Nationalists.

Teodoro and the other teachers were handing out food when a handful of Communist soldiers arrived and requested that Juan go with them. They wanted him to mediate between them and Segismundo Casado, the Republican general who had led the coup to oust Negrín. The Communists did not want this internal Republican conflict to become advantageous to the Fascists.

"Juan, don't go," I pleaded.

"I have to, Bárbara. It may keep more blood from being spilled within the Republican ranks."

I shook my head, "No, it's too late for that. That's what you've been trying to do for the last three years."

Juan looked at me gravely. He thought I was throwing in his face everything that had happened politically, but that was not it. I knew better than anyone else that he had never stopped working for peace from within the more moderate side of his party, but no one had wanted to hear it.

"The war is lost, honey," I added, as gently as I could.

"I know, I know. It's been lost for a long time. But if we massacre one another here in Madrid before Franco gets here, I'll never forgive myself for not trying."

He went with the Communists, and I went to our rooms to give Jaime something to eat. I felt so alone, like I had no friends left in Spain. I broke down crying.

Someone must have heard my sobs. There was a knock at the door, and I opened to find Elfriede, one of Teodoro's cousins.

"Oh, my dear, I'm so sorry about everything you've been through. Teodoro told me what happened with little Jaime. Thank God he's all right." I nodded and tried to wipe away my tears. She hugged me and said, "A good cry does everyone good. But what brings you to tears at this particular moment, Bárbara?"

"I'm exhausted. We've lost everything, my husband just left to go on a really dangerous mission, and I feel so alone."

Elfriede led me to the couch and sat beside me. She stroked my hair and with a singsong voice said, "This, too, shall pass. Life is one trial after another. If we pass them all, at the end we receive a prize, a crown. These past few years have been truly terrible, and the worst part is that they've managed to dehumanize us. Don't hear me wrong—here at El Porvenir we've been able to help hundreds of people even with practically nonexistent resources. But at our core, we've all grown used to suffering, desperation, and other people's pain. It's become normalized, but it isn't normal. I can promise you that through the comfort of his Word, God always sends us the answer for every problem."

Her words filled me with peace.

"I feel like such a coward," I whispered.

She laughed loudly. "A coward? I've never met a woman who was. We bring children into the world, so we can't afford to be cowards. As soon as they're out of the womb, we're capable of doing anything in the world for them."

"Are you a mother?"

Elfriede smiled. "No and yes. God has given me hundreds of children. I remember your stint as a teacher here. What if"—here she cocked her head and raised her eyebrows—"you started helping out at the bookstore and a bit at the school until all of this war nonsense wraps up?"

Her offer was a gift straight from heaven. I needed something to keep my mind busy.

At that time, the Fliedner bookstore, the Librería Nacional y Extranjera, was located in the Phoenix building off Caballero de Gracia and at the corner of Alcalá. When I arrived for my first day, I was timid and felt overwhelmed. It scared me to leave Jaime even for a short time. He had not been out of my sight since we rescued him. But I knew that I needed to get involved with books again. They had always saved me, like driftwood during a storm at sea.

The bookstore had been broken into a few days before. The vandals had ripped up a few volumes, knocked down some bookshelves, and trampled the Bibles, but nothing had been taken. People did not usually steal books.

I spent the day cleaning up and getting things put back in order. I was pleasantly surprised to see a few people watching from the sidewalk, eager for us to reopen. Perhaps I was not the only one who felt like books could save us from our shipwrecked country.

The next morning I had the place looking tolerable. I checked the stock and opened the store to the public around noon. It was a clear day, a precursor to spring, cold but bright. It felt like the light was a promise that beauty and peace would soon return to the country. It made me miss the Madrid I knew before the war.

A tall, thin, disheveled man wearing Coke-bottle glasses entered. "When the bookstores reopen, it's a sign that the world is waking up," he said in a slow voice.

"We can only hope," I answered.

"Are you a Fliedner?" he asked. "I haven't seen you before. I met the grandfather, Federico, an incredible man. My family and I attended his church. I'm an atheist, you know, but I've always admired the Fliedner family. Their work here in Spain has been incredible."

I shook my head and clarified that I was just a friend who worked with them.

"Ah, well. What I came in here for was an almanac."

I handed him the most recent one, and he left after paying.

Half a dozen people came into the store that day. Though few, it was enough to make me feel active and useful. I was contributing my little grain of sand for things to change for the better.

The next day, Juan returned, unshaven and discouraged but alive. We hugged for a long time, then took a walk around the school grounds after a bite to eat.

"The Communists have surrendered. Some are still holding out, but Casado has won this round."

"So what's going to happen now?"

Juan paused and took my hands in his.

"Casado plans to go to Burgos to surrender. We've lost, Bárbara. All this suffering has been for naught."

We held each other in a long embrace. I thought back to when we met in Berlin. Juan was the best-looking guy in town, and I was a girl living on the dream of opening a bookstore. Now we had a child, and the war had made us grow up so fast we felt like an aged couple. What bowed us over was the weight of the war on our backs. As soon as it was over, surely we would get our strength back. But what awaited us would be a trial perhaps more difficult than any yet.

Chapter 39

Madrid
March 27, 1939

The sound of marching filled the air. Worn-out rubber boots from too many years of war resounded over the cobblestoned streets of Madrid. We peeked out of our window and saw the moonlight glancing off the guns. None of the Republican troops were talking, and their heads hung low. They had lost. From the start, their leaders had betrayed them. At its core, this war, as all the others, was a face-off between elites who could not get along and wanted to control the country.

"Well, it's over," Juan said. Casado's envoys had been rejected time and again, as Franco would accept nothing but unconditional surrender. Even his terms for demobilization and treatment of the wounded were humiliating.

"Where will the soldiers go?" I asked. They were headed up the street to Cuatro Caminos, but I did not know where they would go after that.

"To the front to turn in their weapons," he said.

Part of me felt relieved. After the fighting between Republican factions in Madrid's streets over the past few weeks, I had feared that we would have a long war throughout the city. It was better this way. Though it was humiliating for all of us, too many people had already died.

Sleep eluded us that night. We wondered if the Francoists would come for us, but nothing happened.

The next morning, the streets rang with the sound of triumphal cheering. We did not know if the euphoric din was to welcome the Nationalist troops or to mark the end of war, hunger, and cold.

The old flags of the monarchy were flying from many banisters.

Juan and I went up to Teodoro Jr. and asked what he wanted us to do.

"Well," he replied, "it's a Wednesday, so let's do whatever we do on Wednesdays."

"But we've heard that the Nationalist army is going to march from Ciudad Universitaria to the Puente de los Franceses."

He shrugged. "I've not concerned myself with what the rest of the city was doing throughout the war, and I don't think I'll start now."

I still did not understand that for the Fliedner schools, the Francoists posed much more of a threat than the Republic. Franco had made it clear that his war was a crusade and that his regime would be indubitably one of National Catholicism. We would remain the age-old heretics. While tolerated for a time during the Republic, we would become easy targets for anyone to squash like cockroaches.

We passed out the food to the older people and were about to start serving the children when a tall, blond man dressed in a long, shiny black leather coat walked in. He was holding a wad of red fabric in his hands.

The speechless porter followed him in helplessly. Finally, I asked him if we could help him in some way.

"I'm Thomsem. Where's the minister, Fliedner?"

He was clearly a Nazi and probably a Gestapo agent. I had seen very few Gestapo agents during the war. It suddenly occurred to me that this was at least one bright spot in those difficult years.

"Follow me," I said and led him to Teodoro Jr.'s office.

As soon as he saw Teodoro, the blond man spat out, "Why haven't they shot you?"

Teodoro's eyebrows rose and he shrugged. "We decided to stay put and try to help out."

"I want to see the building."

Teodoro handed me the keys and asked, "Bárbara, would you be so kind as to give our visitor a tour?"

Spending time in that man's presence was exactly what I did not want to do, but I held out my shaking hand for the keys and nodded.

We went to the second story, and after I had opened several rooms for him, he asked me to show him the street-facing rooms. I took him to the room with access to the main balcony. He went in and exclaimed, "Yes, this is perfect!"

He unfurled a large flag and secured it to the balcony. It hung down nearly to the level of the door. Then he sighed and stood there taking in the street, as if he personally had conquered Madrid.

"Are you German?" he asked me.

His question made me jump. I had hoped he would not notice. "Yes, I was born in Berlin."

He frowned and studied me carefully. "This place will be hearing from me soon." With that, he went back down the stairs and was on his way.

I returned to Teodoro's office and told him what had happened.

"So there's a Nazi flag hanging out front now."

His face did not change. "If God has allowed it, there must be a reason."

Teodoro detested the Nazis, but he also knew that the Franco-ists would not tolerate a non-Catholic school in the city. We had heard stories about what happened in other parts of Spain once the Nationalists took over, and we had very low expectations.

Chapter 40

The war had ended, which may have been reason enough to celebrate, but a civil war is not like other wars. It is citizen against citizen, neighbor against neighbor, family member against family member. It allows people to act out their long-held resentments and eliminate their adversaries. Many intellectuals were harassed or directly murdered by the Nationalists. Federico García Lorca did not come out in favor of either side, but that did not spare him from being assassinated. Miguel de Unamuno at first spoke in favor of the Nationalists' coup but then condemned its barbarian repression of innocent people whose only crime was thinking for themselves. Amparo Barayón, the wife of Ramón J. Sender, was shot to death.

We had heard stories about what happened among the rebels during the war, but we clung to the ridiculous hope that perhaps, once the war was over, the military would be content to lock up the dissidents for a time. We did not want to admit that what they were after was revenge, whether revenge for *checa* victims or for personal disputes.

The end of the war was more bitter than happy. We felt defeated in every way possible, including morally. Juan would not venture outside of El Porvenir's gates for fear of being detained. And any group of even two or three people who paused to chat in the street would be separated forcibly by the military.

Teodoro Jr. went to the presiding general to request permission to hold Sunday services, and he was told to ask the person in charge of civil matters. He managed to get an appointment with that employee but, with zero explanation or apology, was forbidden from holding any Protestant services. Teodoro explained that the church had been there since 1870, but to no avail. Teodoro kept up his requests, and a few days later, another general agreed to discuss the matter with Franco himself. Finally, Teodoro received verbal permission to hold Protestant services. It was more because of his German origin than an expression of religious tolerance on the regime's part.

In mid-April, the Falange detained Luis Moreno, a worker in the children's home run by the Fliedners in El Escorial. That made us all feel like the sword of Damocles was dangling overhead.

Along with all my compatriots who had remained in Madrid throughout the war, I was summoned to the German embassy. They suspected we were potential collaborators with the Communists. I went with Teodoro and his extended family. We were called one by one. I was shaking when my turn came. I was holding Jaime, but that seemed to make no difference to the Nazi employee in front of me.

"Bárbara Spiel, yes?"

"Yes, sir."

"Why did you remain in Madrid, in disobedience to a direct order from Adolf Hitler?"

His question was so direct and aggressive that I paused before deciding how to respond.

"I married a Spaniard and was pregnant."

"But you are German?"

"Yes, sir. I never renounced my nationality. I left our country voluntarily."

"With what intention?"

"To open a bookstore and sell foreign books here in Madrid."

He frowned, as if the word *bookstore* were distasteful and suspicious.

"I'll issue you a German passport for the moment, but you may not leave the city without communicating first with us. Is that clear?"

I gave him an annoyed look, but he simply jotted something down and barked out the next person's name.

I spent most mornings and some afternoons in the Librería Nacional y Extranjera. I missed Luis terribly. We were not selling any books, but the German soldiers of the Condor Legion that had fought with Franco bought postcards to send back home. Those were the main things we sold in those days, and we used the money for food. The new ration cards administered to the citizens of Madrid were good for a pitifully small amount of very low-quality food. Yet even that was more than we had been getting in the last two years of the Republic, when food was extremely hard to come by.

A group of somewhat disheveled Condor Legion soldiers came into the store. They eyed me and made lewd comments, but they shut up quickly when I spoke to them in German.

One of them stepped forward and said, "Forgive my comrades, ma'am. It's been a long time since they've seen a pretty woman."

"I'm married and have a child," I answered.

"Oh, I—I'm so sorry," the young man said, turning red. He gave his comrades a withering look of reproach before turning back to me. "I'm Sigmund Müller and have been in Spain for two years, long enough to pick up a bit of the language."

"I'm Bárbara," I said, shaking his hand.

"I enlisted to do away with Communism." He was speaking in Spanish, clearly desirous to try out his linguistic skills with someone who could understand even if he made a mistake. "But I didn't like this war. There's too much hatred and too many crimes. It's not what I learned at home or in the army."

"Sometimes we have to play roles we never imagined," I said. I did not want this boy to feel judged, but the Condor Legion had mercilessly bombed the civil population.

"I want to go home, forget all of this, get married, and have a normal life. Now I understand the value of everything I left behind. It's odd, but you have to lose what you love most to realize how much you need it."

"Here," I said, handing him a postcard with a Bible verse on it. He struggled to read it aloud in Spanish: "'Remember now thy Creator in the days of thy youth, while the evil days come not, nor the years draw nigh, when thou shalt say, I have no pleasure in them,' Ecclesiastes 12:1."

Tears welled up in his eyes. "Thank you," he said. "I won't forget this. If you ever find yourself in Stuttgart, my parents have a bakery in Schlossplatz, the Castle Square."

Müller gave me a military salute and left the bookstore with his companions.

The enemy had just been humanized for me, and it was disconcerting. We would prefer to think of our enemies as inhumane demons, but most times they are just people who have lived through different circumstances from ours, which have led them to make different decisions than we have.

When I got back to El Porvenir, I went to find Juan. I gave him a kiss and told him what had just happened.

"Don't fraternize too much with the enemy. Franco has not forgotten those who opposed him, and he'll find a way to make us pay one way or another."

His words were depressing, but I knew Juan was right. Vengeance is a dish served cold, and that was exactly what was about to show up on our table.

Chapter 41

Madrid
April 30, 1939

The days were passing quietly enough. It seemed like life was attempting to return to humdrum monotony. El Porvenir had received several invitations to attend the embassy's celebration of spring for Tanz in den Mai, German May Day. That afternoon, several of us got dressed up, and I managed to convince Juan to come with me. We left Jaime in El Porvenir with one of our Spaniard colleagues.

The embassy grounds were beautiful, every corner bursting with spring flowers. After a few words from the ambassador, servers made the rounds offering sandwiches and beer. It had been ages since beer was available, and the sandwiches tasted divine. Juan went and sat down once the music started.

I pulled at his arms. "Come on, come dance with me."

"It's too hot," he complained but eventually gave in. When the band started playing traditional German songs, Juan went for another beer. I joined a group of my female colleagues from El Porvenir to continue dancing. Then I heard a chillingly familiar voice behind me.

"Mrs. Spiel, how nice to see that you made it through the war."

Terrified, I turned to find the Gestapo agent who had recruited me at the beginning of the war. It seemed he, too, had survived the war and had returned to Madrid now that the conflict had ended.

"The war is over," I said as a preemptive no.

"Well, there are some loose ends to tie up. I see your husband is with you. Juan, isn't it?"

I tried to swallow but my throat was dry.

"What, may I ask, is a Socialist doing sullying German soil? Has he perhaps repented of his crimes?"

"Juan never killed anyone. On the contrary, he helped loads of people escape certain death. There are lots of people who would testify to that."

A condescending half smile played at his lips. He stared at me for a few uncomfortable moments.

"I can denounce him to the authorities, or you can continue working for us. We're aware that the Communists and Socialists are trying to secretly regroup. Names. We just need names."

It was like a nightmare I could not wake up from, and we had nowhere to go to get away from it. We had heard about the in- humane treatment of the French toward the Spaniards who crossed the border before the Nationalists took over. There were no more boats to the Americas out of Valencia. And the Portuguese dictator was deporting anyone who sought asylum in his country or used Portugal as a stepping stone for Brazil. Spain had become one huge barracks for those who supported Franco's regime and a huge jail for the rest of us.

Juan came up when he saw that I was uncomfortable with the person I was talking to, but the Gestapo agent quickly dis- appeared into the crowd before he got to me.

"Who was that man?" he asked. I tried to make my face relax into something other than a look of terror, but I could not tell if my muscles responded.

"He works for the embassy. I ran into him at the Lutheran church before the war."

Just then the new pastor of that church came up to us. He greeted us warmly, and we began talking of other things. The matter dropped from Juan's mind. I was relieved that on his first venture beyond the school grounds he did not comprehend the danger he was in.

Chapter 42

Madrid
May 19, 1939

The night before had been horrendous. The Condor Legion marched through the streets with torches, and all I could think of was the day Hitler rose to power. Fascism now reigned in Spain. It had the unique Spanish flavors of nationalism and Catholicism, but at least in aesthetics and ideology it was of the same ilk as Nazism and Italian Fascism.

Juan and I spent most of the morning walking the grounds. The Fliedner family had gone to Franco's victory parade, more to keep the school out of trouble than as a show of support for a regime that, from the beginning, had persecuted minorities and anyone who held different beliefs.

"We've got to flee the country," I blurted out. I had not told him anything about my conversation with the Gestapo agent in the embassy. Nearly three weeks had passed, but the fear still coursed through my veins.

"The more time that passes, the more things will calm down. So far no one has detained me or even called me in for questioning."

I frowned. I could not understand why Juan refused to see that the delay was just an administrative matter. The military courts were overrun with the death penalties and prison sentences handed out in droves on a daily basis. The jails were so full that the new government had opened concentration camps all over the place.

"Juan, things aren't going to get better, at least not for us. These people are thirsty for vengeance, and Franco wants to wipe out all dissidents. I'm not talking about semantics. He wants to get rid of them physically."

"I'm the Spaniard, and I know how things work around here. Spaniards aren't Germans, Bárbara. We're unreliable even when it comes to killing people. Most of the condemned prisoners have family in the Nationalist camp. Franco can't go around killing half the country."

I was so worked up that I went on a walk outside the school grounds. I did not want to argue with Juan, but I was a refugee. I had already left my home once and I had a pretty good radar for knowing when it was time to get out.

I thought we might have a chance if I worked for that despicable Gestapo agent. I would agree to get him the names he asked for in exchange for safe passage to Portugal and from there to the Americas by boat. I would actually give him false information so that no one would get hurt, but we would already be far beyond his reach once he realized it.

I went to the embassy and asked for him. Shortly, I was led to his office. When I went in, he stood and held out his hand. "How nice to see you here, Mrs. Spiel."

He opened a street-facing window, and the noise of the crowds reached us. The transition Madrid had undergone in a matter of months still shocked me. The city had been the bastion of resistance, of red strength, and of the rallying cry, "They Shall Not

Pass!" Now it was all "Franco, Franco, Franco!" Having already lived through it in Germany, I felt it was a bitter sight to behold.

"I'll work for you. I'll get you the information you want in exchange for safe passage out of the country for my family and me." I spoke firmly and met his gray eyes the entire time.

His smile was more like a wolf showing his teeth than a friendly gesture.

"You'll have the letters within a week, but I want the report as soon as possible. Is that clear? Remember that your friends at the school are also in the embassy's sights. If you pull any stunts . . ."

My chest was threatening to collapse. I had not considered that the Nazis might punish the Fliedners and others at El Porvenir.

"They're innocent," I eked out.

The agent came up so close that his face was an inch from my own. His disgusting features and the smell of vinegar on his clothes repulsed me.

"No one, Mrs. Spiel, no one is innocent. I thought you would have learned at least that lesson during the war."

"But those people are. They've dedicated their lives to serving others. Because of them, the lives of dozens of older citizens and hundreds of children, not to mention families who got food distribution from the school, have been saved. They could have left, but they stayed in Spain to help."

"To help keep reds alive," he spat out.

"To help keep innocent people alive," I corrected him.

"They disobeyed Hitler's orders. People like them are a cancer. They gave hope to our enemies, which helped them hold out longer. Their schools have produced freethinkers and Communists. What kind of religious school is that?"

Debate was futile. I simply walked out. He ordered me not to return to the embassy. I was to bring the report to the Hotel Ritz, one of the city's finest, where he was lodging.

I walked through the streets crowded with the people who had turned out for the parade. I was trying to cross when someone tugged at my arm. "Ma'am? Excuse me, ma'am?"

I turned, nervous. Though I was surrounded by people, I was not safe. But it was Müller, the young German soldier from the Condor Legion.

"I just wanted to tell you that our conversation the other day changed me. I've requested to be discharged. I don't want to use a weapon ever again."

"Oh!" I was floored. "I . . . I'm so happy for you. I hope that works out."

"If there's anything I can do for you, I'll be here through the end of the month, at the barracks near Cuatro Vientos."

"That's wonderful that you get to go home, though it won't be easy. You know what's going on there," I said.

He nodded. "I've been thinking about going to seminary. I could at least help people that way, and they wouldn't draft me. I don't think Germany will really go to war; people don't want another disaster like in fourteen."

I looked around and leaned in closer. "Seriously? Look around, Mr. Müller. All these people you see, just a few weeks ago they supported the Republic. People change on a dime, especially if you give them bread and circuses."

He studied me pensively. We all want to believe that the world will be a better place and that things can change, but sometimes things just are the way they are, and the best we can do is survive, to try to keep from being trampled by the crowd.

"I hope things work out for you." I poured my heart into a

smile and squeezed his hand before resuming my walk through the throngs.

I had never felt so alone even though people pressed into me from all sides. The smells, the cheers, the tears of the spectators with their arms raised in a Nazi salute—I took it all in. The Falange in their standard blue shirts did not look as fierce as the SA Brownshirts did in Germany, with their greased-back hair and little toothbrush mustaches. Yet inside, they were driven by the same hatred and disdain for anyone who was different.

The world around me had gone insane, and I felt like I was the only one with sight in a crowd of the blind. When I got to Cuatro Caminos and away from the multitudes, I could breathe a little easier. So now I knew what the consequences of lying to the Gestapo agent would be. The only way out was to somehow find safety beyond the border.

Chapter 43

Madrid
May 25, 1939

Jaime was playing with the little box where I kept the few pieces of nice jewelry I still owned and a few other important things. He pulled out a silver key and waved it around and suddenly I remembered—the safety deposit box at the Banco de España! I had not thought even once about Alan Hillgarth's promise to store identification and money there to help us get out of Spain if it became necessary. I gently took the key from Jaime and put it in my pocket. Without giving any details about where I was going, I took the trolley to the bank. I had admired the building's impressive exterior countless times but had never been inside. It was right by the Cibeles Fountain and the Palacio de Comunicaciones. The geography of that particular area had somehow been spared in the bombings, though the wounds of war were as present as ever throughout the city and in the famished, impoverished look of the population. The country had no money for reconstruction, having spent nearly all its resources on weapons.

At the main door to the bank, a policeman stopped me.

"Where are you headed, ma'am?"

I showed him my key. "To my safety deposit box."

He examined the key and, annoyed, pointed to a side door. Once inside, I went down a set of stairs to what looked like an armored door. An employee was listlessly standing guard, clearly bored. Apparently some things in the country had not changed. I showed him my key. Sighing as if I had just ruined his morning, he took me to the back of the room and up some metal stairs, then pointed to my box. He inserted his key and I put mine in. He pulled out a metal box and placed it on a nearby table.

When he walked away, I took a deep breath and looked inside, squinting to protect myself from potential disappointment. But there was the money: francs, pounds, and Republican pesetas, which of course were now useless. And nestled underneath were two passports with our pictures but false names. Supposedly we were British. I did speak English, but Juan understood only a few rudimentary words. I just hoped that the people at the border would not speak English either. I left the Republican money in the box and put everything else in my purse.

I walked away from the bank with the air of someone for whom safety deposit boxes were a normal part of life and then went straight back to El Porvenir. I did not want to say anything to the Fliedners and potentially get them into trouble. They already had enough to deal with in their attempts to rescue several Spanish teachers who had been detained, reclaim Fliedner properties that had been requisitioned, and keep El Porvenir open.

Juan was playing with Jaime when I returned. I showed him the passports and started packing our bags.

"Have you lost your mind?" he asked. "They'll stop us at the border and then we'll all end up in jail."

"We've got to get out before things get even worse. The regime is still getting things organized, and the Portuguese border isn't as strictly guarded as the others."

Juan shook his head adamantly. "My parents couldn't get out of Valencia, and no one has bothered them yet."

Anger boiled up inside me, and I finally shot straight with Juan. "Look, that man you saw talking to me at the party in the embassy—he's a Gestapo agent. He wants me to denounce your Socialist comrades who've gone into hiding. He threatened me before the war too. I'm telling you, we need to leave."

For the first time in a very long time, I saw rage flare up in his eyes, a fire I had thought the war and his arrest had extinguished. He got busy helping me pack.

"How are we going to get to the border?" he asked.

That brought me up short. I had not thought that far ahead. Travelers had to be granted permission to be driving on Spanish roadways, and very few passenger trains were working anymore. Thousands of people were trying to either return to their homes or flee somewhere no one knew them.

The only thing I could think of was to try to find Alan Hillgarth at the Palace Hotel. He could get us a car with gas and letters of safe passage from his embassy.

We picked up our suitcases and Jaime and all went to the hotel in a taxi. Though gas was still limited, some taxis had resumed service.

We walked in, and I asked for Mr. Hillgarth. I was told he no longer had his lodgings there. We tried to find him at the British embassy, but they said they did not know of an Alan Hillgarth. Despair was starting to win out when I remembered the German soldier.

An hour later, we arrived at the Cuatro Vientos airdrome base. They called for Sigmund Müller, and within a short time he met us in a small room off the main door. After everyone had been introduced, Müller asked how he could be of service. He listened intently as I summarized our situation.

"In a couple of days we leave for Vigo and then sail to Germany," he said. "My request for discharge has been denied, though I'm no longer officially in the army. Something big is in the works. They're gathering all the troops."

I nodded. "Is there any way you could arrange a transport for us to Portugal?"

He thought for a moment, nodded to himself, then left the room to talk with a superior. When he returned a few minutes later, he said, "Since you're a German citizen, we can help you. We're not all Nazis. A transport will get you to Fuentes de Oñoro, a town near Ciudad Rodrigo. From there you'll have to cross the border on foot."

I nearly collapsed with relief. "Thank you so much," I said, giving him a hug. That young man had just saved our lives.

Chapter 44

They allowed us to spend all day and that night at the airdrome, and Jaime was mesmerized by the huge planes. The next morning, a truck with military supplies parked at the entrance. Müller hid us in the back of the vehicle, behind some crates. Neither the Nationalist police nor army would dare to stop a German transport, but Müller decided to go with us to make sure we reached our destination. We did not know what shape the roads would be in. In the province of Madrid, the roadways were in terrible shape because of all the bombing, but the driver managed to navigate around the craters. Bombed-out cars lined both sides of the road, where they had been moved to make room for the military transports that brought Franco's troops into the capital. As soon as we got into the hills and into Segovia, the going was a bit smoother. The roads were old and not well maintained, but they were basically in one piece.

Several times Jaime got dizzy and looked like he would vomit, but we did not stop. We wanted to get to the border before nightfall, when it would close until the next day. Juan, Jaime, and I enjoyed looking out at the countryside. Cattle were few and far between, but the fields were sown. And the forests of both Madrid and Segovia were a comfort to see.

Passing through Ávila, we noted that its beautiful wall was intact. We had breezed through three checkpoints with no problem. The military and police presence on the streets diminished the farther we got into territory that had been under the Nationalists' control for a long time.

We stopped in a small town to eat. Müller and the driver shared their supplies with us: canned meat, sausages, and other luxuries we had not seen for years, like condensed milk. It was delightful to see Jaime's face light up at the taste of something sweet.

Back on the road, a military control run by African legionnaires—those vicious troops who had been crucial for the success of the military's coup—stopped us near Ciudad Rodrigo. We held our breath hoping they would not look in the back of the truck.

"Good afternoon. Where are you headed?" the African corporal asked Müller.

"Good afternoon. We're eventually bound for Zamora."

"This road goes to Ciudad Rodrigo and then to Portugal." The legionnaire's voice was firmer now than in his initial greeting.

"Oh yes, we just wanted to take a turn through the city first. We've heard it's beautiful."

"You're out for a tourist drive?" The legionnaire was skeptical.

Müller lied like it came naturally to him. "Yes, while you legionnaires get to stay for a while, sadly the Condor Legion has only a few days before we're sent back to Germany, so we probably won't get another chance to see this amazing country."

"Ah, you should've started with that. You want one of our guards to go with you? We can tell you all the good places to eat."

"Oh, thank you, but we don't want to be any trouble. Plus, we're planning to eat at a spot in Salamanca."

Müller handed over the form signed by his superior officer authorizing the trip as well as the endorsement from the Spanish army.

"Everything's in order, comrades. Thank you for all you've done for Spain. You Germans aren't like the Italians—we've had to go around fixing a lot of the messes they've made."

"*¡Arriba, España!*" Müller shouted the Falange slogan, and the legionnaire responded with the Nazi salute.

In the back of the truck, we let out a collective deep breath. The truck continued on its way, and half an hour beyond Ciudad Rodrigo we came to the last Spanish town before the border.

The Germans let us out on the main road just over a mile from the border. They did not want the border guards to see their vehicle.

"Thank you for everything," I said to Müller. "We can never repay you." In response, he gave me and Juan a tight hug and then stroked Jaime's cheeks.

"I hope you don't run into any trouble," he said in his valiant attempt at Spanish. Then he got back in the truck, and our strange German saviors drove away.

Our papers were in order, and we had enough time to get to the border before nightfall. Hope started to rise up in me, but I refused to feel it yet.

After twenty minutes of walking, we reached the border. There were no other travelers leaving Spain but several crossing from Portugal into our country. Most were dealers bringing goods into Spain that they would be able to sell at top price.

A border guard came out of the sentry box to stamp our passports.

"Good afternoon. Where to?"

"To Lisbon." I spoke in Spanish with a strong British accent.

"You've come on foot?"

"No, a car let us out a few miles back."

Something about that must have struck him as odd. He went back to the sentry box to show the passports to a supervisor. A few minutes later, they both came out.

"You're British?" the supervisor asked.

I nodded. The problem was that Juan looked every bit the Spaniard.

"Well, your passports are in order, but there's no mention of the child. He could be a Spanish citizen, and for the time being no citizen is allowed to leave the territory. We just had a war."

"I understand, Corporal, but this is our son."

The man leaned toward Jaime, who had my blue eyes.

"They do look alike," the first border guard said.

"Shut up, Ramón," the supervisor snapped. Then he went up to Juan. "Are you mute?"

"No." Juan said it as quickly as possible.

"You don't look English."

Juan attempted an accent in his response. "My parents were Spaniards. I was born in London."

The corporal frowned, went back to the sentry box, and made a phone call. Eventually he came back and said, "You'll have to wait here. SIPM is sending an agent. They've got a base in Salamanca. You can't leave until you've talked with them."

My heart sank. SIPM was the army's information services department, a critical arm in the Francoist repression machine. I forced myself to keep up the accent and act unconcerned as I said, "We've got a young child. We'll go back to the town and will return in the morning."

The supervisor shook his head. "You'll stay right here. Is that clear?"

We waited for more than two hours with the gnawing terror that our chance of escape had now been reduced to nearly non-existent.

Unlike the Gestapo's trench coats or leather jackets, the two SIPM agents were dressed in suits. They introduced themselves cordially as if we were clients they were courting.

"Hello, I'm agent Triviño, and this is García-Jurado. We're so sorry to bother you; it's just that so many people are trying to cross the border illegally."

"It's no problem, sir," I said.

"Your accent sounds more German than British." He said it as casually as an observation about the weather.

"I lived for some time in Germany," I explained.

"Does your husband speak Spanish?"

"A bit." I was begging God that Juan would not have to talk much.

"The passports are authentic, but the child will have to be registered at the embassy in Madrid. We do not know if he is British or Spanish. Children belong to the nation they were born in and cannot be taken out without the proper paperwork," Triviño explained patiently.

"I understand, but with the war, our embassy has been closed for a long time."

"Where are you coming from?"

I thought it best to be truthful on that point. "From Madrid."

The agent's eyebrows rose. "We'd like to speak with your husband."

"He doesn't speak very much Spanish."

"Oh, that's not a problem." Triviño stepped back and smiled at García-Jurado.

García-Jurado began chatting in English, making banal comments and asking Juan polite questions. Juan stared at him blankly.

García-Jurado nodded and stepped back. "This man clearly isn't British," he said. "You three had better come with us to Salamanca and tell us who you really are. The longer you keep up the charade, the worse it'll go."

The threat sparked different reactions in me and Juan. I started begging them to let us cross the border, while Juan pleaded for them to let me and Jaime go.

"Please, she's a German citizen, and this is all my fault. Just take me in, but let them go, please!"

Triviño held out his hands for silence and quite amicably said, "We'll sort all of this out with the consul, never fear."

Never dropping the façade of friendly helpers, the agents led us to their black Citroën and drove us to the offices of their base. They questioned Juan first and then me. Hiding the truth was pointless. We were given something to eat and told that the next day we would be returned to Madrid and taken into custody. We had opened Pandora's box, and there was not a shred of hope inside it.

Chapter 45

Madrid
May 28, 1939

We were treated very well during the two days we spent detained in Salamanca, but on the ride back to the capital it was clear that things were about to change. We were seated on the side benches of a police van. It was so old that our return journey to Madrid was twice as long as our trek to leave it. They made only one stop, and we were given a meager portion of bread and something that seemed to be rotten bacon. We were not allowed to go to the bathroom at any point.

We spent the first night back in Madrid in the government building at Puerta del Sol. The cell was damp and cold, but at least we were together. They gave me food for Jaime, and Juan and I were given sandwiches. We were not given access to a lawyer, nor was I allowed to contact the German embassy.

An agent appeared and called for Juan and me.

"I can't leave the child alone," I argued.

An older guard who had been kind to us stepped forward. "Don't worry, ma'am, I'll look after him." I had no choice.

The agent took us to an office that faced an inner courtyard. I feared the worst.

The agent inside had bushy black hair and a funny-shaped chin that made him look like a gorilla. "So you've tried to escape the country using false identities. That's a very serious crime. Furthermore, you, sir, are Juan Delgado, a Socialist activist, deputy, and member of Negrín's government."

"I've done nothing wrong," was all Juan offered in response.

"A judge will see about that. For now we just want to know who supplied the foreign currency and British passports. We can tell that they're real."

"Some friends," Juan said. My husband was nearly knocked out of his chair when the agent's open hand met his jaw.

"This is how this is going to work. We're going to play nice. You two tell me the truth. You'll go back to your cell to sleep, and tomorrow you'll be taken to pretrial detention. If it turns out you haven't committed any crimes, you'll be cleared. But if you don't cooperate, things won't be very pleasant."

Juan had already had a taste of torture, and he wanted to protect me at all costs. The agents hit Juan again, this time with their fists, and I begged them to stop.

"So you think you have something to tell us?" he asked.

I told them that a British friend had gotten them for us and stored them in a safety deposit box at the Banco de España. I did not mention Alan Hillgarth's name or specify that he was a spy.

"This friend must have a first and last name."

"Thomas Green," I said, hoping that would be enough. "He left Madrid several months ago. He went back to London."

The agent stared a hole though me. He drew so close he could have kissed me.

"Don't play around with me. You may be German, but you're a whore and a spy."

"Don't speak to my wife that way!" Juan barked, jumping up. But the other agent slugged him in the stomach and, before Juan could straighten up again, kneed him in the face. Juan fell to the ground, where the two agents started kicking him.

"Please, please, stop!" I begged, sobbing.

The men seemed to enjoy their game of kicking a defenseless man on the ground. Then they turned to me and one said, "You're going to live through hell for being a spy. You'll be lucky if they hang you. They'll shoot your useless idiot husband and give your kid to a decent family."

His words shook me to the core. I helped Juan to his feet, and they took us back to our cell, Juan limping the best he could.

The older guard opened the door immediately when he saw us returning. As soon as the other agents left, he brought us clean towels and a small bottle of rubbing alcohol. I cleaned Juan's cuts the best I could, but the deepest wound was to his pride.

"They're going to split us up," he said.

"No, they can't," I said stupidly. I refused to believe what was happening.

"They'll send you to the women's prison and me to the men's. They'll court-martial me."

"Why? You haven't done anything wrong."

"I was part of the government to which they attribute crimes against humanity. Try to get in touch with Teodoro Jr. If he puts pressure on them, he might be able to get you and Jaime out."

I shook my head ferociously. None of this was happening. "No. Everything will get cleared up, and all three of us will be out of here in a few days."

Juan touched my tearstained face.

"Bárbara, we were apprehended at the border with false passports. If the government had suspicions about us before, now they've no doubt. They're not going to believe a story about a British friend helping us. I'll say that I was working for the Brits."

Terror closed up my throat, and I could barely whisper. "They'll execute you."

"If they find out it was you, they'll torture you or hang you or both."

"I'd rather die than—"

Juan kissed me and then whispered, "You have to take care of Jaime. Our son needs you."

"I love you," I wheezed between tears and gulps of air.

"I love you too. That's why we've got to convince these people that you're innocent."

"But they wouldn't kill a German citizen . . ." My voice trailed off in ridiculous excuses.

"You're forgetting about that Nazi. No one in the embassy will lift a finger to help you."

We tried to get some rest, but it was impossible. We had no idea what the morning would hold, and we feared that it would be our last night together as a family. I was wrapped around Jaime all night, and Juan's arms cradled me like when I was a child and the only safe place was the tender lap of one of my parents.

Chapter 46

Madrid
May 29, 1939

Juan and I kept watch all night, willing morning not to come. Though the sun's rays would not reach our dark cell, we knew that our fate would be sealed when it crested the horizon. We were prepared for the end. *Paseíllos* were the extrajudicial killings so common during the Republic's years. Those were the "walk-abouts" in which victims were taken by night and shot by the walls of cemeteries. Those had given way to the Francoist judicial system, a farce in which not even the most basic legal guarantees and standards were met. We had heard that all the courts would function as military courts since Franco had not lifted the state of war and could therefore act with complete impunity.

The older guard had been on watch the entire night. He brought us coffee, which was the only thing we had had for hours. I had no appetite or thirst, but Juan insisted that I drink it.

"They'll come for you first, sir, and then for your good wife," the agent said, holding out a napkin. "I hope all three of you get out of this mess."

The agent's kindness took us by surprise. He was trying to make that fateful hour a little less terrible for complete strangers.

Thirty minutes later, two policemen came to the basement, opened the cell door, and took Juan by the arms. I clung to him, pleading, "Please, let us stay together!" But my cries went unheard. I could not even give him a final kiss.

I slumped to the floor, weeping. Jaime's sobs echoed my own.

Twenty minutes later, two other policemen took me and Jaime from the cell to a garage and loaded us inside a car. From the small window I glimpsed the city. I could not believe what was happening to me. All the people on the street and in the shops were going about their business as if nothing had happened, but I was a prisoner for the simple reason that I had tried to leave the country with my husband and my son.

I started crying again. The policeman with the pockmarked face frowned and snapped, "Shut up, you whore! Or we'll throw the kid out the window!"

I bit my lip in silence and barely breathed until we pulled up in front of Ventas women's prison. We drove through two gates and into a large courtyard where we got out of the car. The jail's officers were all women. I was foolishly relieved at first. In time I came to see that they were as inhumane as male officers.

One of the prison guards pushed me toward a room. They made me put down Jaime and get undressed. Their insults rained down ceaselessly.

"Come on, slut, we haven't got all day! You act like a little daddy's girl, some bourgeois red. Those are the worst kind." That scolding came from a jailer named Eloísa.

Another guard made me bend over. She forcefully examined my private parts and caused needless pain. Without allowing me to get dressed yet, they sat me down and shaved my head. As the locks fell to the floor, I willed myself to stay strong and not let those harpies scare me.

"Grab your stinky mutt of a boy and get through that door."

Finally allowed to dress, I followed their orders, and another guard led us down a long hall. The prisoners were silent in their cells. Many were too weak to stir as we passed. I soon learned that the food was scarce and the beatings abundant. They put me in a cell with a woman with straight, dark brown hair. Though her eyes were swollen and bruised from being beaten, she had a kindly air about her.

"Oh God, your poor child is here too," she said, holding her hand out to Jaime. She smiled at him and touched his cheek, but he burrowed deeper into me and cried.

"Poor thing, this is no place for a child. I'm Matilde Landa, delighted to meet you," she said, dropping her hand from Jaime to shake mine.

"I'm Bárbara Spiel," I answered.

"German?" she asked. "I wonder if we've seen each other before. I was married to the reporter Francisco López Ganivet, but we divorced. Welcome to your luxurious new lodgings. Don't worry, the director is actually a very decent woman, Carmen Castro. She was a student of mine at the Institución Libre de Enseñanza—oh, the ironies of life!"

"I'm so pleased to meet you," I said.

"I've managed to start a sort of defense council for the prisoners here. We'll try to get you out as soon as we can, and the boy too."

I sat on the cot, weak with exhaustion and hunger. Matilde sat beside me.

"If you haven't been accused of violent crimes, you've got less to fear. The rotten hypocritical pigs who call themselves Christians are in charge now, but there's a shred of decency in a couple of them. I'm an atheist, but I'll tell you something: If they follow Jesus, then call me a cloistered nun!" She burst out laughing at her own joke. I was too bewildered to react. She went on, "There are two ways to take things in life, for better or for worse. The pigheaded guards here want to keep us alive but deadened. But they're not going to win."

Jaime was famished, but I had no food or milk for him. I asked the guards, but they said food was served in the afternoon. He finally fell into an exhausted sleep in my arms. I was dirty, worn out, and hungry, and I could not stop thinking about Juan and wondering what was happening to him.

The next day the prisoners were made to line up in the courtyard. The guards did not seem to care how hot it was. The one named Eloísa came up to me and demanded, "Hand the boy over. They'll take better care of him in the nursery."

I refused to let Jaime go, and two of the guards started punching my stomach until I reflexively loosened my grip. Jaime screamed and held his arms out to me, and I wanted to die as I watched him be taken away. We had already been separated once, and I could not bear it again.

A young prisoner came up to me, put her hand on my shoulder, and said calmly, "My name is Adelina García Casillas. Come over here with us. It's going to be okay. They'll bring him back to you at night."

She led me to a group of girls her age. The oldest among them could not have been even twenty. I looked around, confused. "What are you all doing here? You're just kids."

Adelina shrugged. "A jerk in my neighborhood accused me of trying to reorganize the Communist Youth, but I wasn't even in Madrid at the time. My dad had sent me and my sister to the country."

We sat down in the shade. Breakfast had been cold coffee and one piece of hard bread, but now I was no longer thinking about my stomach. I just wanted Jaime to be with me.

The early days in that inferno were terrible. I only saw Jaime at night, and all day the prisoners were forced to sew uniforms for the army. I did not know what my sentence was or how long I would be in jail. I had no way of getting word to anyone outside of the prison until one day I got an idea and went to Mass. At the end of the service, I went up to the nicest-looking nun, Sister Susana. She gave me a warm smile.

"Sister, I have to get in touch with someone. No one knows I'm here in jail."

The young nun wore glasses, and a few blond hairs had escaped her coif.

"I understand that the prisoners aren't allowed to contact anyone on the outside for the time being."

"Please, it's a message for a Protestant pastor."

She looked at me in surprise and then added, half to herself, "Of course, you're German."

I handed her a letter for the Fliedners. I did not know what might have befallen them, but I hoped against hope that they might be able to advocate for me.

The next Sunday, after Mass, I went up to Sister Susana again.

"Hello, Bárbara. I gave your friends your letter. They are very nice people. They gave me this for you." She pulled an envelope from her pocket.

"Thank you, Sister," I whispered, tears in my eyes.

Sister Susana led me and the rest of the prisoners who had attended the service to a table where they served chocolate bars—the reward for voluntarily attending Mass. As I scarfed down all that I was allowed, she spoke.

"I don't like what happens in this prison, but I thought it would be a good place to serve. At first I despised all these reds, but you seem different."

I looked up in surprise. "Why did you hate them?"

Sister Susana struggled to regulate her voice. "I belonged to the Hermanas Adoratrices, an order that works among prostitutes and women in vulnerable situations. Our house was on Princesa Street in Madrid. After the coup, a militia group attacked the building with their machine guns, and we all ran to hide with friends and family. We managed to regroup in an apartment and keep the order going. We stopped wearing our habits so we wouldn't stand out. A few months later, during a bombing raid, when we were running to the shelter, some militia fighters recognized us. They took us to the Fomento *checa*. Our crime was belonging to a Catholic order."

Her voice had dropped until it was barely audible. But she continued, "They raped the younger members of the Hermanas. It was terrible. They didn't arrest me—I managed to escape the militia fighters that day during the raid. Some good Christians sheltered us, but the militia tracked us down a few months later. They raped us, then shot us at the Almudena cemetery. When they came closer for the final shots, some policemen showed up, and the militia ran off. A policeman noticed I was still alive and took me to the hospital. Then I managed to get into Nationalist territory. I worked as a nurse, and now here I am serving in this prison."

Her testimony floored me. I had heard what some of the militias did to Catholic men and women in religious orders, but I had never met one of the victims.

"I am so, so sorry, Sister Susana."

She gave me a sad smile and wiped her face. "I've forgiven them. It's the only way the soul can heal. Forgiveness frees the one who gives it more than the one who receives it, I can tell you that. Who knows—these women in here may be the wives of the ones who tortured and raped me and my sisters, but I've decided to love them freely. Is that crazy?" That was the only part of what she said in which her voice lacked confidence.

I shook my head, and she smiled again. "I really do wish you luck." She returned to the kitchen, and I squeezed Teodoro Jr.'s envelope that was nestled in the pocket of my uniform. I went back to my cell hoping desperately that he could get me out of prison and reunite my family.

Chapter 47

Teodoro Jr.'s letter had not been hopeful.

Dear Bárbara,

I'm deeply grieved to learn about your circumstances.
We had hoped—prayed—that you three were no longer
in Spain. I imagine you know what's occurring outside
the walls of Ventas. War has broken out in Europe. Germany invaded Poland, and Poland's allies entered the
conflict. Here in Spain, where we have just ended a war,
we know very well how terrible it is, but our German
brothers who still remember the Great War have fallen
once again into the same error. Of course it's the politicians who start the wars. We can only hope that this one
is short and causes little bloodshed.

My sisters and many other family members are not in
Spain at the moment, some in Switzerland and others in
Germany. They are having a very hard time getting back
in the country. The borders are shut with lock and key.

I don't want to trouble you further with my problems. After receiving your letter, I looked into the situation of your dear husband Juan. It seems that his trial will be in a few weeks at the courthouse at Plaza de las Salesas. He's accused of uprising and of supporting the Republic, as well as repressing innocent people during the war and signing death sentences. You're aware that his role in government supports such accusations even though he himself is not responsible for any of that. I spoke with his lawyer, a captain well known to my family. The prosecutor has nothing against Juan himself, but that won't keep them from declaring a guilty verdict. The good news is that the prosecution is not seeking the death penalty. However, I've also learned that Juan is currently ill with tuberculosis.

Regarding your situation, apparently the only charge against you is falsifying information on a passport. I would think that your trial would be held soon enough and that you'll be fined and then released.

I hope very much to see you soon, and together with your whole family. You three are in our prayers daily.

Teodoro Fliedner Jr.

On the one hand, it was an enormous relief to know that Juan was still alive and that his crimes were not considered so serious as to warrant the death penalty. Yet his tuberculosis worried me. I cared very little about my own case, but I did not want Jaime being brought up in Ventas.

A few days later while Matilde and I were chatting, I grew more and more restless the longer the afternoon wore on. The guards had not brought Jaime to me, and it was already getting dark. I called for the closest guard and asked about him.

"Auxilio Social came for him, didn't you know?" she sneered.

"Why? Was he sick?" I did not yet understand what the true purpose of the Falange social aid organization was.

She threw her head back and laughed at my innocent question. "No, idiot. You red mothers are a bad influence on your spawn. Do you want your boy growing up with the stigma of a murderer for a mother?"

I was confused, presuming she was simply seeking to torture me with her taunts.

The guard kept it up. "Dr. Vallejo-Nájera—heard of him? Well, he's researching what he calls the 'red gene.' Look at the bright side: Your problem is a disease."

Her banter was maddening. I started shaking the bars and screamed, "Tell me where my son is!"

"They gave him to a good family so he could be raised the way God commands. Now shut up, you red slut!"

The guard slammed the door shut, and I turned to face my cell. Matilde hugged me tightly to try to calm my shaking. My son had been taken from me again. I wanted to curl up and die.

Chapter 48

Madrid
December 23, 1939

I never thought one could grow accustomed to being dead while still alive, but that is exactly how I felt. Since Jaime had been kidnapped, I wandered listlessly about my cell with no breath of life. It did not help that Matilde had been transferred to a different prison not long after. I hardly left my cell, and I had lost a lot of weight.

Sister Susana brought in sweets to try to cheer me up. "You've got to eat something and keep your strength. Tomorrow is the trial. If you get out of jail, you can petition to have your son back."

I looked at her indifferently. It felt like my brain no longer worked.

"I promise; I myself will vouch for you. I've also written the courts requesting that they set you free as soon as possible. Trust God."

Those words sounded vapid and hollow to me. In the past few years, I had done nothing but trust God, but that hadn't kept my husband from being locked up. He had been in the prison infirmary for weeks. And trusting God hadn't kept my son from being kidnapped, though my captors called it adoption.

"Sister, I've got nothing left."

The nun sat beside me and helped me sit up a bit before answering. "Bárbara, you've got to fight for your family's sake. Life hasn't been easy for anyone. You've got to understand that the only way to get things to change is to fight. You can't give up now."

She stayed with me for another hour. We did not speak, but my resolve grew stronger in her hope-filled presence. That night my sleep was restful for the first time in a long time, and my soul felt a measure of calm.

The next morning, several of my fellow prisoners helped me tidy myself up. I missed Adelina very much. She and twelve other younger women had been executed before the firing squad in August. I could not understand why I might be set free while those teenagers met such a cruel fate.

The guards gave me back the dress I had been wearing back in May when we were arrested. My hair had grown long enough to pull back in a stumpy bun. My shoes had not been kept with my dress, but they gave me another pair. They were too big, but it was better than going barefoot in the cold. I studied myself in the rusty bathroom mirrors. I had aged a frightening amount in the months at Ventas.

"You've got to get out of here," I told the reflection in the mirror. I returned to my cell, and when the police came to take me to the trial, I felt strong and ready.

It was wonderful and terrible to see the streets of Madrid again. I thought back to my sweet old bookstore, the Librería de Madrid, and how hopeful I had once felt. We parked in front of the courthouse, and I was led up the short staircase. The noise and bustle of the street were overwhelming after months of moving only from my cell to the workshop, dining hall, chapel, and bathrooms. My

brain had all but forgotten that the world kept frenetically spinning outside the prison walls.

In the chamber they led me to, there were two clerks, the judge,
my lawyer—whom I had seen only once—and the prosecutor.
There was an audience of one: Teodoro Fliedner Jr.

I sat in the dock for the first time in my life. I knew I was innocent and hoped the judge would see this, but I had little faith in
the regime's justice system.

My accuser was named Captain Álvaro Soto Burgos. He
glanced my way, then addressed the judge.

"Your Honor, the case before us today is very simple. Bárbara
Spiel, the daughter of a well-known Social Democrat in the German parliament, is a traitor to her country and a spy. She escaped
from Germany in 1933, surely due to her Communist militancy.
In Madrid, she married the Socialist deputy Juan Delgado, who
is accused of war crimes, and then opened a bookstore. Furthermore, she is a Protestant, a follower of that fornicator Luther. But
these damning facts are merely decorative. The real issue is that
the accused was apprehended at the Portuguese border attempting illegal entry. Why was she fleeing? First of all, because she was
a spy in the service of the British government; second, because
her husband was a criminal; and third, because she had amassed
a hefty sum of money thanks to her work against the legitimate
Spanish state. For these reasons, we seek the maximum penalty,
the death sentence, as applied to all spies and traitors."

Just as the prosecutor took his seat, my lawyer stood.

"Your Honor, Bárbara Spiel may be some of the things the
prosecutor asserts, but she is neither a spy nor an accomplice to
crimes. Her husband confessed and took full responsibility for
the falsified passports for which they were apprehended in their

attempt to escape. The defendant herself could have taken their child and left the country whenever she chose due to being a German citizen. The great fault of the accused is that she fell in love with the wrong man. I submit to the court two statements testifying to her upstanding character: one regarding her behavior prior to incarceration and one addressing her time as a prisoner. Sister Susana of Ventas women's prison fervently sustains that the defendant is an upright Christian and a wonderful mother who should not be incarcerated. Furthermore, Sister Susana sustains that the defendant's child, who was adopted by another family a few months ago, should be returned to her."

The prosecutor attempted an objection, but the judge did not allow it.

My lawyer continued. "The other statement is from the director of the organization that runs the school El Porvenir, where the defendant taught German. The director, Teodoro Fliedner Jr., is the grandson of Federico Fliedner, a German who came to Spain for the purpose of founding schools. The Fliedner family has served the city of Madrid for generations and they are universally held in high esteem. Mr. Fliedner states in his testimony that Bárbara Spiel at all times conducted herself in an exemplary manner and that she should not be imprisoned on unfounded accusations. We will now turn to these unfounded accusations. What proof exists of her supposed collaboration with the British government? Falsified passports and a few sterling pounds. Both can be procured on the black market with relative ease; even so, her husband has already confessed that both the money and the passports were his. To what crimes has the accused been an accomplice? She has been a teacher, a caretaker for children and older citizens during the war, a bookseller, and a mother. I request her immediate release and recognition from this court of her aptitude as a mother, such that her child should be returned to her."

The judge stroked his chin and turned to me.

"You understand that you are under oath?"

"Yes, Your Honor."

"Is it true that you carried out no espionage in favor of the British government?"

I looked straight into the judge's eyes. He was on the upper end of middle age and had the demeanor of someone who could read the mind and conscience of anyone he saw.

"I have not given information of any type to the British government," I said. My voice was steady and clear as I spoke that carefully worded truth.

"You have not collaborated with your husband in the crimes for which he is accused?"

"My husband was in charge of food supplies for the Republican side. He never took up arms or gave orders for anyone to be put to death."

The judge lifted the gavel and, before the smack that indicated the session was closed, pronounced his sentence: "I declare that Doña Bárbara Spiel de Delgado is innocent of all charges, and I order her immediate release."

The prosecutor tried to argue, but the judge ordered him to be silent.

My lawyer spoke. "Will you give her a certificate allowing her to reclaim her son?"

The judge's look was apathetic. "We aren't here today to argue the maternal merits of the accused. Court is adjourned!"

The bailiff untied my hands. Sister Susana had slipped in late. She ran up and hugged me. She greeted Teodoro, whom she already knew from having given him my letter. I left the court building with Teodoro.

"Thank you for everything," I told him when we got into the car.

He shook his head as if it were nothing. "We'll help you get your family back."

The words of that good man filled me with hope. He drove me to a small apartment the Fliedners had rented for me to demonstrate to the judge that I could take care of Jaime. When we entered, I was delighted to see Elfriede and other workers from El Porvenir. For the first time, it hit me that they were family to me.

The next day, we filled out the paperwork requesting the reinstatement of my parental rights. We took it to a courthouse as well as to the offices of the social welfare organization, Auxilio Social. We were told that in the best interests of the child, children were never taken from the "good families" who adopted them and returned to their families of origin.

I studied the government employee who refused to receive the form I held out to him and replied, "Don't worry; I'm used to miracles happening."

Elfriede suggested that I go back to helping her in the bookstore while I worked on trying to reunite my family. Once again, books were going to save my life.

Chapter 49

It was wonderful to be back at the Librería Nacional y Extranjera again, but we were not able to keep it open much longer.

The year before, there had been a huge book-burning event in Madrid, at the Universidad Central. The Falange's secretary of education, Antonio de Luna García, organized it together with several notorious Falange leaders. Books by well-known authors—Communists or just freethinkers—fueled the pyre that terrible day. One of the saddest parts was that there were many priests and bishops among the instigators of this and other book burnings. It was like an attempt to resurrect the Inquisition.

During the war and after it ended, dozens of booksellers, editors, and writers had been relieved of their positions or executed. A few had managed to flee the country. Librarians faced the same fate. The librarian Juana María Capdevielle San Martín was jailed, miscarried her son in prison, and then was shot. The highly influential María Moliner was demoted and remained under surveillance, but at least she was not killed.

Finally it was our turn. The authorities did not burn the books of the Fliedners' bookstore, but they did shut it down. At first,

Teodoro Jr. thought about selling the books to the Anglican cathedral on Beneficencia Street, but Elfriede and I thought that would be too risky. A bookseller from the old days came to the Librería Nacional y Extranjera to take a few volumes. We transferred, organized, and stored the rest in the basement of El Porvenir.

The Spain that the new regime inaugurated was, without a doubt, the most conservative, retrograde version of the country in easily two hundred years. Part of the repression ended when the Republic surrendered; other aspects began in earnest. There were still thousands of families separated in disparate territories and tens of thousands of people crammed into jails and concentration camps.

Juan was sent to work on building the Valle de los Caídos. It was a sort of megalomaniacal mausoleum General Franco dreamed up and wanted built on the mountain range outside of Madrid. The monument was in honor of those who had fallen in the war efforts against the Republic.

Juan's assignment to the prisoner work crew was good news in a way. It meant that I could visit him on Sundays. Yet the demanding physical effort of the forced labor threatened to do him in. He was still weak from his bout of tuberculosis.

That Sunday in late April, Teodoro agreed to let me join him on a visit to the Fliedner children's home in El Escorial. It was not far from the construction site in Cuelgamuros where Juan was working, and we would visit Juan afterward. It was the first time I would see my husband since being separated after our arrest nearly a year prior. Before going into the visitation room where Juan was waiting, guards frisked us and examined the package of food I had prepared.

As soon as the door opened, Juan jumped up and rushed to

hug me. He was thinner than I had ever seen him, and the mountain sun and air had darkened and toughened his skin.

"Oh my God, I can't believe it—it's really you!" he exclaimed. Then he shook Teodoro's hand. "Thank you, thank you for everything you've done for us."

Teodoro waved it away and said, "What matters now is getting you out of here. We're trying to appeal your sentence."

"Thank you, thank you," Juan kept repeating. Then he took my hands. "What about Jaime?"

His question stabbed into my heart, as happened every time anyone mentioned my son.

"We haven't made much progress. They won't tell us where he is or anything about the family that took him. I don't even know if he's in Madrid."

He shook his head. "This is unbelievable."

"It just requires patience," Teodoro said.

"One of our ideas is to try to get a bishop to intercede on our behalf with Auxilio Social." I glanced nervously at Juan. I still could not believe he was standing right there in flesh and blood. "The bishop Leopoldo Eijo y Garay . . ."

Juan shuddered and blurted out, "But he spoke publicly and adamantly against the Republic and was even part of the Mass during Franco's victory parade in Madrid! There's no way—"

"Which is exactly why a word from him could get you pardoned and get Jaime back at the same time. He and Teodoro have a mutual friend, and we're hoping to get an audience with the bishop tomorrow."

The Catholic Church had not enjoyed the degree of power and influence it currently had since the days of the Habsburg dynasty. Yet it had come at a high price of priests, monks, and nuns being murdered—more than six thousand known deaths, and the count was not final.

Juan and I hugged again before we had to say goodbye. It was impossible to put into words what happened inside me to feel his body pressed against mine again. I cried and held him as tightly as my arms allowed.

"We'll be together again soon," he murmured, stroking my hair.

I felt deep inside me that he was right. I would go to any lengths to get my husband back. I dragged myself away from him and followed Teodoro out of the visitation room. Teodoro gently respected my silence on the ride back to Madrid proper. I stared out at the forests of pines and meadows dotted with holm oaks. Though there was still a shortage of nearly everything in Spain, at least there were cows once again grazing on the pastures as the country ever so slowly recovered.

More than half a million people had died and spilled their blood over that beautiful landscape. Spain would never again be the same. If the wounds of war last for generations, those from a civil war never scar over.

Chapter 50

Our hoped-for visit with the bishop never materialized.

I had gone to the Auxilio Social office countless times since my release in December, but the answer was always the same. They would not give me any information about my son whatsoever. In my desperation, I visited Sister Susana, hoping she would be able to discover where Jaime had been sent.

"That information is confidential, and I doubt I'll be able to find out anything," she told me over coffee at a café near her convent.

"I've got to see my son." It was not a plan, but it was the truest reason I would ask this of her. "Please, I'm desperate. I've tried everything the legal and correct way, and it's gotten me nowhere. I don't know what else to do. I need help."

Sister Susana shrugged in consternation. She had followed the rules all her life and was torn over this dilemma. She took a deep breath, gave a little shake to clear her head, and said, "This is what I can do. I can go with you to the office and try to distract the receptionist while you do whatever you need to do."

"Thank you, yes, yes, that will help!" I clasped her hands in gratitude. I understood how difficult it was for her to put herself at risk to help a near stranger, a supposed collaborator with the side that had hurt her so badly.

The next day we went to the Auxilio Social office. It was unbelievable to me that an organization founded supposedly to help the needy, especially children, was now stealing children from certain families to give them to others.

When she saw that I was in the company of a nun that time, the manager changed her typical dour tone and invited us in warmly. I had the office layout memorized by then and knew that the files for the children were kept in a filing cabinet along the wall of her office. With luck and a few seconds alone with that filing cabinet, I could find Jaime's file and the address of his adoptive family.

Sister Susana was chatting up the manager in her peaceful way and gladly accepted the offer of some tea. The manager stepped out to get the tea, and I seized the chance to open the filing cabinet. It took me just over a minute to locate Jaime's file, but then we heard the door from the back room open. Sister Susana deftly glided to the hall to meet the manager and offer to help carry the tea tray. She took her time praising the teapot and fussing about how the manager really should not have gone to so much trouble. I jotted down the names and addresses I needed, slid the drawer closed as quietly as I could, and returned to my seat. I just had time to catch my breath and look tired and thirsty by the time they returned.

"Again, thank you so much for this lovely spread," Sister Susana said as they came in.

The manager poured the tea, and I took the cup she held out to me, willing my hand to be steady and my smile to be serene.

"I really am sorry I can't help you ladies," the manager said, speaking directly to Sister Susana, "but I can't give you any information without a judge's orders. I hope this little matter gets cleared up soon. Doña Bárbara seems like such a nice woman, and it's clear that she loves her son."

Her comment made my blood boil.

"I haven't met many mothers who don't love their children and who aren't willing to do anything in the world for them," I said. "Stealing children from their mothers is the worst sin I can think of. God will not forget it."

Sister Susana gave me a warning look, but the manager seemed unfazed.

She said, "These reds aren't like the rest of us. Dr. Antonio Vallejo-Nájera has helped explain it all in his research."

"God shows no partiality. Have you never read the Bible?" I said, straightening to my full height in my chair.

"Well, the world isn't perfect, is it? And we can't follow all the precepts of our Lord to the letter," the manager replied.

"Like loving our enemies." I really was trying to contain myself, but it was not working well.

The manager's face hardened, and she got to her feet to signal that our meeting had come to an end.

I took my time draining my teacup, stood at my leisure, and we made our way back out to the street. Sister Susana was rattled.

"I'm so sorry," I told her. "I just—"

"I understand; I can put myself in your shoes and imagine what this must be like. But that attitude won't help you get Jaime back. Your side lost the war, and now, for people like that woman, you and the people you represent are vermin. You have no rights in their minds, because before, the Republic had taken away all the rights of people like her and me in Madrid."

"In other words: People like her hate me." The nun nodded. "And, in a way, with good reason," I added, "since they can't tell the difference between the Republicans who committed the crimes against them and the rest of us who witnessed it all in silence."

Sister Susana nodded again, then gave me a hug. "I wish you all the best, Bárbara, and you and your family are in my prayers daily."

"Thank you, thank you so very much," I said. In a different scenario, we would have been good friends. But the world around us demanded that we be irreconcilable enemies.

I walked away from Sister Susana with tentative hope in my heart. I had no faith in Franco's regime, but now I could start making a plan for how to change my future. I would not stop until I carried it out and got my family back.

Chapter 51

I had not wanted to involve my friends from El Porvenir in the plans I was concocting, but I needed their help. Because of the children's home in El Escorial, Teodoro Jr. knew a lot of people in the mountains outside of Madrid. I needed a trustworthy guide to lead me and Juan through the mountains from Cuelgamuros to the area of Segovia. I had found a man to drive us to Zaragoza, where Jaime lived. After rescuing him, we would try to get across the border into France. The French were too tied up trying to hold out against the Germans to watch the border with Spain as closely as they had during our civil war. Teodoro knew people in Navarre who could get us into France. After that, only God knew what might happen.

The plans seemed simple on paper, but I knew it would be a different story to carry them out. Anything could happen to derail us.

Sundays were pretty slow in Cuelgamuros. The prisoners who were building the huge cross in the Valle de los Caídos went to Mass and were allowed to spend the day with family members who visited. Roll was not called until evening. If we managed to escape and get to the other side of the mountain in about four hours, by the time they realized Juan was gone, we would already be in Soria and, in another few hours, in Zaragoza.

Teodoro drove me to Cuelgamuros, but I got out and started walking a long way before we got to the area where the prisoners were working. I had a backpack and, under my skirt, pants and boots for hiking. Juan and I spent half an hour in the visitor's room, ate a little of the food I had brought, and then walked around the monument site. The man who was going to guide us through the mountain had cut a hole in the fence surrounding the prisoners' area. As soon as we got to the wooded area where the far end of the fence was, it was easy enough to climb through the hole. The guide was waiting about two hundred yards north of the hole.

"Hello, I'm Marcos. I grew up in the children's home run by the Fliedners in El Escorial. I'm so happy I can help you escape."

"Thank you," Juan said, shaking his hand.

Marcos handed Juan a pair of hiking boots, and we set off.

"We should go as fast as you can here at the beginning. It's uphill and may seem tough, but going down is much harder," Marcos warned.

We followed his advice. An hour later we reached the mountain pass and started the descent. It seemed easy enough at first, but the going got harder when we entered the gorge. The rock was loose and it would be easy to lose one's balance and fall into the rushing water of the creek, swollen at that time of the year.

We followed Marcos's steps and picked our way through the difficult terrain without too much trouble. Then I slipped. I slid down the polished rocks like a child on a playground slide, and I could not grab onto anything quick enough to stop my fall. As I hit the freezing water, I groped for a branch or a rock, but the current was too fast.

Marcos and Juan sprinted downstream. The water tossed me up and down mercilessly, and I lost strength as I took in more water than air. I felt myself sinking, and then a strong hand grabbed me and pulled me out. It was Juan. He immediately pulled off my jacket and wrapped his around me.

"We can't take time to dry off. The sun will do it." Marcos sounded confident, but I could not stop shaking with cold. Yet an hour later, I was completely dry.

We reached San Rafael at the designated time. We were exhausted, but the hope of escaping and reuniting as a family gave us the strength we needed.

"Thank you so much for your help. Be careful," I said to Marcos.

"May God watch over you," he answered with a wave.

Juan and I got into a car driven by a man named Cosme. He also knew Teodoro Jr. and the Fliedners. Cosme's son had been a boarder at El Porvenir. He was a taxi driver in Segovia and had taken the day off to drive us to Zaragoza. The fact that there were no longer checkpoints along the road was a point in our favor, though the Civil Guard could stop a vehicle at any moment. Cosme was taking a great risk. Juan had just broken out of prison and was a fugitive from the law.

"We won't stop till we get to Zaragoza," he said. "You'll spend the night with some friends of the Fliedners."

Juan and I were eager to put as much distance as possible between us and Madrid, and the drive went by fast. We reached Zaragoza at dusk, and Cosme dropped us off at a house near the cathedral. He shook our hands and wished us well, then started the drive back to Segovia.

We knocked at the side door of the three-story building, and a woman opened the door. She invited us in and led us upstairs to the living quarters. There was a change of clothes waiting for each of us in the bathroom.

By the time we were cleaned up and changed, the aroma of soup beckoned us to the dining room. Our stomachs growled in response. A short, balding man was sitting at the table reading the newspaper.

"Good evening, my new friends. I'm Federico Escartín. Please consider this your home."

"We're so pleased to meet you and grateful for everything," Juan said.

"We're part of a church congregation that is no longer allowed to meet, but Teodoro got word to us. As soon as he told us your story, we were eager to help."

The bewilderment on Juan's face showed what he was thinking. Why would these people put themselves at risk for us? Juan was not a Christian, but he could tell something motivated them that was beyond his understanding.

Our hostess, Teresa, came out of the room where she had put their children to bed. The couple were watchmakers, and the floor below was their workshop and shop.

"We figured you would need transportation to the Pyrenees. Teodoro talked with a driver, but the man backed out. I'm going to take you. It's a five-hour drive from here. We'll leave as soon as you get the boy in the morning, and then the mountain guide will get you across the border tomorrow before nightfall."

"Thank you. We're so grateful—we don't know what to say," I said.

"Bárbara, we know what it's like to be parents. You'd do the same for our children," Teresa said.

After filling our stomachs with as much soup as they could

handle, we went to bed. We were exhausted after day one of our escape plan, but the riskiest part was still ahead.

Jaime had been adopted by a high-ranking Falange official in Aragon. Every day they took our son to a Jesuit school, and that seemed the best place to try to get him and escape to France.

As Juan snored beside me, I could not stop thinking about Jaime. I hoped he would recognize me. We had been separated for almost nine months. I was afraid that once Juan's absence had been noted, the police would get in touch with the adoptive family, but perhaps they were still searching for him on the mountain. Time was of the essence.

That night stretched on forever. I could not sleep a wink, though when morning came I was not tired. My mind and body were sharply attuned to one thing and one thing only: rescuing Jaime and getting out of the country.

Chapter 52

Zaragoza
May 27, 1940

The Jesuit school where the Falange family sent Jaime, the Colegio del Salvador, was just over a mile from Federico's house. That day, Teresa took their children to their school and Federico drove us to Jaime's school. We were amazed that he was willing to help us though it could cost him his life.

We arrived at the school right as parents were dropping off their children. Dressed as we were thanks to Federico and Teresa, we did not stand out or look suspicious. The porter let us in with a kind smile. In the office, we asked after Jaime, and the monk at the front desk did not hesitate to tell us which room he was in, but he did ask why we wanted to know.

"We've come from Madrid to see him. We're good friends of the family," I answered as if that explained everything.

"Oh, of course. Well, you won't be able to see Jaime till his parents pick him up. Don Fermín comes to get him with his bodyguard."

"No problem at all. We just hoped to give him a little surprise, but we'll see him this evening at dinner."

We made as if to leave but went down the main hallway instead.

Fortunately it was empty, and we found Jaime's room easily. At the door, we put our plan in motion.

Juan pulled the fire alarm, and in under a minute the hall was full of children and teachers leading them to the front yard. As soon as Jaime stepped into the hallway, I scooped him up. He gave me a startled look and then began to cry. A teacher came up and asked what I was doing.

"Oh, he's sick, so I came to pick him up."

The man looked at me questioningly but, in the midst of the confusion of the alarm, only responded, "Well, hurry up; the fire alarm has gone off."

I walked out holding Jaime. Juan followed a few yards behind so as not to raise suspicion.

At the door, the porter told me to stop, but I did not. He ran after me, but Juan tripped him, and a minute later we were in the car racing down the road.

Federico took the main highway toward the Pyrenees, but a few miles out of the city switched to back roads. Jaime's adoptive father was a powerful man, and soon the highways around Zaragoza would surely be closed.

I was hugging and kissing my little boy nonstop. He cried in fear and confusion until suddenly he stopped. He looked me straight in the eye and said, "Mamá."

That was the sweetest sound I had ever heard. How I had longed to hear his voice and see his little face again!

Juan stroked his hair and kissed his forehead. Jaime responded with "¡Papá!"

Tears poured out of my husband's beautiful eyes. We were finally together again. We heard Federico blowing his nose and saw him wiping a handkerchief across his face as well.

Out the window, the landscape slowly changed. The desertlike region around Zaragoza gave way to fertile meadows that were followed by hills and lovely woodlands.

In Navarre, we drove by huge fields of grain. After Pamplona, the landscape changed again, this time to forests full of beech trees that stretched over us in a protective embrace.

We began the ascent to Urtasun, the town where we were to meet our next guide. Yet just a mile or two from the town, a Civil Guard patrol car stopped us.

Federico's hand was shaking as he turned off the car. This could mean the end of everything for us and jail for him.

"Good afternoon. Where are you headed? You're awfully close to the border."

"It seems we've gotten turned around," Federico responded.

"Where are you wanting to go?" the guard asked again, checking us all out carefully.

"We're heading for Roncesvalles, but I think I've taken a wrong turn."

"Yes, you have," the guard said. "You're not from around here?"

"No, we're from Huesca," Federico answered. His voice was calmer than I knew he felt. "One of our aunts has passed away."

"But your tags are from Zaragoza," the policeman responded.

Just then Jaime started crying. The guard looked in the back of the car again and, inexplicably, said, "Well, go on, but don't get too close to the border. On both sides you're liable to end up shot. Things are pretty tense in France right now. They're losing the war, and people say they'll surrender any day now."

That news hit me like a punch to the gut. The country we hoped to enter was about to fall into Nazi hands, but we had no other choice.

My old bookseller friend Françoise Frenkel had escaped from Berlin to Paris in 1939. When war broke out with Germany, she went south to Avignon. As a Polish Jew—not to mention a progressive, freethinking bookseller—she was well aware of what could happen to her if the Nazis caught her.

Federico drove away slowly until we were out of sight of the patrol car, then quickened his pace until the town lights came into view. He stopped the car and pointed to a path.

"This is where I leave you. That path will take you to the spot where the guide will meet you."

We got out of the car. I squeezed Federico's hand, hoping that the gesture communicated the depth of my gratitude. But fear of what awaited us choked me such that I could not speak.

He nodded at me and Juan and said, "Take care." Then he turned and took a different route back to Pamplona.

As soon as the three of us were alone, a new fear came over me. What if the guide was not at the meeting place? We would have to cross the border the best we could. There was no going back.

We walked just over a mile to the place Federico had described to us. No one was there. We sat down on a rock to wait. The weather was nice, but dark clouds were gathering on the horizon. It would not be long till the sun set.

We heard a whistle and, turning, saw a young man. He was blond and covered in freckles. He studied us with curiosity and then, apparently convinced that we were who he wanted to see, introduced himself in a very thick Navarre accent.

"*Kaixo*! I'm Ander."

We returned his greeting but said nothing more, as we could not be sure that he was our guide.

"Let's be on our way; night is coming. We've got to get to the shelter first."

So that was that. We followed Ander along the paths, leaving the town behind.

"How long until France?" Juan asked.

The young man flicked his glance at Juan. "Depends on how fast you walk! It's five hours to the next town, but four to get to the border."

We were going fast. Juan carried Jaime, and I had the backpack. We circled a beautiful lake and passed several lookouts, only stopping once for Ander to say, "See that over there? That's France."

Chapter 53

France
May 27, 1940

An hour later, we were in France, though we could not tell exactly when we had crossed the official border. The invisible lines that human beings draw to divide people are a mirage against the backdrop of real mountains, trees, rivers, and animals.

"You're not safe yet. My family has been doing this for hundreds of years, though the borders have moved countless times. But the French are on edge more than ever right now and anyone might turn you in. Urepel is the first town we come to, but I need to get you at least as far as Saint-Jean-Pied-de-Port. There, with a bit of money, you can hire someone to drive you as far as Pau. From there, it should be simple enough to get to Avignon."

At the shelter, we had a simple meal as the weariness of the past forty-eight hours settled into our bones. We cuddled up and, despite the uncomfortable floor, were asleep within minutes. Jaime had been a complete angel on the hike. He nestled into me as if not a day had gone by since our life together in the apartment.

We resumed the hike the next morning and made good, uneventful progress. Avoiding inhabited areas, we reached Saint-Jean-Pied-de-Port five hours after we set out.

Ander spoke some French, though the people of that region could also communicate in both Basque and Spanish.

He stopped a local baker with a gray Citroën van and asked, "How much would you charge to drive these good people to Pau?"

"I'd lose a day's work and might meet trouble with the gendarmes. We aren't supposed to be helping the Spaniards."

"You'll be well paid, and the risk of being stopped is pretty low."

"All right. My granny was from Spain, so . . . Just don't say a peep if we get pulled over," he called in our direction.

We nodded, as if to show him how well we could hold our tongues.

Ander turned to us. "I wish you luck. My grandfather helped the old Federico Fliedner out once. May this war end and the world go back to the way it was."

"Thank you so very much for everything," Juan said, shaking Ander's hand.

We got into the baker's van and drove away. Three hours later, in Pau, we started to breathe a bit easier. Juan bought a newspaper and we understood how serious the situation was in France—they would cave any day. The Allied plan to contain the Nazis in Belgium had failed. King Leopold was about to surrender; Calais had already fallen; and the general consensus was that the tide would not turn against the Germans anytime soon.

From Pau, we took the first train headed to Marseilles. Avignon was en route.

We disembarked in Avignon after a restless night on the train. We found Françoise's small, one-story house without too much trouble and knocked. From her face it was clear that she had not been awake long, but she threw herself onto me.

"My God, you pulled it off!" she cried in German. Her embrace was tight as the delicious smell of fresh coffee and toasted bread wafted out of the kitchen.

"I'm so glad to see you!" I choked out, unable to stop the tears.

"And this is Jaime? What a darling!"

"Do you remember Juan?" I pulled him into the circle of our reunion.

"How could I forget him? In my nightmares I still hear the shouts of those horrible SA beasts breaking into my bookstore in Berlin. Then I wake up and thank God that Juan was there that day." Françoise beamed at Juan and wrapped her arms around him too. Then she said, "But do come in, come in, all of you!"

The hallway led to a small, cozy kitchen. Waiting on top of a pretty floral tablecloth was a carafe of coffee, steamed milk, and piles of toast. All three of us eyed the food hungrily.

"Go on, sit down, eat! I'm making more right now."

We downed the toast as soon as Françoise refilled the plate, several times over, until Jaime finally sat back against me with a contented sigh.

"So how are things around here?" I asked.

"Absolutely terrible. The French have no clue how to fight. The damned Nazis are steamrolling them. It's a matter of time before the government surrenders."

"But they can't!" I shook my head to chase away reality.

"Hitler's little pets are all fiends. The French don't know up from down."

I was quiet for a while, sipping the coffee.

"It's all delicious," Juan said in French.

"Oh, thank you."

"So what will you do if the French lose?" I asked Françoise.

"I've heard from my family how things have gone in Poland. If the same thing happens in France, it's over for us. The only options are trying to get into Switzerland or get to Marseilles and jump on the first boat headed across the Atlantic."

Juan's eyebrows rose. "Is it really that bad?" he asked. The war had not even been going on for a year, and the German offensive in France had started only a few weeks ago.

Françoise shrugged. "I don't know, but it's always smart to have a plan B."

A nap after breakfast restored our energy. I wrote Teodoro Jr. to let him know that we had arrived safely in France. Knowing that the Fliedners had many friends and family members in Switzerland, I also asked if he could get in touch with any of his contacts there.

In the afternoon, we walked around the beautiful ancient city of the popes. Françoise served as an excellent guide for the papal residency and the main streets. Though we were removed from the Mediterranean Sea, its influence was all around. Those first days in Avignon felt like a family vacation, a restorative pause before a new storm broke.

Chapter 54

Avignon
June 14, 1940

The Nazis had bombed Paris and taken Dunkirk, though much of the Allied army had managed to escape. German troops were on an unstoppable march toward the capital, and everyone was in a state. Rumors flew about the French government's retreat to the south and of the imminent surrender.

My letter to Teodoro Jr. had arrived in a timely manner, and his answer came shortly thereafter. The same day he wrote me, he also wrote to his contacts in Switzerland.

We were just over two hundred miles from the border with Switzerland. It was not that far, but no one could enter the country without a visa. If the Avignon region of France fell to the Germans, it would no longer be possible to get out.

A few days later, we were notified by mail that we had been granted the visa to go to Switzerland and should appear in person at the consulate in Lyon. Françoise had not been so lucky, but her spirits were unflagging.

"Take the first train today to Lyon. I'll figure things out. You know I'm a survivor," she said. But her words did not comfort me.

The Nazis were about to take over, and she was in a very precarious situation.

"As soon as we get to Geneva, I'll request a visa for you. My friend Teodoro Jr. is well connected."

Françoise walked us to the train station. Everyone else was trying to get farther south in France, so we had no trouble finding tickets to Lyon. Françoise stayed with us on the platform as we waited to board.

"Oh, these past weeks with you three have been so wonderful. The loneliness of recent years has been hard. Books are the only friends that have joined me as I bounce from place to place. I had hoped to open a bookstore here in Avignon, but war is at odds with culture. It's the pinnacle of human barbarism."

Her commentary was sad but on point. We hugged, and our tears mingled. I whispered, "Take care of yourself. Don't let them win."

When it was time to board, we went to our compartment and sat close to the window, waving to Françoise until the train was going too fast to see her anymore.

The two-hour ride was so quick and easy compared to the other modes of travel our journeys had required. Even so, it was disorienting to arrive in a new city in a foreign country.

The city was clearly not at ease. Lyon was the major city in the region and a likely target for the Germans. The streets were busy with people scurrying to and fro, packing up and heading to their country homes or to smaller towns nearby.

We went straight to the Swiss consulate, but it had closed at noon for lunch. We went to a nearby restaurant to eat and wait until it reopened. When we returned, we were dismayed to see an interminable line of people who had gathered during the interim.

Juan approached a soldier guarding the door and asked if we had to wait even though we had been granted our visas.

"I'm afraid so, sir. Everyone here is in the same situation."

So we waited in line for three hours until it was finally our turn. Jaime was worn out by then. When we were finally inside the building, an employee greeted us apologetically.

"I'm so sorry you've had to wait. We're completely overwhelmed by the number of people trying to get out of France."

"We understand, and it's no problem," I said. We were just grateful to be among the privileged few allowed to escape in time.

The man stamped and folded all the necessary documents and wished us luck. He also warned us that there were no buses or trains going to Switzerland at that hour. He told us where we could find lodging but clarified that we should be at the train station first thing in the morning if we wanted to try to get tickets.

That was one more night of stewing internally instead of sleeping. At least Jaime was able to rest. At the first light of dawn, we went to the station, but there were no seats available on any of the trains. We found the same at the bus station—not a single ticket. Juan tried to hire a private driver, but all the taxis were already booked by other people also trying to get out. The rumor was that the Nazis were just a few days' march from Lyon. There was no time to waste.

We wandered throughout the city amid the chaos. Fear had taken hold of the people. Eventually we decided to try our luck on foot. The closest Swiss town was less than a hundred miles away. It would take us several days, but it was better than waiting for the Germans to come.

We walked for five hours and reached the town of Chalamont in exhaustion. It was overrun with people doing the same thing we were doing. We saw a car that was not completely full, driven by a woman. There were only two children in the back.

Holding Jaime, I stopped the woman and asked, "Please, ma'am, could we ride with you, even if only to the next town?"

She frowned but agreed to take us as far as Poncin. That would be halfway there. It was dark by the time we arrived. Though the town was less crowded than Chalamont had been, we still could find no place to spend the night. The priest had opened the church for the travelers thronging the roadways and small towns of France. So we stretched out on the pews after a light supper of bread and milk.

We were up early the next morning, knowing that the twelve remaining hours of walking would end up taking longer since we had Jaime with us.

At Saint-Martin-du-Frêne, we stopped to rest and eat. Our ears pricked up at the sound of Spanish. A nearby group of men was talking in hushed tones but still loud enough for us to pick out their Madrid accent.

Juan hung back since we could not be sure what side they might have been on in the civil war. I went up and asked, "Are you from Spain?"

They looked up, surprised to find compatriots in such a remote spot on the map.

"Yes. We were Republican diplomats but escaped to Paris last week. Now we're headed to Switzerland. Because of international treaties, they can't deny us entry."

I caught my breath. With hesitant hope, I asked, "Could you get us to the border? There are three of us, but the boy can sit on my lap." By car it would take only an hour or so.

"Sure, we can make room," the man answered.

It was hot in the car, but that mattered little as each rotation of the wheels solidified the hope of leaving the inferno of European war behind and entering an island of peace.

The border was several miles beyond the Génissiat Dam, across the Rhône, but traffic was bottlenecked starting there.

After waiting for some time in the unmoving car, one of the Spaniards said, "We'll get there faster on foot."

We joined many others who abandoned their cars on the side of the road and set out walking. An hour later, we were in line at the border.

We were all nerves when it was our turn. What if something about the paperwork was not in order? The border agent was an older gentleman with an enormous mustache. He took our papers and studied them silently. Then he looked up, beamed at us, and handed them back. Stroking Jaime's face, he said, "Welcome to Switzerland!"

And with that, we started across the bridge. We looked back and were dismayed to see that our Spaniard diplomat friends had not had the same luck. Desperate, dramatic scenes were unfolding on the bridge. It was too much to watch, so we hurried across. On Swiss soil, we stopped long enough to rest on a bench. We still had to get to Geneva, but finally, after so long and after so much suffering, we were safe.

Chapter 55

Geneva
June 16, 1940

The Martins came to pick us up and drive us to Geneva. Their house was on the outskirts of the city, shimmering atop a hill of luscious, thick grass. Juan and I had the sensation of walking into paradise. Afra and Finn Martin were a delightful older couple who lived alone. Until retirement, both were doctors at the local hospital and everyone in town knew them. We learned all of this over a simple, delicious dinner.

"I hope the food sits well with you. We know it can be difficult to try new cuisines," Afra said when I came back to the kitchen after putting Jaime to bed.

"Thank you so much for everything," I said. Two tears escaped and trickled down my cheeks. Something about Afra reminded me of my mother.

Juan and Finn were having coffee at the dining room table, and we went to join them.

"It's hard to believe that on the other side of those mountains there's a war going on," Finn said.

I had felt the same way when we walked into Switzerland, as though the invisible lines people call borders were strong enough to hold back the good and the evil that humans are capable of.

"I'd like your help with something. I'm hoping to get a visa for a Polish friend, Françoise Frenkel. She's in Avignon right now."

Finn shook his head and sighed. "I'm afraid the government is being very stingy with visas at the moment."

"She's in danger because she's a Jew."

"Yes, we've heard what's happening to the Jews. We've spoken out about it with the Vatican, our own government, and the United States. We get the feeling it doesn't matter to anyone," Afra said.

The next morning I woke to sun spilling in through the window and lighting up the soft white sheets. Juan was sitting in a wrought iron chair on the deck off our room, contemplating the mountains. I slipped up behind him and kissed the top of his head.

"Jaime is already having breakfast," he said. "I didn't want to wake you."

"I haven't slept like that in years. No bomb sirens, gunshots, screaming, or crying. I think I could get used to this."

In the kitchen, Jaime beamed at us with milk-covered lips. Afra's clear blue eyes sparkled with delight as she looked at our son. She turned to us, smiled, and invited us to sit down for breakfast.

"I've been thinking, Bárbara my dear, that you could maybe work at the bookstore that's beside the cathedral." I was delighted with the idea but did not want to leave Juan alone. She went on, "And you, sir, could help out in my son Antoine's law firm. They deal mostly with business matters."

"Oh, you don't have to go to the trouble to set that up. I'll look for a job."

"Well, you could at least start out there, get your feet wet. There's no hurry for you all to leave our home. We feel like our own children have come back for a visit. We want you to stay as long as you'd like."

The weeks we spent with the Martins were blissful, though we knew the storms were raging over Europe and spreading to the rest of the world. I thought constantly about my extended family in Germany and what they must be going through. I was relieved that my father was in London, but the Nazis were bombing the city mercilessly.

I had no news of Françoise for three long years. Then one day, when I was working at the bookstore beside the cathedral, she walked in the door. She was frightfully thin, and the war had aged her terribly. But I recognized her half smile and practically jumped over the cash register to get to her.

We did not speak. We only held each other and wept. All the worry that had weighed me down about her flooded out as I had to prove over and over to my eyes that she really was there in the shop with me.

I took her back to the little house Juan and I were renting. We had had a little girl, and Juan was already back from picking the kids up from the nursery and school. The war had stretched on and on. From the safety of our home, school, and work, we read everything we could about it in the newspapers. We had all been relieved when the United States joined, though in 1943 the outcome was still up in the air.

The five of us sat down at the table for supper, and the adults just looked at one another for a moment. Françoise raised her glass for a toast.

"To books! May they reign again in this crazy world and undo the terrible power men have given to hatred and death!"

The sound of glasses clinking brought me back to my first Christmas in Madrid—to the dreams and longings of youth—and settled me in the present: aware of the life ahead of me now that I understood that people do not drive their own destiny. Around that table, the rudder of our existence was true love.

Chapter 56

Berlin
June 12, 1946

We could not return to Franco's Madrid, but Switzerland was a kind of wonderland that we knew could never be our forever home. So we decided to put down the Delgado family roots in Germany. Berlin was a rubble heap that the ever-industrious Germans were rebuilding with their customary zeal for perfection.

Juan and I opened a small bookshop in the American zone. We stocked a wide variety of books in English but also in German and French. For the first time since Hitler rose to power, publishing houses could now print what they wanted to. The German reading public had been kidnapped by National Socialism for years, and bookshops became places to dream again after awaking from the nightmare of the Third Reich.

Malleus Maleficarum rested in a glass display case in the back room where I kept the most valuable books. It was there as a reminder of the degree of hatred human beings are capable of. Beside it was the manuscript about my years in Madrid and my early dreams about the bookstore. I did not know if that collection of typed pages would ever see the light of day, but I liked to see it there and hoped that the stories it held would not fall into oblivion.

Juan helped me at the store, and the children spent the afternoons there with me as well. There was a small but growing community of Spanish expatriates, and they were our source for news from Madrid. The repression and hunger had not stopped, and censorship continued stunting people's minds. Even so, Juan and I still dreamed of returning someday. We had faith that a new world would arise from the ashes of the old one, though the powerful victors of the civil war were determined not to allow it.

As the last rays of sunlight filtered through the front window of the bookstore and I read a new arrival, an image of the Madrid sky flickered through my mind. That sky held a blinding clarity that made one feel so small and yet so lucky at the same time. It brought to mind Antonio Machado's words: .

Madrid, Madrid! How beautiful your name sounds,
breakwater of all the Spains!
The earth is torn apart, the sky roars,
you smile with lead in your belly.[*]

---

*Original translation of Antonio Machado, "Madrid," poem I, November 7, 1936, in *Madrid, baluarte de nuestra guerra de independencia* (Servicio Español de Información, 1937), public domain, https://www.cervantesvirtual.com/obra -visor/madrid-baluarte-de-nuestra-guerra-de-independencia-7-xi-1936--7 -xi-1937-1158000/html/36062030-9dc0-47d8-a234-65c984b9a0f8_2.html.

Epilogue

New York
September 2023

From the sidewalk, Kerri caught sight of her face reflected in the bookstore window. Her name was not on the front cover of the book with copies piled on the table inside, but she was bursting with pride. Alice had gotten her imprint to release it as the big reveal of the year. Before hitting the bookstores, it had already received high praise in the most respected outlets.

The young editor went inside and watched the shoppers who stopped to pick up the book and flip through it. The jacketed hardback was a magnet for many people. The story it held appealed to the souls of readers from all walks of life.

Kerri glanced at the other new releases and wondered why, among all the wonderful options, people might buy the particular book she had edited. The answer was not long in coming. A university student picked up the book, started reading the first few pages, then waved away her impatient friends so she could keep reading. She could not put it down.

Kerri thought about how good books were the ones that stayed with a person long after the cover was closed, like the lingering taste of a delicious meal or the splendor of an unrepeatable sunset behind a beautiful landscape.

She went back to her apartment. She had sacrificed many things for her dream of seeing that book come to light, but it had been worth it. She fixed a cup of tea, woke up her laptop, and started writing. Bárbara Spiel had given her the courage to cross the fine line that separated her from the world of authors.

As her fingers danced over the keyboard and the sounds of the city lullabied the afternoon, Kerri entered her own Palacio de la Novela, her own book temple, and forgot everything else as her soul dissolved between the pages of her book.

References

Cela, Camilo José. *The Hive*. Translated by James Womack. 1950.
Reprint, New York Review of Books, 2002. Page 16.

De Cervantes, Miguel. *Don Quixote*. Translated by John Ormsby.
1885. Project Gutenberg, 2004. Vol. 2, chap. 16. https://www
.gutenberg.org/cache/epub/996/pg996-images.html.

Luther, Martin. "A Mighty Fortress." 1529. Public domain.

Machado, Antonio. Poem I in *Madrid, baluarte de nuestra guerra
de independencia*. 1937. Original translation.

Merriam-Webster. "Lasciate ogni speranza, voi ch'entrate." Accessed
December 7, 2024. https://www.merriam-webster.com/dictionary
/lasciate%20ogni%20speranza,%20voi%20ch'entrate.

Clarifications from History

The fictional story of Bárbara Spiel is woven against a background of real people, places, and events.

The French bookstore run by Françoise Frenkel in Berlin was real, as was the famous bookstore run by Sylvia Beach in Paris. The story of the Fliedner family, the *tertulias*—literary discussions— in Café Gijón, and the existence of the Palacio de la Novela are likewise real.

Luis Fernández-Vior was in fact a famous author of detective stories who worked as a police officer before becoming a full-time writer. Joaquín Guzmán worked at the Librería Nacional y Extranjera, the Protestant bookstore associated with the Fliedner family's work in Madrid. The details about the beginning of the Madrid Book Fair and the story of its founder, Rafael Giménez Siles, are true to life.

Every attempt has been made to accurately portray the primary setting, Madrid, as well as the other cities in which the drama unfolds. The description of the physical and political reality of the Madrid of the Second Spanish Republic, the Madrid besieged by Fascism, and the Madrid controlled by the *checas* that terrorized a vast number of citizens aligns as closely as possible with documented history.

The Buenavista *checa*, its directors, and the savage treatment of prisoners held there were real. Likewise, Ventas women's prison as well as some of the characters described herein, including the director and Bárbara's cellmate, were also real. Some of the details regarding the timelines of these characters have been telescoped for the sake of the novel's plot.

According to the diary of Elfriede Fliedner, the Librería Nacional y Extranjera was shut down between October 23 and 26, 1939. The books and other materials were taken to the Anglican Cathedral del Redentor on Beneficencia Street, and also to the basement of the school El Porvenir. The date of the bookstore's closing has been altered to accommodate the storyline of the novel.

The construction of the Valle de los Caídos—Valley of the Fallen, renamed in recent years the Valley of Cuelgamuros after the area where it is located—is without a doubt one of the monuments to horror that best describes the character of Francisco Franco, a pitiless megalomaniac who controlled Spain with an iron fist for nearly forty years. The Falange and other Fascist movements, in conjunction with the organized violence of the Francoist army, destroyed the lives of tens of thousands of people. Meanwhile, hundreds of thousands were forced into exile, and the cultural and educational fabric of the country languished for decades.

May this novel pay homage to the booksellers who kept alive the flickering flame of hope that a better world was possible.

Timeline

1936

February: The Popular Front wins the national elections, paving the way for Azaña to take over the presidency of Spain later this year.

March: The extreme right-wing party Falange Española de las JONS (Juntas de Ofensiva Nacional-Sindicalista) is outlawed.

March–May: Riots, strikes, and generalized anarchy break out in several regions of Spain.

July: There is a military uprising in Spanish Morocco and some areas of mainland Spain. The government dissolves the regular army. Franco arrives in Morocco to take control of the army on July 19. Hitler agrees to help the Nationalists. Stalin decides to support the Republicans. German and Italian aircraft transport Franco's army to the Iberian Peninsula.

September: The military cabinet names Franco head of state and supreme commander of the armed forces of Spain.

October: The first volunteers of the International Brigades arrive in Spain. Aid from Russia arrives for the Republican side.

November: Germany and Italy recognize Franco as the legitimate head of the Spanish government.

1937

February: The Nationalists begin another offensive attempt against Madrid. The International Brigades play an important role in rebutting the attempt.

March: The Battle of Guadalajara occurs. Italian volunteers are defeated, leading Franco to abandon the attempt to take Madrid by direct attack.

April: Guernica is destroyed by aerial bombs.

April–May: Infighting among Republican factions in Barcelona seriously weakens the political and social order of the city.

June: The strategic city of Bilbao falls to the Nationalists.

August: The Vatican recognizes Franco's government.

1938

April: Republican-controlled territory in Spain is divided in two by Nationalist military advances.

May: Franco declares that the Republicans must surrender unconditionally.

July: The Republican army begins to collapse after the Battle of the Ebro.

October: The International Brigades leave Spain.

1939

January: Barcelona falls to Franco.

February: Great Britain and France recognize Franco's government.

March: Madrid falls to Franco.

April: The Republicans surrender unconditionally to Franco.

Discussion Questions

1. In the opening note to readers, the author claims novels can help us "reconcile with the past." In what ways does *A Bookseller in Madrid* seek to do this? How has the retelling helped you gain a new understanding of history?

2. The fictional protagonist Bárbara Spiel, as well as the real-life women Sylvia Beach and Adrienne Monnier, are bookstore owners who sought to change the world. Do you think they achieved their goal? What impact did these bookstores have on the cultures surrounding them?

3. In the novel, bookseller François Frenkel says, "There is no real art without suffering." What does she mean by this? How is *A Bookseller in Madrid* a testament to that statement?

4. Do you think Bárbara made the right choice when she fled Germany? What was her bravest option? Which might have allowed her to effect more change?

5. Throughout the novel, books are described as a refuge, a source of freedom, and true companions. Why do the characters view books in this way? What role do books play in your own life?

6. Luis challenges Bárbara with the perspective that books can spread evil as well as offer redemption. What evidence

do you see of this throughout the story? In what ways does the good of literature outweigh the inherent danger in the spreading of ideas?

7. In the story, theologian Dietrich Bonhoeffer argues that stupidity is more dangerous than wickedness. Do you agree with this statement? What means do humans have to combat wickedness? What about ignorance?

8. At Juan and Bárbara's wedding, Indalecio Prieto says that he wishes love ruled the world. If love does not rule the world, what does? How might Juan's and Bárbara's answers differ from yours?

9. Bárbara says that "when we open a book, the world is re-created, as if we were back in the paradise we lost." How can the return or transportation to another world impact the world we are living in?

10. Bárbara is approached to act as a spy on behalf of the British embassy, and she is also manipulated by a Gestapo agent into becoming a spy for the Nazis. What about Bárbara's unique position made her a candidate to act as a double agent? What would you have done in her position?

11. What is the role of safety in the story? At what point would you say Bárbara and her family are truly safe?

12. How much did you know about the Spanish Civil War before this story? What were you most surprised to learn?

About the Author

Photo by Elisabeth Monje

MARIO ESCOBAR, a *USA TODAY* and international best-selling author, has a master's degree in modern history and has written numerous books and articles that delve into the depths of church history, the struggle of sectarian groups, and the discovery and colonization of the Americas. Escobar, who makes his home in Madrid, Spain, is passionate about history and its mysteries.

Visit him online at marioescobar.es
X: @EscobarGolderos
Instagram: @marioescobar.oficial
Facebook: @MarioEscobar

About the Translator

Photo by Kristen Stewart

GRETCHEN ABERNATHY worked full-time in the Spanish Christian publishing world for several years until her first child was born. Since then, she has worked as a freelance editor and translator. Her focus includes translating and editing for the *Journal of Latin American Theology* and supporting the production of materials related to the Nueva Versión Internacional and New International Reader's Version of the Bible. Chilean poetry, the occasional thriller novel, and a book on Latin American protest music spice up her work routines. She and her husband make their home in Nashville, Tennessee, with their two sons.